The HATE ZONE

GIGI BLUME

SODASAC PRESS
PUBLISHING HOUSE

FIRST EDITION

Library of Congress Cataloging-in-Publication Data has been applied for.

ISBN: 979-8-9861828-0-3

Editing by Allusion Publishing

Cover design and illustrations by Once Upon a Cover

The HATE ZONE

CONTENTS

Chapter One

JANUARY

Gentlemen. Boys. People of the male persuasion who call yourselves 'dude'. Unless you're Dwayne 'The Rock' Johnson, please! For the LOVE. Keep your shirt on.

Seriously. Nobody wants to see that.

You may think you're the sexiest beast known to womankind. But no. Just no. Trust me when I tell you, no matter how ripped, how tan, how waxed your torso is… we're not impressed.

I mean, we are, but not in the way you think we are. Let's just say we're very selective. So, boys, keep it on and we'll tell you when it's okay to take it off. Capisce?

Good. Thank you for coming to my TED talk.

So here's the thing. I have this bodyguard named Ugo. Had. He's totally fired now, and here's why. When he found out I split from my boyfriend, he decided to declare his love for me. Shirtless. Slathered in oil. Wearing jeans so tight, I'm surprised he's not singing soprano. And the guy seriously couldn't take no for an answer. I'm already having a bogus day thanks to the aforementioned boyfriend. So when Ugo completely lost it, my eyeballs turned the act of rolling backward into an extreme sport. Ugo went completely ballistic. I'm talking Lou Ferrigno *Incredible Hulk* vibes, spitting and grunting and throwing things. He does not take rejection well, folks. And he's a big guy. Enormous, really.

Thank my lucky stars I'm not at my own house right now. My dad insisted I stay with him at the hotel penthouse suite for a few weeks, or at least until the whole thing blows over with my washed-out popstar ex. He says it's for my safety, but I suspect he just wants to keep an eye on me. Here, I'm surrounded by hotel security that burst in a minute ago. There are three of them trying to wrestle Ugo into submission. But Ugo is slipping and sliding out of their grasp. Did I mention he's covered in oil? Think pig wrestling at its finest. Yeah, that bad.

My dad and his assistant are crouched behind the grand piano being absolutely no help at all. Scratch that. The assistant is calling for more security guards, so at least she's doing something, unlike Dad, who's the biggest coward of the bunch. We wouldn't want him to wrinkle his Armani suit, now would we?

I stand my ground in the face of this psycho freak show because I'm not afraid of Ugo. I just don't want him to break more stuff. And I wish he'd put a shirt on—although, the human slip and slide effect from all that oil is working to his advantage. I give him points for creativity.

As soon as the security guards have a hold on Ugo, he slithers out of reach, coming at me with a hint of caveman in his stride. What is he even thinking? If he throws me over his shoulder, I'll most definitely slide right off.

"You stop right there, Ugo." I hold up my palm like a 1950's backup singer. Surprisingly, he stops. "I want you to go now."

He regards me with these sad puppy dog eyes, although the rest of his face is extremely frightening. Veins are popping out of his forehead, but there's something in the way he looks at me that cracks my heart a teeny tiny bit.

"But..."

He doesn't complete his thought because the guards finally get wise and bind Ugo's ankles and, because of those tight jeans, they are able to get a pretty good grip on something other than greased-up flesh. I'm tempted to cry, "Timber," as Ugo tumbles to the floor. Five more guards rush in, one of them using a Taser to immobilize Ugo even as he's pinned down like a WWF wrestler.

"Good gravy, what took you so long?" Dad emerges from behind the piano, tugging on the hem of his suit. Nice to see he's finally found his courage behind that piano.

"We came right away, Mr. Madison, sir."

"How did he get past the guards in the first place?" Dad continues. "He's half naked."

"He has a fob," I say, stating the obvious. "And full security clearance."

Dad couldn't be more annoyed, but something tells me it has more to do with the disruption of his schedule than concern for my safety. He turns to his assistant.

"Have the digital codes changed." And as he stomps into the other room he barks over his shoulder to the security team, "And take this *thing* out of here. He's ruining my floors."

The security guards nod like the glorified Boy Scouts they are, and drag Ugo by his tied-up feet toward the elevator. A streak of oil tracks on the marble floor like the slime trail of a slug. If it wasn't for the yuck-factor, I might find it funny. Okay, it is a *little* funny.

I go into the media room for my purse while Dad's assistant calls for housekeeping to bring a mop. She better come with some grease-cutting cleaner to get that grease stain up. I don't notice Dad behind his laptop until he calls out to me.

"Where do you think you're going?" he says accusingly.

"I have a hair appointment."

"Have your girl come to you."

I sigh inwardly, pinching the bridge of my nose. I have the best hairdresser in the business. She only takes on a handful of clients—all high-profile celebrities like me. And she'll do almost anything for me. But she won't do house calls when color is involved.

"And I don't want you to sleep at your house until we can find a replacement for Guido."

"Ugo," I correct him.

Dad scowls at me over his laptop. "January, I am extremely busy this morning. Can you please keep your drama on the other side of this penthouse? I don't need to deal with your ex-boyfriends or your meathead bodyguards. Lord knows we're still recovering from your last romp in the tabloids. I only ask that you stay here until your latest dumpster fires die down."

My last romp in the tabloids? As if I enjoyed getting sold out to the paps by my shallow friends. Dad seems to forget I left that party hours before the police arrived. The life of a hotel heiress, slash reality TV star, isn't as easy as it looks. And trust me, in these heels, it looks darn good. But no matter. I'm so over these stupid arguments he likes to start. And after a week's vacay in the pit of Mordor, I don't have it in me to deal with yet another man's hooey.

I will concede, however, that compared with the breakup with my boyfriend and whatever this was with Ugo, I feel marginally less crappy about my personal chauffeur's retirement. Thomas was the best part of my life. And with two living parents, hundreds of glamorous friends, and over eighty-million Instagram subscribers, that probably says a lot about my life.

So yeah. I'll pass on Daddy's battle royale.

"I have a talk show appearance on Monday, otherwise I'd cancel my hair appointment. If I could just get a ride, I promise to stay here in your tower for as long as you like."

Dad flings his reading glasses off his face, letting them land on his keyboard with a metallic clink. His eyebrows lurch down, giving him a decidedly indignant appearance, and the frown he's wearing seems to fit him like a well-loved pair of shoes.

"Why do you have to do that?"

"Do what?" I ask, genuinely having no clue what he's complaining about now.

"Act like that." He swishes his hand around. "Play the victim. Poor January Madison, locked in a tower with nothing but Daddy's credit card. You sound just like your mother."

He says that last part under his breath, but he fully intended for me to hear it. In his world, a negative comparison to my mom is the worst insult imaginable. And although it stings a little, I'm laughing at him inside my head because honestly, I'm more like him. Not like that's a good thing. But at least, unlike my mom, I can get through the day without flirting with the pool boy in a martini haze —if memory serves from my youth. Come to think of it, that might be the root of my olive aversion.

Deep breath.

There must be a solution.

I turn on my heel to go figure it out on my own, but Dad stops me with his voice.

"Wait." He sighs, checking his watch. "I don't trust you. Give me twenty minutes."

Uh, thanks?

Worst. Day. Ever.

Chapter Two
ENRIQUE

"Stop! I can't… breathe." My little sister, Francesca, is laughing so hard, she's getting a case of the hiccups. I wish I was there to grab her a glass of water, but I'm driving, so I give the best advice I can over the phone.

"Pull on your tongue," I say much louder than I ought. I don't need to shout because my new limo has state-of-the-art Bluetooth tech, but I do anyway. I'm turning into my dad.

"Now you're just making stuff up," she says, still laughing. "I'll… *(hiccup)* be… *(hiccup)* fine."

She won't be fine. But in my defense, I didn't mean to make her laugh.

"Okay, change of subject," I say, trying to sound serious. She called for a reason, not to hear about my crazy morning. "Don't tell me you called to weasel your way out of a ride later."

She's performing tonight at a fancy Hollywood thing and there's no way I'll let her drive that *carcacha* she loves so much.

"Wait, wait," she says. "I need to know the rest. Did you really call her Barf Girl?"

"Not to her face." Seriously, Francesca needs to let this go or she'll hyperventilate. Besides, I need to get off the phone soon. I'm on my way to meet with my new client—Matthew Madison of Madison Luxury Hotels. This is big. I should have spent the morning putting another waxy shine over the sexy black finish of the limo. I love this car more than I'll ever love a woman. But when Academy Award-winner, Dame Stella Gardiner, asks you to drive an unknown musical theatre actress to the same fancy Hollywood thing your sister's singing at, you don't turn her down. Especially after Stella awarded Francesca with a full-ride college scholarship five years ago. But when Stella's young unknown musical theatre actress friend almost barfs in your gorgeous limo, she's gonna get a nickname. Barf Girl. For some reason, my sister finds that hilarious.

"Hold your breath and swallow three times."

"What… *(hiccup)* did Stella do?"

"When I tried to gun it out of there, Stella came running after us in her designer digs."

It was pretty funny, actually, but I try to downplay it for my sister's sake. "Then she took Barf Girl into the mansion. My upholstery is safe."

"Oh man. I'm going to find out who that is when I get there."

"Don't you even repeat what I said."

"You can't see me, but I'm crossing my heart," she says sweetly.

"What's up, *Panchita*? Why did you call?"

"Soooo… *(hiccup)* charming."

"Will you just try the tongue thing? Hold it with your fingers and tug. It's science."

"Fine."

A few moments of silence follow and I wait for her while cruising down Santa Monica Boulevard. She coughs and there's a scratchy sound like she's fumbling with her phone. After a minute she's back on.

"All good?" I ask.

"That was weirdly gross but I think it worked."

"And you doubted me."

"Anyway, I was actually hoping you'd come early. I want to go over my song with the musicians before guests arrive at the Gala."

I go over my schedule in my head. This meeting with Mr. Madison shouldn't take too long. I think it's just going over the schedule and protocols. I can still get in a quick workout before picking up Francesca at our parents' house. She's the only one of us eight siblings still living at home if you don't count our youngest brother who's at college most of the year.

"Okay. See you at five."

"Four," she says.

"Four. Got it." So it will be a mini workout. It's all good. I'll just do arms.

I hear the muffled voice of my mom in the background shouting something in Spanish.

"And Mom says to pick up Tía Lucy on the way over. They're making *Rosca de Reyes* tonight. Well, Tía Lucy's making the bread, and Mom will just put in the plastic baby Jesus dolls."

I sigh. I do love *Rosca de Reyes*, that sweet, milky bread we only get on Three King's Day. But seriously! Tía Lucy has a huge truck. She can drive herself. I know she wants to impress her neighbors, so I told her she could cash in on one limo ride from me. Why she doesn't save it for a special occasion is a mystery only known to crazy Tía Lucy.

I suppose I'll get in a tiny workout. A fifteen-minute cardio sesh.

"I'm sorry," says Francesca. "I tried to run interception for you, but you know how they are when they get an idea in their heads."

"It's all good. Listen, I'm almost at the Madison Hotel. See you at four thirty."

"Four!"

I laugh and disconnect the call before Mom makes any more demands.

It's a bright, sunny day for the week after New Year's—unseasonably warm even for L.A. The midday sun sparkles off the gleaming surface of the Madison Towers Hotel, promising to blind out the other hotel competition just by existing. I've heard, out of all their hotels worldwide, only their Manhattan sister property rivals this one. I also hear that's where Matthew Madison's wife, the illustrious Mrs. Madison, keeps her residence—unless of course, Mr. Madison is in New York. Then she jets off to Paris or someplace tropical that serves martinis poolside. That's what I've read, anyway.

I pull around the back to the VIP garage as instructed in my contract. I can only assume I'll be picking up the bigwigs and financial partners of the Madison conglomerate from their offices somewhere across town, but Mr. Madison himself gets picked up here. From what I understand, it's also a heavily guarded entrance for celebrities and politicians to come and go without drawing attention. I flash my badge and the guard lifts the gate for me. My heart pounds as I take the parking spot reserved for me. ME! This is getting real. I'm a good fifteen minutes early, so I take an extra moment to run a lint roller over my suit. It's a simple uniform, but classy—something I'd picked out for myself in case I needed it for a non-work thing like a wedding or the hundreds of quinceañeras I'm obligated to attend to represent the Precio family. My brothers and I always turn heads when we walk into a church—like the guys in *Reservoir Dogs*. Mom's all about making an impression, which isn't hard when six imposing men in suits flank all four-foot-eleven of her. She likes to stop in doorways like a mob mom —arching a brow at any onlookers—while the seventh son, Memo, floats in wearing his white priestly robes, shaking hands, smiling, kissing babies. Mom's favorite son. If it weren't for my brother Memo and his vow of poverty, people would begin to gossip that the Precio brothers were embedded in the Mexican Mafia. Maybe they think that anyway. It's a matter of respect in these communities.

I finish with the lint roller and check my teeth in the rearview mirror when something catches my eye. Four burly security guards are carrying what looks like a dead man. They're joined by three more guards who open the back of an SUV, where they plunk down the body. Just before they shut the hatch, the man comes back to life, flopping around, kicking one guard in the assets with bound feet. He's gigantic. And holy cow, how can he breathe in those teeny-tiny jeans? Also, he'd lost his shirt somehow (not a story I care to know) and from where I'm sitting, he's not a happy camper. I sure wouldn't be if I had to stuff *my* junk in those tight jeans.

He's roaring and cussing—spit flying out of his mouth. The guards attempt to wrestle him into submission, but he evades them and hops out of the SUV, getting closer to my car than I'm comfortable with. Hello, shiny wax job. None of them see me, though, and I'd like to keep it that way. Always best to never get involved in anything sketchy going on in this town. I check my watch.

Freaking A, this better not make me late.

I hear one of the guards say, "This is above my pay grade." Meanwhile, the burly shirtless man hops into the alley, giving them the bird without looking back. Glad I missed *that* altercation.

I wait for the guards to meander inside the building before heading up the glass elevator, which shoots straight to the penthouse. I'm one of the few people not directly employed by Madison Corp. who owns a fob for this elevator. It's pretty freaking cool.

I'm deposited into a vestibule of sorts, which is roughly the size of my entire house. There's a small, extremely hard sofa, and a couple of sleek chairs where I sat to sign the contract a week ago.

I check the time. Five minutes early. Good. I go over to sit on the uncomfortable sofa, my butt inches from touching the rock-hard seat cushion, when Mr. Madison's assistant blasts through the double doors, high heels clicking fiercely over the marble floor. She's a sleek woman in her late forties—always the picture of confidence and control in designer pencil skirts and perfectly coifed hair. She's the last person of contact before meeting with Madison himself and presents herself as such with equal parts grace and ice. If I didn't know she'd had work done, I'd even go so far as to say she's an attractive woman. Right now though, I can tell by her intense frown that something's amiss. It would take a heckavalot to downturn that much plastic.

She sees me (mid-squat) and halts. "Oh, Mr. Precio. I'm so relieved you're here."

I straighten, flashing her my most charming smile. It's my best feature, and I can't help but use it to my advantage around powerful women. It's a self-preservation tactic, I guess.

"You can call me Enrique." I nod respectfully, and I can tell the exact moment when her eyes snag on my signature dimple wink. She clears her throat and rolls her shoulders back just enough to assert her position.

"Very good. Unfortunately something's come up which

demands Mr. Madison's immediate attention. I've been charged to instruct you to wait for him in the garage."

Ay que la fregada.

"Does he need me to drive him somewhere? He hadn't mentioned it."

Actually, he hasn't given me any kind of schedule at all. I thought that's what today's meeting was about.

"I'm sorry, I don't have any other information for you right now, Mr. Precio."

"Enrique."

She ticks her head. "Yes, of course. All I know is that you are to wait in the garage."

Right. Dismissed from the penthouse.

I'm ushered out with a wave of her arm like those people who give too-long speeches on awards shows. She waits for me to enter the elevator and pushes the G button, lest I get any ideas to make a pit stop at the buffet.

It's here I realize I don't even know her name and, for some reason, that triggers my flirtatious instincts. I think I'll call her Judy. I bring my pinky and thumb to my face and mouth the words "call me" just as the doors slide shut. In the minuscule second when there's only a sliver of an opening left, a crack of a smile forms on Judy's lips.

Twenty minutes later I'm leaning against Black Beauty scrolling mindlessly on my socials and bored out of my mind. I could be on my way to the gym by now. Free weights, maybe a few minutes on the treadmill. Shower. Protein shake. Pick up Tía Lucy with enough time for her to show off in front of her neighbors. Meet Francesca. Disapprove of her dress and wait for her to change into something with a high neckline and ankle-length hem. Drive her to the same Bel Air mansion I dropped off Barf Girl. Go to the movies by myself. Resist popcorn.

I'm roused by the arrival of the elevator car. Doors swish open and out walks Mr. Madison in his usual crisp business suit. He's followed by two security guys who stand as sentinels, holding the doors open for a woman giving more attention to her phone than anything else. I slip my own phone in my pocket and stand at the ready near the limo passenger door. All eyes are riveted on this woman. She's all apathetic casual as she reluctantly saunters out of the elevator like there are a million other places she'd rather be. She's shabby and glamorous and high fashion all at once. The world is her own personal catwalk. And as she steps into my direct line of vision, I recognize her. January Madison. Hollywood socialite and heiress to the Madison Hotel fortune. Nobody has any idea what she's famous for other than having loads of money and tossing her blond hair for the paparazzi. I've never really paid much attention to those things. But seeing her in person, I can see why the cameras love her. She has got to be the most effervescently beautiful, breathtaking woman I've ever seen. She glows. She very well might be a goddess, which quite frankly is against my religion to believe. But I'm ready to believe it as her eyes fall over me in a blatant once-over of my entire body. (Thank you, gym membership.) Her gaze dawdles on my chest for a moment before moving down. I forget myself. My tongue is lodged in my throat. My signature dimple-wink escapes me. I think this may be love at first sight—until she opens her mouth.

"Where's the Bentley?"

Mr. Madison grumbles, "We gave the Bentley to Thomas, my dear. As a retirement gift."

"So why didn't you buy another Bentley? I can't be seen in this."

She pulls a sour face at my car. My perfectly sexy car. My brand-new gorgeous Cadillac.

Mr. Madison clears his throat and addresses me. "Do you have any Bentleys in your fleet, Mr. Precio?"

My *fleet*? I ain't got no stinkin' fleet. What do I say to a question like that without looking like a dummy? "Not at this time, sir, but I will take a note of that for our next purchase."

Do I sound like a professional business guy and not like a clown? No, I didn't think so, either.

"You hired a rent-a-limo? Eww. Seriously, Dad?"

"We have an exclusive contract with Enrique," says Mr. Madison, and then turning to me adds, "It's well maintained, isn't it?"

"Less than a week old, sir."

"There we have it. No one else has sat in that backseat, January."

Other than my mom, about twenty of my cousins, and that girl who almost barfed, of course.

January stares me down, like she somehow knows I use this thing for all my friends and relatives.

Mr. Madison slips me a Benjamin, as if he wasn't already paying me extremely well for an exclusive contract.

Maybe it's for the added pain of letting his daughter tag along.

"You'll take January where she needs to go," he says to me, almost conspiring. "We'll have an itinerary for you once we know our schedule."

"Looking forward to it," I say with the most genuine smile I can muster. I'm supposed to be driving the executives. The important guys. Mr. Madison himself. Not his bratty offspring.

Mr. Madison gives me a formal nod, turns to his daughter with a knowing look, and heads back to the elevator, disappearing behind the sliding doors with both guards. He just bamboozled me. Did the old bait and switch. And now I'm stuck with this girl who's eyeballing me like she just scraped me off the bottom of her shoe. I tick my jaw because it's taking every bit of willpower I possess not to find a hose and spray her down with it, hoping the water's ice cold. Restraint is not my strong suit. I open the door for her and she inspects the interior before sliding in.

"You better not be a psycho," she huffs.

This contract is going to test every ounce of poise I can muster. At this rate, I'd trade this spoiled socialite for Barf Girl in a hot second.

Chapter Three

JANUARY

Oh joy. Our new chauffeur (Rico or Ringo or whatever his name is) is a hot, scowly grump. Emphasis on the grump.

And the hot. Ugh! *No, no, no, no, no.*

I'm just in a salty mood, that's all.

I miss Thomas. Couldn't he have waited a year—or ten —before retiring? I'm glad he got the Bentley, though. He deserved it.

Presently, hot grump has murderous eyes on me by way of the rearview mirror. If they discover my body in a ditch somewhere, I'm going to be a really pissed-off ghost.

"Well?" I say with extra sass because that's the kind of day I'm having. Why isn't he moving?

He brings his arm up across his seat and cranes his neck around. "A destination would be nice," he bites. He's such a treat.

There's something about those inky black eyes that send a shiver across my skin. I should have taken my dad up on his offer to bring along one of his rent-a-cop security guards. Then again, based on the way they handled slippery Ugo, they're pretty much useless.

Breathe in. Find your happy place.

Why does this guy not have the GPS already programmed? This is the kind of thing he should have on his daily itinerary. Sighing, I rattle off the address and add, "Did you get all that, or do I need to say it slo—"

My words are cut off by the swish of the partition window slowly closing as I catch a glimpse of him slipping on his mirrored sunglasses. Grrrr. The partition is heavily tinted and looks to have an airtight seal. One thing it's *not* is soundproof. This guy is obviously not used to dealing with famous people because every partition window should be soundproof in a luxury vehicle. I know it's not because some kind of heavy metal music blasts from the front.

"Turn that down," I cry. I know he hears me. "You are the worst driver I've ever known. And we haven't even left the parking lot yet."

I roll down the partition using the controls in the back. "I said, turn that down."

He tilts his sunglasses down and glares at me in the rearview mirror, eyes twinkling with amusement. "Not a fan of Iron Maiden?"

I don't think I've heard an Iron Maiden song in my entire life.

"No," I say. "Can you just turn it off, please?"

This is an exercise in futility. Tomorrow he'll be gone and maybe Dad will have relaxed his hold on me by then so I can go back to my house.

Breathe out. I'm in a flower-covered meadow. No. I'm shoe shopping. Yes.

He tips his chauffeur hat and shuts off the music. "If you insist on declining the entertainment portion of our services, I will do your bidding."

He's mocking me now. I find myself disliking this man with each passing moment.

"I don't have time for a smartass. Just shut up and drive."

He salutes me and raises the partition once again, pulling out of the garage. At least we're on our way to my stylist's house now. Sans thrasher music. Chez Marie is a high-end, full-service salon on my hairdresser's residential property. She services celebrities there who prefer a private setting. Despite the new car and infuriating driver, the familiar route calms me. Whatever sunlight filters through the heavily tinted windows soothes me enough to get on with my socials. I open Instagram and decide to go for a 'before' post. I click a selfie and put it through a filtering app and I've got my hashtags ready to go in my notes app. Copy. Paste. Caption.

On my way to the fabulous @chezmariesalon for her VIP

treatment. Stay blonde or go darker? #januarymadison #selflove #positivevibes #glossitup

Likes and comments flood my post almost immediately.

"Please stay blonde."

"Go red."

"I want to be just like you, January."

"Promote it on @totallyascamaccount to gain thousands of follows."

I block the scam account and smile at the rest, liking a few. People literally go nuts when a celebrity likes their comments. It's a rush, and who would I be to not give them what they want?

I'm so lost in the land of perfectly pretty snapshots of people's lives that I don't notice at first we're stopped. He cut the engine and is just sitting here in the silence. I look out. We're in the right neighborhood, but my stylist's residence is still half a block down the street. Is he lost?

I tap on the glass.

"Hello."

tap tap tap

"Hey, Ringo. Why are we stopped?"

It's quiet for a while, and I'm just wondering if he's ever going to answer me when the partition window slides just as slowly down as it did going up.

"We're here, Sunshine."

He doesn't turn around to face me this time, but I feel his eyes on me through the rearview mirror, even if I can't see them past his aviator glasses.

"No, we're not. The house is down there."

I point, but he's not paying attention anymore. I hear a

bleep bleep. Then the sound of celebration balloons indicating he just typed "Congratulations" on Facebook.

"Are you kidding me right now?"

This snags his attention back to the rearview mirror and I detect a sliver of a smile as the glass slides back up.

He's quiet for some time, and I'm thinking he's just going to sit here forever. I'm fuming... justifiably. But then he charges out of the car and has my door open in a flash of fury. I can almost imagine flames in his eyes, but it's probably just the reflection of the sun off his mirrored glasses. And why do I find this so hot?

Gah. Breathe in.

For a thousand seconds, or what feels like it, we just look at each other. It's a staring contest to the death, apparently. And I don't like to lose. I figure my sitting position puts me at a disadvantage here so I slide out of the car, standing as tall as I can. I'm not a short woman, especially in these heels, but he still towers over me, and he seems to enjoy every second of this weird standoff.

He smiles. Dimples form like deep trenches of warfare. One is slightly larger than the other, which is only accentuated by the day-old stubble all over his jaw. Didn't this guy think to shave on his first day on the job?

"Listen, April," he says, breaking the silence.

"January."

"Right. I think there must be some kind of misunderstanding."

I level a hard glare into his glimmering sunglasses. "In what way?"

He licks his lips, choosing his words carefully. "Is this going to be a regular occurence?"

"Is *what* going to be a regular occurrence?"

"Me. Driving you. I'm going to be driving the executives from now on, right?"

"What executives? There are no executives."

"You're telling me your father runs a multi-million-dollar hotel conglomerate and there are no executives?"

I snort. "Not in LA. They're all in Manhattan or... wherever." I wave my hand around.

"So why take the limo, then? Shopping trips and nail salons? Is that it?"

"You are to replace Thomas, my old driver. He retired. And I go to a lot of places besides the mall. I'm not a teenager."

He mumbles something under his breath that sounds suspiciously like, "Could have fooled me."

But I let it roll off my shoulder. Who is this guy anyway? I plant my hand on my hip and toss my hair back because I am Wonder Woman.

"So what's the name of your illustrious, executive driving limo company? Snarks R Us?"

"You know, I had my heart set on Snarks R Us, but that one was taken." He shakes his head solemnly.

"How unfortunate for you."

"Yeah. So I settled for Enrique Precio Limousine." He holds up his palms. "I'm just glad I don't have to change my name now."

"Okay, Enrique Prosecco, I'll tell you what. Take me to my hairdresser's house down the street. The end."

He points at the house in front of us. "You mean this isn't it?"

"You think you're hilarious, don't you?" I say.

"A sense of humor will take you a long way," he replies.

I snort. "Like all the way to my stylist's house, maybe?"

He glances briefly down the street and back to me. He just shrugs—and even *that* gesture drips with foxy confidence. "Maybe."

Breathe out. I will not give in. I will not.

"It is your job to take me to my destination. Door to door." I cross my arms, projecting dominance and wealth. Who's the boss? I am, fools. Who pays this man's salary? My family does. Mic drop.

He doesn't need to know my dad is the actual boss, here. This seems to do the trick because he kinda nods. Very tiny nod, mind you. Then he gets back in the driver's seat and starts the engine. *Starts the engine!* With me still standing outside. Clearly he's not getting the door for me.

I scramble inside, shutting my *own* door. I really hate this man.

He stops just shy of my stylist's house and cuts the engine.

Seriously?

At least he doesn't keep me waiting this time. He gets out, adjusting his chauffeur hat just so, and opens my door. He even makes a grand point to sweep his arm out.

"Madam," he says, all proper with a slight bow.

This man is purposefully making my life difficult. Just like my dad. Just like my ex. And Ugo. And every other man in my life.

"Ugh," I growl. "Fine."

I collect my purse, put on my game face, and exit the limo. His head is still bowed, but I can see that smirk on his scruffy face. I have a sudden urge to touch it, feel the sandpaper of his whiskers under my palm. Poke my finger in that infuriating dimple that's just hiding under the surface.

Poke poke.

But no. I'm a butterfly over the meadow. Wisps of a dandelion floating in the breeze. My therapist would be so proud. Let go of the anger. Be one with nature.

I lift my chin and straighten my spine, giving that horrible man my power-look before making a sweeping departure from his presence.

But something on the car door snags on my purse strap, yanking me backward. This, combined with the heel of my stiletto sinking into the grass, causes me to lose my balance and... down I go. What's worse is it happens in slow motion. Not just in my head... but really in slow motion, and all the while I'm sinking down, I can't do anything to prevent it. And neither does the infuriating man with a Cheshire grin spread across his face. It seems to get wider with every inch I fall, until I'm on my butt. On the grass. With my skirt bunched up almost to my panties. I imagine he's stifling a full-blown laugh, but he turns his head away so I can't see his face. Then his hand appears out of nowhere, extended in a show of chivalry to assist me. But I already made a fool of myself and I'm hoping that the neighbors of my stylist aren't home peeking through windows.

I slap his hand away, furious and mortified.

"I can manage," I snap.

But he doesn't buy my pseudo feminism, and his bear-like paw swallows my hand as he helps me to my feet. His palm is solid and warm, his touch sending trickles of awareness up my arm.

Once he's satisfied I'm standing on stable ground, he squeezes a fist at his side, then flexing his fingers says, "Should I come back later? Or…"

I adjust the purse strap on my shoulder and do my best to regain my composure, clearing my throat. "It will be a couple hours. Don't be late."

Chapter Four

ENRIQUE

January's hair appointment is on hour three. Not two, as she estimated. I could have gone through my workout twice over by now. But we got off on the wrong foot, and I don't want to do anything else to jeopardize this contract, so I stay and wait outside the moderately posh house that January disappeared into over three hours ago.

I don't need this job. I have enough money saved to live

comfortably for another year or two without working. And then there's my dad's restaurant chain. I could do very well for myself if I give in and take over one of the locations as he had hoped. He still hopes it, actually–bringing it up almost every week in his grumpy, guilt-trip way. I suppose I just like the idea of being an entrepreneur. Making my own path.

I don't have the success Dad has yet, what with his eight restaurants–it's just me and one limo. White-glove treatment. And that's the way I like it for now.

I'm leaning against the back panel of the limo when January finally emerges with a coif so perfect, she glows. Her hair is silky and full, cascading over her shoulders in brilliant, gleaming waves. I have to look away–it's like staring directly into the sun.

I dip my head as I open the door for her. I am not going to say a word. I'm consciously pressing my lips together lest something come out of my mouth that I'll regret.

She stops right next to the open door, striking a pose even I can see with my eyes cast down.

"How do I look?"

"Very nice," I mumble, still focusing on the ground.

She clicks her tongue. "You're not even looking."

For heaven's sake, why doesn't she just get in the car already? Does she not get enough attention from every single hot-blooded male on this entire planet? Why does she need approval from me?

"I saw you walking toward the car," I say with a tone as even as possible.

"Thomas would always give me his opinion," she says.

I grit my teeth. "Well, I am not Thomas as we have already established."

She huffs with a definitive pout and I find myself slipping off my sunglasses and ever so slowly raising my eyes to meet hers. My heart catches in my throat from her beauty. It's one thing to see photos and videos of gorgeous celebrities from a distance—when there's no danger of internally combusting from the sheer magnitude of their good looks. Here, inches away from this exquisite woman, I'm struck with a strange feeling in my chest I don't particularly care for. My pulse pounds in places I didn't even know I had a pulse. My belly stirs, off-kilter. It's a sensation akin to losing control of the wheel and free-falling off a bridge to certain death.

I don't like this, getting caught in her enchantment—sucked into idolizing the glittery life she leads. And then I realize this is her thing. She almost can't help herself, like she feeds off of admiration. And that both irks me and saddens me at the same time.

My gaze falls over her, soaking her in like sweet bread dipped in milk. She looks good. She doesn't need me to tell her that. She knows it as a universal truth—a scientific fact, if you will—like Newton's law of motion. But she's fishing. She's fishing because she can. Because nobody has ever told her otherwise. Telling her otherwise would be a lie.

And I may be a lot of things, but I'm no liar.

"You look…" I swallow hard, suddenly very aware that whatever I say would just be one more compliment for her to collect. One more among a sea of others. I could say, "You're stunning. Your beauty is unsurpassed. Kings fall down at your feet from sheer awe."

But I can't bring myself to make my mouth work other than to say, "You look… fine."

It's the truth. She does look fine. Oh so very, very fine.

She pulls a face, clearly displeased with my answer, and settles inside the car. I can't shut the door fast enough.

Sliding into the driver's seat, I activate the ignition, and through the open partition, I ask in a professional tone, "Back to the penthouse, Miss?"

She digs into her purse and produces a tube of lip gloss, taking her time unscrewing the top, lathering it on her lips, back and forth, back and forth. Once she's effectively drenched her mouth in a pink, frosty glaze, she smacks her lubricated lips together with exceedingly wicked delight.

"No. I don't think so," she says finally, whipping her hand around. "I think I do need to do some shopping after all. Rodeo Drive, please."

Of course she decides to go shopping on a whim. I should push back. I really should. Tell her she needs to schedule her transportation in advance. But I'm mildly intrigued by her. Besides, as we pull in front of Louis Vuitton, she tells me she'll only be about twenty minutes picking out a new handbag. I'm sure there's no shortage of handbags in her life. But hey. Why not buy another one? I imagine her to have one of those walk-in closets with remote control drawers and hidden compartments of jewels and shoes just like in that *Princess Diaries* movie my sister would watch obsessively.

True to her word, January's back in eighteen minutes with two shopping bags on her arm. She's quick when she knows what she wants, I'll give her that. Relieved we got that out of the way, I'm ready to take her back to the hotel, but she insists on stopping at a few more stores. I check the time. This is cutting it too close for my taste. She doesn't buy anything else, though. Just window shops for another half hour.

"Shopping can be so boring," she announces.

I couldn't agree more.

"Well," I say. "It's been an educational afternoon, but I think it's time to head back to the hotel."

"The hotel?" she cries. "No. Have you seen the state of my fingernails? I can't be interviewed on *Breakfast Hollywood* like this."

Breakfast Hollywood? She's going on that ridiculous morning show hosted by the most plastic people in Tinseltown?

"And when will this interview take place?" I ask.

"The day after tomorrow, silly. Don't you have access to my calendar?"

Apparently not.

She rattles off the address of her nail place, and now I'm getting nervous. How long is this going to take? I have just under an hour before I have to pick up Tía Lucy, and she better not lollygag, either. Knowing her, she'll want me to make a few laps around her neighborhood while she waves like the Queen of England at the busybodies on her street.

As I let January out of the car, I'm reminded of the three-plus hours I waited for her to get a blow-out. This nail thing could possibly take forever.

"I'll return shortly to pick you up?" I ask.

She shrugs. "Half-hour, forty-five minutes."

As soon as she's out of sight, I'm in my car, flying across town. I dial Francesca on the Bluetooth.

"How long does it take to get your nails done?"

"Hello to you, brother," she says.

"Please just answer the question." I'll apologize later; for now, I need answers.

"I don't know. Am I getting toes, too, or just fingers?"

How the heck am I supposed to know this? I suppose someone like January would get the works.

"Uh, toes," I say.

Francesca hums, calculating beauty equations in her head.

"Well, if I'm going to get paraffin wax, a foot massage, and gel nails… I'm gonna say at least an hour and a half."

"Really? Are you sure?"

"Absolutely. Everybody knows it takes over an hour for a mani pedi."

I guess that makes sense considering it took over three hours just for the hair.

"Thanks, *hermana*."

Before I can hang up, she says, "You'll be here at four, right?"

My heart races as I check the time again. My spur-of-the-moment plan was to pick up Tía Lucy early, drop her off at my parents' house, rush back for January, take her to the hotel, and bolt back again to my parents' house for Francesca. It would mean she'd be later than she wants, but she'd still make it on time. That is, if the little princess doesn't want to shop for more handbags.

"I might be a little late," I admit. "But I'll get you to the Gala on time. I promise."

Even if I have to tow January Madison along with me.

"Enrique, I'm doing 'The Hair Song' by Carner and

Gregor. It goes to an E-6. I can't go into that cold. It's all sorts of coloratura arpeggios and syncopated rhythms."

I'm getting a huge headache. "Francesca, I know you're speaking English, but I have no clue what you just said."

She sighs. "I guess I'll just take my Pinto."

"Nope. No. You're not driving that thing to a Bel Air mansion just to break down halfway there."

Google Maps wizzes through my head, I'm playing back the route to the Gala. Maybe I could make this work.

"Can you be ready in twenty minutes?"

Francesca laughs. "I'm ready now."

Of course she is.

At this point, I'm halfway to Tía Lucy's house. I know I'm risking traffic and all sorts of things, but what choice do I have? Francesca agrees to call Tía Lucy, making sure she's waiting for me outside so we can get a move-on. When I arrive, my aunt is nowhere to be found. In fact, when I park the limo and knock on her door, she takes what seems like forever to answer.

"I'm on a time crunch," I remind her. "Didn't Francesca tell you?"

"Yes, yes. Let me just grab my fascinator."

Her fascinator? What the heck is a fascinator?

She disappears inside her house for another minute or two and emerges wearing a flowing cape and a hat-like thing, which looks like a peacock died on her head. She struts out; gliding down the walkway like it's her own personal red carpet.

I usher her into the limo. "Tía, I thought you were just making *Rosca de Reyes* tonight."

"Por favor de Dios," she replies. "I like to dress fancy for the three kings. *Los Reyes Magos* deserve it."

Oookaaay.

I break more traffic laws than I care to admit while dropping off my aunt, then driving Francesca to her Gala. I don't even have time to complain about her neckline. I suppose it's modest enough for a glitzy Hollywood Gala.

Miraculously, I make record time. With all the back and forth, I've managed to return to the nail salon an hour and twenty minutes after dropping January off. I imagine her sitting under a fan or something while her polish dries, and I'll be casually waiting for her with a smile on my face.

But when I pull up, she storms out of the front door like she'd been watching for me from the window ready to pounce. I barely have a moment to jog around to the passenger side.

"I specifically told you half-hour to forty-five minutes, Mr. Progresso. Where the heck were you?"

She is positively fuming, stomping her foot. And did she just call me Mr. Progresso?

"I… did you finish early?"

"Do you even know how to tell time? I have been waiting for over an hour. Thank goodness the salon owner keeps basil iced tea stocked for me. I would have fainted from dehydration."

Okay, I know I messed up, but she's being a tad dramatic here. And grossly exaggerating her wait time.

"So, if you've been waiting over an hour, then you were done in what… fifteen minutes?"

"I didn't check the exact time, dude. You're late. That is all."

"Everybody knows it takes over an hour for a mani pedi," I say, quoting my sister.

I know, I know. It's not a good idea to argue with the client. They're in charge. And as far as January's concerned, I'm just the help. A lowly, inconsequential peasant. The downstairs staff. A minion whose sole existence is to bow before the greatness of her charmed life. I knew a lot of girls like that at Berkley—if you don't have a trust fund or belong to a country club, they look down their noses at you.

"What would you know about mani pedis?" she says, getting in my face. We're toe-to-toe, and her little hand is perched on her hip while she stares me down. So freaking close.

This woman is making me lose my ever-loving mind. Between the Barf Girl incident, getting the bait and switch treatment from Matthew Madison, Tía Lucy and her fascinator, and now, with this heiress pushing every button she can, I'm basically dry brush in Calabasas during fire season.

And is she getting my name wrong on purpose? Mr. Progresso? Hilarious.

And I can't help it. Her little reactions to me are too delicious. I meet her glower head on, closing the gap between us until her nose is less than an inch from mine. She is trying so hard to maintain a scowl, but I can tell that the proximity of our faces—of our lips—is breaking down her moxie.

"Well, here's the rub, February," I say, tilting my head ever so slightly as if angling to kiss her. "I happen to know a lot of things that would surprise you."

Her nostrils flare. "Doubtful."

Call me crazy, but I get the feeling January Madison,

heiress to the Madison Hotel fortune and Hollywood socialite, is enjoying this little tête-à-tête. Just as much as I am.

Leaning in closer so my breath caresses the shell of her ear, I whisper, "So. Many. Things."

Her body shivers in the wake of my near-touch, and I'm thinking she'll forget all about my tiny time mishap. That she'll consider me worth the wait. Maybe driving little miss won't be so bad after all.

I feel the cool weight of her as she places her delicate palm on my chest. Her fingernails graze the fabric of my shirt, freshly sharpened like a small, feral animal. She gives me the tiniest of scratches. Then shoves me.

It doesn't hurt—the scratching—but I clutch at my collar just the same.

"Watch the raccoon hands, sister."

She laughs. Even her laugh is like a feral animal.

"I knew you'd be a psycho," she says, sliding in the limo.

I shut her in as I say under my breath, "And I knew you'd be a pain in my ass."

Chapter Five
ENRIQUE

"You said *what?*"

"Nothing, Ma," I say over my shoulder. Didn't realize she was listening to me tell the story of yesterday's debacle to a couple of my brothers, Nate and Ignacio. My mother has ears like a wolf.

"You don't speak that way to a lady," she says, sweeping into the kitchen to grab plates for our weekly family dinner. She insists on using her fine china. With seven sons and a husband with butterfingers, I've told her many times to just use paper, but she insists. That's why the place settings are a hodgepodge of several sets. Mostly chipped. And mostly due to Dad's aforementioned butterfingers.

"Haven't I taught you better?" she adds.

"That elite school I paid for better have," Dad shouts from the living room. Apparently the whole family's listening to my conversation. Mom just rolls her eyes because we've been through this a thousand times. Dad was never on board with sending us to private school, but Mom never backed down. Whenever Dad complains that the 'elite' school didn't tame his wild-mannered kids, Mom comes back with, "We got a priest out of the deal." To which Dad responds, "A priest and seven demonios."

They have this exchange at least once a week.

I purposefully came into the kitchen to avoid contact with the rest of the family.

"We missed you at church," she continues, ignoring Dad. "You went earlier, then?"

I sigh. "No, Ma. I slept in."

I don't add how I was so upset from yesterday's fiasco with January, I didn't fall asleep until four AM. Mom shakes her head solemnly as though I've dashed all her hopes and dreams.

"I failed you," she laments. The mom guilt is strong with this one.

"You haven't failed me. I was just tired, that's all." Also, I really didn't feel like going. I'm a disappointment to all Catholic moms everywhere.

She brightens. "You're lucky Memo is coming tonight. He'll hear your confession."

"Not gonna happen."

The last thing I want is for my big brother to know how messed up I am. Let's just say I have a less-than-stellar conscience.

My eyes snag on one of Mom's junk sculptures. I don't know where she finds so much junk metal and broken knickknacks, but my mother has made a hobby out of what she calls 'art of discarded things'. We all humor her efforts.

"Ooh, what's that?" I'm laying it on extra thick just to change the subject.

"You like it?" Her face beams at seeing me take in an eyeful of her latest masterpiece.

"It's… interesting," I say, turning my head to the side. "What is it?"

"Can't you tell? It's Don Quixote. The wisk is his sword."

"Oh. Yeah." I can kind of see it if I squint my eyes and turn my head to the side.

"Anyway, I'm glad you like it. I made it for you."

"ME?"

Nate snickers in the corner like the weasel he is. "It's gorgeous, Mom. It'll look perfect in Enrique's house."

I throw him my death glare. "I can't wait to see what she has in store for you."

I kiss my mom on her cheek. "Thanks, Mom."

"Ignacio, do you like it?" she calls out.

My brother stops his chopping for a second, looks over his shoulder, and grunts. "Yeah. Wasn't Don Quixote insane? That's why he went after those windmills? Then it's perfect for Enrique."

Mom smiles adoringly at Ignacio. "Don Quixote was at least chivalrous to women. An attribute my sons would do well to learn."

Ignacio snorts and returns to his chopping. He's preparing the meal today only because Dad can't bear to leave his lucky chair while the Rams are winning. Otherwise, it's Battle of the Top Chef every Sunday between them. Usually, Mom actively avoids the kitchen, which makes me suspicious that she's even in here.

Dad lovingly calls her *chismosa* (because it's way more fun to say than 'nosey') when she finds her way into a private conversation. Now Tía Lucy is sticking her nose in the kitchen, which pretty much guarantees the whole neighborhood will get wind of this before we can say grace.

"*Que descraciados*," she says in typical Tía Lucy fashion. "Kids these days."

My Uncle Enrique—yes, we share the same name—grunts his agreement from the living room.

Thank you, peanut gallery.

I was named after Tío Enrique, but that's where the similarities end. Currently, he's on his eleven-hundredth beer, so it seems. When he's like this—like this meaning three sheets to the wind—he agrees with anything people say and laughs at everything.

Nate pours himself a bowl of cereal, which earns him a smack in the head from Ignacio. "Can't you wait ten minutes?"

"I'm hungry." Nate shoves a spoonful into his mouth

and slugs me in the arm on his way out of the kitchen. "Good luck, buddy."

Thanks for your support. I'll remember you having my back.

I level my eyes with Mom, which means I have to squat about three feet. "January Madison is a spoiled rich brat. I was just suppressing her expectations."

She throws me the disapproving mom face. "She can't help being born rich any more than you can help being born with big feet."

"*Que grande piesotas* ever on a baby," chirps Tío Enrique, laughing with a mouthful of chips. "Chupacabra."

Why is he even listening to this conversation?

"I grew into my feet," I say. "Besides, I don't go around flaunting my feet for everyone to see. And walking all over people with them just because I feel entitled to do so."

I wouldn't mind using said foot to kick January's perfect little butt, though. Great. Now I have that image in my head.

"Nevertheless," says Mom, using my proximity to sneak in a one-arm hug. "I want you to be nice."

She winks at me and takes the dishes out to the back patio where we have a big farm table set up for our Sunday dinners.

"Why don't you do quinceañeras? There's lots of money in quinceañeras," says Tía Lucy. She clicks her tongue disapprovingly and follows Mom out.

"I'm with *you* on this one," says Ignacio, tossing me a reassuring smile before getting back to his cooking. It's some kind of Indian tikka masala, curry fusion dish and it smells divine. But Ignacio's telling Dad it's mole. "She sounds like a piece of work."

At least I have one person on my side. I leave the kitchen to go find Francesca to ask how her concert went last night after I dropped her off. I didn't have it in me to hear about it when I took her back home afterward. I have to pass the Precio testosterone convention to get to the staircase leading to Francesca's room. There's Dad and Uncle Enrique in the La-Z-Boys shouting at the TV, and I'm almost home free when my uncle slurs, "*Oye*, bigfoot. *Da me una chela.*"

Yeah, no. He can get his own beer. I just flash him a peace sign and he sloppy grins.

My phone pings right when Francesca opens her door for me and I sit on the end of her bed to check the email. I curse at my phone when I see the contents.

"Language," says Francesca. I roll my eyeballs to the back of my head.

"Uh, I mean... oh, gosh darn."

She scrunches her cute face in a satisfied grin. "Better."

She goes back to what she was doing before I walked in —restringing her guitar—but the suspense is killing her. She can never get a hold of her FOMO. She tosses her guitar on her pillow and scoots right up against me. "Are you going to keep me wondering what that outburst is about?"

I stretch my arm far, far away from her. She'd have to climb over me to get to my phone. It's driving her nuts. She's practically shaking with curiosity.

"Ah, just some boring work stuff," I say.

"Lemme see. Is it a girl? What's her name?"

It's about a girl. But not in a fun way.

Francesca pokes my side, and I hate that she knows my only tickle spot. I cave and surrender my phone. She snatches it like a hungry monkey, reading the email from Mr. Madison's assistant: VTaylor@madisonindustriesinc.com.

Her name's obviously not Judy, then. Well, not that I thought it was, but still. I wonder what the V stands for. Vicky? Veronica? Wouldn't the signature line show her full name instead of just Ms. V Taylor? I must know.

"I don't get it," says Francesca. "What's got you all worked up over this? It's just dates and addresses. And what's JM?"

"Give me that."

I snatch my phone back and smooth Francesca's imaginary fingerprints away with my sleeve. I guess I'm a little protective of my stuff.

"JM stands for January Madison." Francesca's jaw drops, but I hold up a finger insanely close to her nose. "And before you say anything, I'm not thrilled about this. I was supposed to have an exclusive contract with Matthew Madison and his fancy executives, but instead he's got me shuttling his brat around all over the city."

I swipe up to reveal the details. "Fashion show. Photoshoot. Pedicure. Bleh! Look at this. Five days in Palm Springs."

"Sounds like fun to me." My baby sister winks at me with dimples that match mine. Out of all my siblings, she's the one who looks like me the most.

"You wouldn't say that if you met her."

"How bad can it be? She's in the back seat. So don't talk to her."

Ah, Francesca, ye know not what ye sayeth. Something about that spoiled rich girl makes me want to say exactly what's on my mind, and say it right in her face. No one's ever gotten under my skin like that. Maybe it's the ridiculous dose of beauty God gave her, mixed with the personality of a T-Rex. It's unnatural. It's warm, gooey chocolate chip cookies right out of the oven topped with garlic paste. It's so jarring it makes my skin prickle with an acute awareness of her every move. Anything that comes out of her mouth shoots straight up my spine. Even those pouty sighs.

"Tried that. It's like she's trying to push my buttons and I can't help but spar with her.

Francesca wrinkles her nose in thought. I can tell she's trying to sympathize with me but inwardly laughing at my plight.

"Kill her with kindness," she says, like it's the simplest thing in the world. Judging by what I know of January, she'll see right through that and make my life in hell even hotter. I mean, burning. No. Grrr. Nothing is hot or burning when it comes to January. Nothing at all.

"So how did your hair song coloring pages do?" I ask, grateful for anything to bring up to change the subject.

"Coloring pages?"

"You know." I mimic an opera singer, floating my hand up.

She shoves my shoulder. "Coloratura. It's basically a musical term for insanely high notes."

"Okay. How did it go?"

"Amazing. And I made a new friend."

My crazy sister. She makes friends everywhere she goes. Sometimes I wonder if we're related.

A boom of intense shouting comes from the living room. Uncle Enrique is the loudest of them all, but Mom is a close second. That could only mean one thing. Mom finally broke and I'm not about to miss it.

Francesca widens her eyes in delight. "Let's go."

We run downstairs to see what all the racket is about, and there's Mom, chasing Tío Enrique around the living room. Ignacio, Nate, and our other brother Mateo are standing to the side watching with amusement. All they need are 3D glasses and a bowl of popcorn and they'd be that Michael Jackson meme.

I only caught the tail end of the show before Tío Enrique goes to the back patio, flippantly saying over his shoulder. *"No pasa nada."*

My siblings collectively gasp.

"No pasa nada?" cries Mom. *"No. Pasa. NADA?"*

Oh boy.

My mom is pretty chill most of the time, but there are just some things one simply does not do.

Never get out of the car to direct Mom's parallel parking as if she were landing a plane. If you do, she'll gun it and run you over. Second, never tell her to calm down. This includes variations such as. *"tranquila,"* *"calmate,"* and "Take it easy."

Trust me. It won't end well.

And finally, never, *ever* say, *"No pasa nada."* Unless you have a death wish. Also, any combination of the above will result in cataclysmic wrath. For example.

"Tranquila, mujer. No pasa nada." Which translates to "Calm down, woman. Nothing's going to happen." Which, ironically is the exact same thing Tío Enrique said to Mom

years ago when he gave my little brother Sebastian mango slices with the peeling still attached. Right before Sebastian almost choked.

Presently, Mom's in the backyard ripping my uncle a new one. I kinda feel sorry for the guy, but knowing him, he probably deserves it.

"What did he do?" I ask my brothers. But it's Tía Lucy who answers as she hobbles past us toward the kitchen.

"Your mamá caught him cutting his nails on the coffee table."

Francesca fakes throwing up.

"Toes or finger?" I ask anyone who will answer.

"Does it matter?" says Ignacio. "It's disgusting either way."

Nate bobs his head to the side considering Ignacio's statement. "One is considerably grosser than the other, you have to admit that."

"Agreed," says Francesca. "Either way, I think I'll stay out of that room until it's had a deep clean."

Mateo shrugs and takes a seat next to Dad, who is blissfully watching the game and out of the line of fire.

"Where did Tía Lucy go?" Ignacio asks, looking around.

"I think she went in the kitchen to doctor your tikka masala," I say.

Nothing gets Ignacio to move faster than when someone is in his kitchen. Technically it's Dad's kitchen, but Ignacio took it over today, and he is just as protective of his cooking space as Dad is. I'm glad one of us took after our dad because who would run all the Dos Panchos restaurants Dad intended for us?

A minute later, Tía Lucy runs back out of the kitchen to the front door. "Your man friend is here, Panchita."

"I'll get it, Tía." Francesca starts toward the front but has to pass me and my other brothers first. I stop her with my arm. Nate and Mateo join me to form a circle around our little sister.

"What's the gringo doing here?" demands Mateo.

Francesca crosses her arms defiantly. "He has a name, which you so rudely forget, and he's practically family."

That boy Edmund. He's been coming around since they were in first grade. What, eighteen years or so. He's indecisive, doesn't have a real job, and he's not good enough for Francesca.

"Just because he comes over every other Sunday doesn't make him family," I say. "We don't want to see you hurt, Panchita."

"If I get hurt... *brother*... it will be on my terms. Not yours. Besides, we're just friends."

Nate snickers at that. "Does *he* know that?"

"What's that supposed to mean?" Francesca says.

"Just make sure he knows we're having a family meeting tonight. He leaves as soon as he's done eating."

"Fine." Francesca hurries off and I can hear her trying to get Tía Lucy to leave Edmund alone.

Who knew I could ever use a lame excuse like *'family meeting'* to get rid of dudes coming after my sister? And what is this so-called meeting about anyway? My parents host a dinner every Sunday. Are they just calling it a meeting to make sure we all show up? Ahem, cough Memo. Cough-cough.

Slowly but surely the rest of my brothers arrive, as well

as Tío Pedro. Sebastian blasts in, making fart jokes. As a college undergrad, he still hasn't grown out of adolescence, apparently. I'm pretty sure he still burps the alphabet, too.

We're all so proud.

Ignacio's tikka masala is to die for. After Dad complained the 'flour tortillas' were too thick, Ignacio finally explained the dish was not actually the traditional Mexican dish, mole, but rather an Indian meal.

"They're not tortillas, Dad," he'd said. "It's naan bread."

Tío Enrique smothered guajillo salsa on his plate and heated himself some corn tortillas, essentially Mexicanizing the Indian food Ignacio had prepared.

Dad thought it a vast improvement to add avocado and practically threw the other half at Francesca. "Panchita, eat the avocado."

She pushed it aside. "I don't want avocado, thanks."

"Then suffer. I don't care."

Then Mom pinched him under the table and he apologized. Edmund, trying to suck up no doubt, ate the other half of Dad's avocado saying he wouldn't want it to get brown. I really don't know what my sister sees in him but I'm glad he listened and left when dinner was over. He's not a bad person, but he's also not the right person for my sister. Unfortunately, Mom and our oldest brother,

Guillermo, love him and that's as good as an open invitation to break Francesca's heart when he changes his mind about what he wants to do with his life… again.

Now that dinner's over, Tío Pedro filled his plastic containers with leftovers, Tío Enrique went who knows where, and Tía Lucy's in the kitchen washing dishes.

All the siblings are together, which is no small feat. Dad chose tonight for the super secretive family meeting before Sebastian goes back to school next week. Guillermo, who's rarely available on Sundays, made an exception at Mom's insistence.

It's just us eight kids, Mom, and Dad at the table now. We're drinking hot chocolate with the king's bread Lucy made. We all fought to get a piece without the plastic baby Jesus inside because whoever gets the baby in their slice has to make tamales on February 2nd. So far, no one is fessing up to it.

Dad clears his throat and taps on the table to get our attention.

"Well, I'm already tired, so I'm gonna get right to it."

We all exchange a worried look. The Precios don't do family meetings. We're not the freaking Brady Bunch. So when Mom and Dad demanded every one of us attend dinner tonight, we feared the worst. Could it be Dad's health? Or worse. Are Mom and Dad splitting?

Dad continues. "When I first came here from Mexico…"

Oh, boy, here we go.

"I didn't have anything but the clothes on my back and a twenty-dollar bill."

"We know this story, Dad," says Sebastian. "You've told us many times."

We're all thinking it, but Sebastian is the only one young and tactless enough to say it. Dad's a little crestfallen at losing the opportunity to tell his origin story… again. He looks around at all of us for confirmation.

"I told you this?"

We all reply in concert, "YES!"

"The first thing you ate when you crossed the border was Taco Bell," says Mateo. "And you said to yourself, 'Self, I can make a better taco,' so you opened your own restaurant."

"No," says Dad. "First, I got a jov as a dishwasher."

"Job, Dad. J-O-B…ba ba ba."

Oh Sebastian, why does he have to be so argumentative? All that lawyering he does at school I suppose.

"Jo-o-o-o-vvvvv," Dad attempts. It's beyond his skillset, let's just leave it at that.

"And you didn't speak a lick of English," adds Nate. "But you worked hard every day until you met Pancho Two."

Everybody groans. Pancho Two is Dad's business partner and start-up investor, and we don't really like the guy. Dad was working as a sous chef at a steakhouse when they met. Pancho Two was a sales vendor and would come around, getting chummy with the cooks. I'm fuzzy on the details as to how they became friends. Maybe it's because they're both named Francisco. Eventually, they partnered together to open Dos Panchos Restaurant and Cantina. The rest is history. Or at least, the Precio family history.

To confuse things more, Dad sometimes calls him Tocayo, which in Spanish is something you call a guy who shares your name. In my case, Tío Enrique is my tocayo but let's not even go there right now, especially after the toenail incident. Since Pancho is a nickname for Francisco, we call Dad's tocayo Pancho Two.

Are you following me so far? I'm twenty-nine and it's taken me my whole life to figure this out, so don't feel bad one bit.

Guillermo, ever the peacemaker in the family, speaks up. "Let's just allow Dad to finish his story."

"If we don't help him along," replies Dante. "We'll be here all night."

"If you guys don't stop interrupting," argues Ignacio. "We *will* be here all night."

Mom pats Dad on the arm. "Why don't you get to the good part?"

Dad pauses for dramatic effect. It's one of his trademarks. "I worked hard for years and years until we could open another location. Then another. And I said to your mother, 'This isn't for us. This is for the kids.' And so we opened a fourth restaurant when Enrique was born. More kids. More restaurants."

"We didn't think we'd have so many," adds Mom.

"EIGHT," cries Dad, crossing himself. "Que Dios me ayude. But I kept my promise. Eight kids. Eight restaurants."

"We wanted each of you to take ownership of a Dos Panchos so you won't have to struggle like your dad did," says Mom with a shrug because she knows how we feel about it. It's been an ongoing argument in our household ever since Dante announced in kindergarten that he wanted to be an astronaut. He didn't become an astronaut, but that doesn't stop Dad from getting salty. We know Dad had plans for us, and we're grateful, but the restaurant business isn't for everybody.

"I wanted to leave each of you a legacy. It's not for me. It wasn't ever for me or your Mom. It's always been for each of you. But no. You don't want it. You all would rather do your own thing."

I really think my dad missed his calling as a Jewish mother. He's got the guilt thing when talking to his kids down like a fine art.

"But…" Another dramatic pause. I'm telling you, he's the master. "We came up with a solution."

"Dad," I interject, "I think I speak for everyone when I say we don't expect anything."

"I agree," says Mateo. "We all have our careers. Ignacio's the one who should take over the business."

"What career, Mateo?" Dad says. "Music?"

"Dad," says Francesca. "You've got years and years ahead of you. Years. Right?"

"I'm not dying, if that's what you're asking. I just want to retire. Ay que la madre! Ignacio, you tell them."

All eyes swoop to Ignacio who's all poise and seriousness. He folds his hands on the table like a CEO at a board meeting.

"Basically, we have two options," he says. "One, sell the restaurants and divide the monies between all eight of us. Of course we'd be selling the Dos Panchos name and concept, so I'd have to sell my restaurant, too. We also couldn't guarantee the new owners will keep the staff that's been working there for years."

Everyone grumbles, saying they hate that idea.

"Option number two," he continues, "is that I buy you all out."

"What do you mean, buy us out?" says Sebastian. "Legally, these are Dad's restaurants. And what about Pancho Two?"

"I told you before," says Dad. "Eight kids. Eight restaurants. It was always for you. Not me. You."

"Pancho Two is willing to take his percentage," says Ignacio. "He's already exceeded his original agreement with Dad. This would be good for him."

"So how would this work?" asks Nate. "Ignacio's just going to take over all Dad's responsibilities?"

I look Ignacio right in the eye. "How are you going to run eight restaurants *and* your fancy catering business? That's a lot."

"Have you ever heard of a thing called delegation? Each location has a manager and executive chef. Just like Dad's been doing for years. Your little limo driving thing doesn't have any employees."

"Let Enrique have his fun," says Mom. "He likes cars. Remember when you had that red toy car, Enrique?" Here she addresses the whole table. "He named that car Leon and took it everywhere."

"Mom!" I cry.

She goes on. "One day, Leon went missing. I was worried he'd get upset. But Enrique just said Leon had gone on vacation. He didn't' seem concerned about it. Then, a few months later, boom. We found Leon at someone's house. Whose house was that, Francisco?"

"Mom, please," I say. "Can we get back on track?"

Dad shakes his head at mom. "It wasn't anybody's house. He left Leon at Sunday school."

"No, you're wrong." She rolls her eyes dramatically. "All I'm saying is if you want to drive a limo, Enrique, you can drive a limo."

"Four years at Berkley," grumbles Dad. "Four years. For what?"

"I'd like to think I'm putting my business degree to good use," I say.

"Okay," says Ignacio. "Let's just circle back to the restaurants."

"I don't want to leave Mom and Dad without their income," says Dante.

"Believe me," says Mom. "We're not hurting at all. And Dad will still work."

"I want to go into business with your uncles," Dad says. "Internet sales."

"We can go to Florence," adds Mom.

"Or Portugal."

"Oh, can we go on one of those river cruises? Like on the commercials?" Mom is off on a tangent, like we aren't even in the room.

"Anyway," says Ignacio. "Dad and I estimate each restaurant would sell for one point five million... give or take, depending on what the market value is today. Obviously, I don't have ten million dollars in the bank to pay all of you, but I crunched some numbers, and we can realistically part with ten grand per month out of each location's revenue. It would go to the bank of your choice, you can set up investment accounts, you can blow it all in Vegas, I don't care what you do with it. In about eleven years, you'll all be millionaires. Unless, of course, you blow it in Vegas."

"No." Memo stands up, shaking his head adamantly. "I can't agree to this."

"I thought he might say that," says Mom.

Dad slams his hand on the table. "It's his legacy. The other kids get theirs, Memo gets his."

"I took a vow of poverty," says Memo.

"Okay, okay." Ignacio holds up his palms and gestures for Memo to sit down. "Memo can give his portion to charity."

"That's *Father* Memo to you," says Mom.

"If we're being technical," I say for argument's sake, "It's Father *Francis*."

I think my Dad feels proud Memo chose St. Francis when he took his vows—after Dad's own namesake. As long as he doesn't start calling him Father Pancho, I'm good.

"I think we should all give to charity," says Francesca.

"So in other words, give it to you and Mateo," teases Nate.

Mateo throws his hands up. "I'm not a charity case. Why is everyone always bagging on my career?"

"It's not a career," cries Dad.

Dante points his finger at Mateo. "You borrowed money from me twice last month."

"It was Christmas time. Everyone's strapped at Christmas."

"Not Dante," says Sebastian. "Even I had money saved from my summer job. And I'm a student."

All at once, everybody's talking over one another, trying

to figure out how Dad can keep the restaurants, or maybe pass them down to just Ignacio because he's the one who's worked the hardest.

A piercing whistle cuts through the noise and we all turn to see Tía Lucy at the door with her fingers still in her mouth. She pulls a face and wipes the saliva from her fingers on her apron.

"I just want to let you know," she says sweetly, "that they can hear you in outer space. Captain Kirk called. He's trying to get some sleep."

My mom has three sisters, but only Tía Lucy can stand the Precio men enough to come over every Sunday. She marches to the beat of her own drum anyway. Shaking her hips side to side, she glides to the table and cuts a piece of king's bread.

"So?" says Ignacio. "Can we come to an agreement?"

Francesca gets up from her chair and goes to Dad, hugging him from behind. "Is this really what you want, Daddy?"

"Sí, Panchita. It is."

She gives Ignacio a resolved look and nods. Dante does, too, followed by every one of us, including Memo.

"There's a town in Puerto Rico where the fathers and nuns go down to work," Memo says thoughtfully. "They could use the help."

"Okay." Ignacio releases a big breath. "Meeting adjourned."

"Aggghh, noooo!" Tía Lucy cries out.

Francesca rushes to her. "What?"

Tía Lucy digs the plastic Jesus doll out of her bread and holds it up. "I got the baby."

Chapter Six

JANUARY

"And we're back with more *Breakfast Hollywood*, your favorite morning show keeping you company with the latest celebrity news. Hold on to your organic Greek yogurt because we have January Madison joining us in our studio. January, we're thrilled you could make it today."

"Happy to be here."

Bright lights. An uncomfortable couch. The two *Breakfast Hollywood* hosts smiling back at me with so much Botox, I wonder if it hurts them to move their faces. Brock Tanner has been doing this show since I was a baby, so that really says something about how he doesn't seem to age. From where I'm sitting, I can tell he's wearing enough makeup to frost a cake.

Cassandra Cross, on the other hand, is only in her third year on *Breakfast Hollywood* after Brock's previous co-host left in a scandalous cover-up. Cassandra swept in as the replacement without anyone batting an eye. That's how confident she is at winning America's hearts with her feathered blond hair and orange spray tan.

Daytime television is a different vibe than other forms of media. Even late-night talk shows aren't as fast-paced as a morning news program. The segments are short and punchy, and being here feels like I'm on a tinsel town assembly line. Hair and makeup. Greenroom. Briefing with the producer. Wireless mic. Five minutes to make my plug. But everyone knows the hosts control the conversation. They want the gossip to boost ratings. I just need two of those five minutes to push my line of dog products.

"So, January," begins Cassandra. "How are you holding up after your breakup with popstar Jonny Z?"

Okay, first of all, we only dated for two weeks. And second, I was the one to break things off.

"Couldn't be better," I say. "It was an amicable split. Completely mutual."

"That's not what I hear," she says with a brow wag. "Here's a tweet from two days ago."

A screenshot of Jonny's tweet shows up on the monitor screen, which I'm sure is what the live audience is seeing right now while Cassandra reads it.

"He tweeted, 'I'm devastated and heartbroken. I'll never stop loving January.'" Cassandra pauses for dramatic effect, hand to her heart. "Wow. Fans are all over this. Here's just one of many fan tweets."

Oh good grief, do I really have to sit through this?

Another tweet appears on the screen which Cassandra reads. "Zoomer1998 tweets, 'Totally unfair. Ruined my week.' What do you have to say about that, January?"

Is she kidding me right now?

"Well, Cassandra, I hope zoomer1998 has a better week soon, and what better way to cheer up our fans than with puppies?"

I wave to the animal handlers my PR group hired to bring a few dogs to model my new line of accessories. Thank goodness Brock chimes in.

"Ah yes, you've brought some furry friends with you," he says.

An assistant director escorts the handlers onto the set while Brock continues. "While we're waiting for the puppies to get into position, tell us, January. Do you think Jonny Z will write about your breakup on his next album?"

"I really couldn't say."

"How will this affect your work going forward?"

"Not sure there'd be any impact at all seeing as I'm not a songwriter, Brock. But I do write checks for Kanines for Kids thanks to generous viewers like yours who make it possible by ordering couture accessories for their pets."

"Is this reminiscent of the falling out you had with your best friend and costar Shauna LeRay on season three of *The Real Babes of Beverly Hills*?"

Leave it to a gossip show to dig up old news. The reality

show was a big mistake, but I stuck it out for Shauna until she could get another soap opera contract. But the producers wanted to spice things up so they cooked up a love triangle that drove a fake wedge between Shauna and me. The show was canceled shortly after.

"That's water under the bridge, Brock. Shauna and I are closer than ever. Speaking of closer, how about we get a close-up of this little guy?"

I scoop up one of the puppies at my feet and make up a name for him. "Noodles is wearing one of our popular Waterford Crystal dog collars encrusted with marcasite and ruby dust."

"Oh, how nice for Noodles," he says condescendingly.

Cassandra chimes in, "It must be comforting to have dogs around to help you cope with your breakup."

"That's not why… I don't need comforting, not in the least bit."

Cassandra pouts her lips and wrinkles her brow as much as she can with the amount of plastic she has in her face.

"Even though you haven't tweeted about it, we know how hard this must be for you."

"Some might say silence is a sign of fault," adds Brock with a knowing nod. Then he looks at the camera. "So the question is, who broke up with who?"

"Whom," I say. Neither Brock nor Cassandra pay me any mind, though. They've already moved on, my line of dog products long forgotten and the clock is ticking on my time slot.

"We're going to take a break, but while we're gone, head on over to our Instagram stories and take the poll. Who's more heartbroken? Jonny Z or January Madison. We'll be right back." Brock winks at the camera as he signs off. And just like that, I'm dismissed. The next segment is a story about a woman who hasn't cut her nails in ten years. She's waiting in the wings with her enormous curly Q nails that sort of make me want to vomit equally as much as I'm intrigued about how she uses the bathroom with nails that long.

Brock gives me a lame shake of the hand which I immediately regret. There's something slimy about him. It's one of those core feelings I sometimes have about people. Cassandra skips a friendly dismissal altogether, in favor of a touch-up on her powder.

When I return to the limo, I have to knock on the window to get Enrique's attention. Thomas used to come inside the studios or wait by the car door. I never figured out how he'd know when I finished with my interviews or appointments, but he was always ever so reliable. This guy, though… ugh.

At least I'm not left waiting this time. He jumps into his role as soon as he sees me, opening the door for me and taking me to my next stop. Lunch with Shauna. I would almost say he's turned a corner and that his manners are…dare I say, pleasant…as he tips his hat and asks me where to go. Almost. He blasts Greenday music on the way there.

The funny thing is, he stands outside his limo, poised to open a door for me, the entire time I'm having lunch. Shauna is there when I arrive, having chosen a patio table. Enrique's parked on the street not thirty feet from us. His presence does not escape Shauna.

"Oooh. Is that your new driver? He's H-O-T hot. Where can I get me one of those?"

She wiggles in her chair and throws Enrique a flirty glance.

"Believe me, they broke the mold when they made him."

Shauna wags her brows at me. "Really now? Tell me… what does his *mold* look like? Is it jumbo-sized?"

"If we're talking about his ego, then yes."

She sips on her straw playfully. "If you say so, bestie."

I don't know why she uses that term with me. I wouldn't consider her my best friend. Then again, I don't really have anyone else I can even remotely call a friend. I grew up in Paris, traveled back and forth from New York to LA most of my adult life, and all the people I know are only interested in the parties and connections that comes with hanging out with me. At least Shauna knows me well enough to order my keto lunch for me ahead of time.

I snap a picture of my food with my phone, and then a selfie holding up my lemon basil iced tea. I see Enrique shake his head from the corner of my eye.

"So spill the tea," Shauna says, scrolling on her phone. She's barely touched her salad. "My Instagram is blowing up with Jonny Z gossip, but I'm like, shut up, people. My girl January will show the receipts."

By 'receipts' she means screenshots of texts with Jonny, and I'm not about to do that. Not like there's anything to screenshot. Like I said. We dated for two weeks.

"I high-key, low-key hate him, you know," she continues, still scrolling her phone. "Oh my gawd. Look at Kenna Sparks."

She turns her screen to show me Kenna Sparks's latest Instagram post. She's holding up her drink making a duck face. Her caption reads *#soyfoamcoconutmachalatte #newdaynewme #risewiththesun*

"I love her, she's so gorge. But she needs to aim lower. But she's so nice. I love her."

Right. I don't know Kenna Sparks well enough to comment, but I'm sure anything Shauna says is a gross exaggeration, even if Kenna really should aim lower. Maybe she'd like Jonny.

We finish lunch and part with air kisses. Shauna waves at Enrique before she goes on her way. He pretends not to notice even though every guy I know can't keep his eyes off her. I think it's her confidence…or how beautiful she is…or a combination of both.

Before I get in the limo, I slow down my pace to finish the caption on an Instagram post. I don't like to post while I'm eating in case someone stalks me at the restaurant. So I always post after I leave.

I can tell by his dramatic sigh that Enrique is growing impatient, holding the door open for me. For some reason that just makes me want to take my sweet, sweet time.

"Are you done, Your Highness?"

I hold up a finger. "Shh-shh-shh. Just a sec." Or maybe a few minutes. I'm in charge, here.

Just to get on his nerves, I add extra emojis, taking forever to pick them out. Enrique slides up beside me, invading my space with his imposing presence casting a shadow over me. He's practically breathing down my neck but I refuse to budge. This spot on the sidewalk? It's mine. However close he gets, I'm not swayed. I am a fortress. He leans in, brushing against my shoulder with his dark, starchy suit. His face is inches from mine, but he's not looking at my screen like he's pretending to. He's looking at me, trying to get me to break. I can feel the heat of his skin. The crackling virility in the air between us. His scent is a delicious alchemy of cedar, masculinity, and clean, French sheets. I breathe it in, infuriated with myself.

"Listen, princess. No one wants to see your avocado toast."

Cold awareness slaps me back where I belong.

"For your information, it's not toast."

"So… just avocado?" He whistles. "You paid, what? Forty bucks for that lunch?"

Actually, forty-eight, but he doesn't need to know that.

"I can take you to a Mexican restaurant for some guacamole that will blow your toastless avocado toast out of the water. And it's only seven bucks."

I sneer at him. "No, thanks."

"Free chips and salsa."

"Can we go now?" I slip into the limo. "And no more music."

Before he closes the door, he leans his elbow on the frame. "What do you have against music?"

"It's not music I'm against, Mr. Prosciutto. It's you."

He jolts his head back as if I'd punched him in the jaw. "Well. Glad we cleared that up."

He closes the door and doesn't make a peep the rest of the ride. According to the instructions I gave him this morning, our next stop is my house so I can pack a few things for my extended stay at Dad's penthouse. Enrique had my address already programmed in his GPS. I can hear every command from the computerized voice loud and clear with the absence of music. LOUD and clear. I'm beginning to wonder if my new driver is hard of hearing or just stubborn.

He parks directly in front of my house and opens the car door for me without a word. I'm already so used to his snarky comments like, "The party awaits." or "After you, October." But none of that comes from his mouth. It's almost *more* irritating.

"I'll need help with some boxes," I say, signaling him to follow me in the house. To be perfectly honest, I have everything I need at the penthouse, but there are a few items I'd like access to, like my camera equipment for my fashion reels, and some favorite shoes. But Enrique brings out the worst in me, so I had planned to select the heaviest objects I own just to watch him strain as he loads them for me. Out of the house. In the trunk of the limo. Up the tower to Dad's penthouse. Repeat. But… after carrying the first load to the car, Enrique comes back into the house with decidedly less clothing than before, and I lament the error in my scheme. He begins his ascent up the curve of my staircase, all swagger and muscle in a white tank undershirt which stretches snugly over every ridge of his chest. The gentle slope of his bare biceps yields to strong forearms—the kind you read about in romance novels when the heroine watches the man slowly roll up his shirtsleeves. A dusting of dark hair covers sun-browned skin; not too much, but just the right amount to prove those forearms are undeniably male.

I swallow. Hard. And then I remember my TED Talk from earlier with Ugo.

"Where's the rest of your uniform?"

He slows down but doesn't stop approaching me. "My jacket? In the car."

"And your shirt?"

He glances briefly over his shoulder and grins devilishly. "Wouldn't you like to know."

Ugh. Such a guy.

"Men who take their shirts off at every opportunity are just begging for attention."

"Or, we're hot from carrying boxes up and down the stairs for their brat client and don't want to sweat all over our nice clothes."

He glides past me at the top of the stairs, the salty heat of his arm barely touching my skin as he brushes by. The cotton fabric of his undershirt stretches across his broad chest, hugging every ab muscle, and straining against his back as he bends over to pick up a box I'd filled with hardcover books. His gaze flickers to me, catching me staring open-mouthed.

"You better not break that," I say, trying to recover and hoping he doesn't realize there's nothing breakable in there.

He scowls at me with those dark eyes and lifts the box over his head with one arm. One glorious arm, bronzed and bulging with muscle. I have a sudden urge to squeeze the Charmin.

"This isn't in my job description, princess. But I'm guessing you're just here for the show."

Oof. He's so full of himself. And so right.

"Somebody thinks more highly of himself than he ought," I say, all aloof and sassy. That's me. Not getting hot and bothered at all. Nope.

Enrique lands a heated stare right into my soul, and one corner of his mouth curls into a sly grin, showcasing a devastatingly juicy dimple. I hate him for it. My hormones think otherwise. Stupid hormones.

I can't do this. Can't flirt with fire when I know it's absolutely ridiculous. I call temporary insanity. This man needs to put a shirt on.

"Just be done soon, okay? And wait for me in the car when you're finished."

This isn't me. I'm just worked up over that interview this morning. All that talk about Jonny. But even I have to admit that Jonny never got me worked up like Enrique, and that's because I don't hate Jonny. In fact, I hardly gave him much thought at all. These strong emotions are clearly rooted in the extreme dislike I have for this man. He knows he gets under my skin, and he's using it to his advantage. What his end game is remains to be seen. Where did my dad find this guy anyway?

With a haughty once-over of his form, I turn on my heel and close myself inside my bedroom suite. Normally I wouldn't exercise in here, but I have to do something to shake off these pinpricks that have formed all over my body. So I kick off my shoes and launch into a robust session of jumping jacks. An activity I haven't done since I was seven or eight. One, two, three... take that, traitorous hormones. Four, five... oooh, my lacy bra is not made for this. Six, seven... dang. I press my hands on my girls to keep them from bouncing. Now I know why grown women don't do jumping jacks. At least not without an industrial strength sports bra.

Chapter Seven

ENRIQUE

Fine. I signed up for this gig. I could have walked away. I still can. Every day I drive to pick up January at the Madison Tower, I ask myself why I do it. Why? Of all the professions I could have chosen, this is the one I landed on. But why?

It's true I love cars. Ever since I could remember I had a toy car in my hand. Some kids slept with a stuffed animal. I slept with a dye-cast limited-edition General Lee. When my classmates were given crayons in preschool, they'd draw hills and sunshine. I'd draw cars and trucks. Especially red ones.

When asked what I wanted to be when I grew up, I'd reply, "Formula One race car driver," without hesitation. Halloween costume? Speed Racer.

Get the picture?

My mom has always encouraged me to follow my passion. I could do anything I wanted if I set my heart on it. My dad? He'd hoped I'd take over one of his restaurants.

According to Dad, we were born with chef's blood in our veins. He calls it *Sangre de Especias*. Blood of spice. That's a little weird if you ask me, but Abuela says Dad was dropped on his head as a baby, so that explains a lot.

But I digress. I don't have blood of spice. I have motor oil for blood. The adrenaline of the engine runs in my veins. Dad doesn't get it.

I never did apply myself to the life of a race car driver. I studied business in college, and for a few years after graduation I worked hard on the books with Dad to increase the revenue of Dad's restaurants. But that is just not my thing. So, here I am, driving around a bratty socialite heiress, but at least it's my own business on my own terms. Mostly.

Over the past several weeks I've had the craziest schedule. Social gatherings. Photoshoots. Beauty appointments. The SAG Awards. I either have to wake up at the crack of dawn or stay up all night. I've come to expect the unexpected when it comes to our interactions. We've fallen into this strange dance where she'll take out her daggers and I'll play along, sparring with her. There's a sparkle in her eyes when I tease her, throwing playful jabs her way. Sometimes she banters with me for hours like we're in a badminton match. Other days she's quiet, or maybe too busy to come out to play with me. Every now and then, I see the woman behind the curtain—just the tiniest sliver. But that girl is very heavily guarded beneath a glitzy mask.

There are several days in a row where I don't work at all. Other times, like today, I'm summoned for a last-minute ride. Of all the exciting places I've taken her, this is the most unexpected. The dentist. I'm in a parking garage adjacent to an unassuming glass building around the corner from the shops on Rodeo Drive, where she went handbag shopping that one day. If I were so inclined, I could walk around while waiting for January to get her teeth whitened or whatever it is she's doing upstairs. As a matter of fact, I've been here three hours and getting sick of watching YouTube videos on my phone. I saw a Subway over on Bedford. Maybe I can head over for a sandwich if this is going to take much longer. I pop onto my Uber Eats app to see if I can get something delivered when there's a tap on my window. A young woman in scrubs is signaling for my attention. When I roll down my window, she asks, "Are you Enrique?"

Hmmm. She doesn't *seem* like someone trying to mug me. If so, I could take her.

"Yes," I say tentatively.

"Can you come with me, sir? Miss Madison will need some help getting downstairs."

I chuckle jokingly. "What, did she break a heel?"

She scrunches her features. "Not quite."

I follow her to the elevator and we go up to the top floor. Inside the lobby, it's sleek and shiny and looks more like a day spa than a dentist. Actually, the gold sign behind the reception desk reads Beverly Hills Dental Spa.

The girl in scrubs leaves me in the lobby while she goes through the double doors where I assume the treatments are done. A few moments later she returns with reinforcements. A man in similar scrubs comes out with January leaning against him, her arm draped over his shoulder. She can barely walk but doesn't seem terribly upset about it. She looks… drunk. When she sees me she flaps her hand around as if she's attempting a parade wave.

"Ricky! Hiiii. Dith you miss me?"

The guy in scrubs approaches me with January.

"I take it you're Enrique?"

I nod, not sure what's going on here.

"Miss Madison says you're her ride home. She'll need some rest, but the recovery time should be minimal. Maybe keep an eye on her for a few hours."

"Recovery time? What did she have done?"

"Just a re-do on some of the veneers," says the girl in scrubs.

January flops her head toward the girl. "I love you. You're the bestest ever."

"We love you, too, Miss Madison."

January squints at her. "My name is Madison?"

Ha! There's an opportunity to mess with her here, but I'm not so horrible as to take it. Even though my tongue is itching to tell her that her name is July because she was born on the Fourth of July, I abstain. I could really have fun with this. But I don't. Why do I have to be so freaking nice when a woman is out of sorts?

"What kind of drugs did you give her?" I ask instead.

"We don't normally use oral conscious sedation for veneers, but Miss Madison… let's just say she got spooked by the needles the last time she was here so we had to do something other than numbing the areas."

I don't blame her. I hate needles, too. Doesn't everybody?

"We're going to let you go with your boyfriend now, Miss Madison," says the man in scrubs.

January's face softens toward me. "You're my boyfriend? Oooh."

Her weight is transferred over to me, and the man seems happy to have unloaded his burden.

"If she experiences any discomfort once the Triazolam wears off, she can take some over the counter ibuprofen. Just make sure she's hydrated and maybe gets some food in her belly. She confessed to not having breakfast, so that is most likely a factor in how she's reacting."

"What did you say it's called? Triatholot?"

"Triazolam. It's a sedative normally used for wisdom tooth extraction, but sometimes it's ideal for patients with… *moderate* levels of anxiety." He and the female nurse share a look as if to imply January's a difficult patient, which I can easily believe, but something within me stirs. I want to defend her for some reason. "It's perfectly safe," he continues.

Sure, it is. I'm googling that later on. But first, I need to get this clingy monkey home.

"Do you need help taking her to the car?" asks the female nurse. I can tell she does *not* want to help but is asking out of obligation.

"I think I can manage," I say.

January bids the nurses goodbye with sloppy waves and air kisses. As soon as the elevator door closes on us, she's all over me.

"You're so strong. Do you work out?" Her fingers are under my suit blazer pinching at my ribs. The little touches tickle me and I jolt from the sensation.

"Yes, I work out. How about we keep our hands to ourselves?" I peel her hands away, firm but gentle.

She pouts her lip out. "You don't like me."

"I never said that."

"But you don't. Where are your sunglasses? They're so shiny."

"We're indoors, princess."

"I like shiny things."

I give her a closed-lip smile.

"Your teeth are shiny. Open your mouth." Her finger comes at my lips, but I enclose my hand around hers, lacing our fingers together. My mind flashes back to what the male nurse said.

"We're going to let you go with your boyfriend now."

The thought makes me chuckle. In what universe would a woman like January ever go out with me?

"What's so funny?" She's gazing up at me with those wide, beautiful eyes. She almost looks… kind. Without thinking, I stroke the side of her face, brushing back a lock of hair.

"Nothing, sweetheart."

My pulse pounds in all the right places. This woman may be the bane of my existence, but I'm a hot-blooded man, and there's no denying she's gorgeous. Still, that doesn't excuse me from leaning down, close enough to kiss her. And it doesn't help when she meets me halfway, tilting her head up with an invitation. If this were any other woman in the right circumstances I wouldn't think twice. When a hot woman comes on to you and you don't take her up on it, you lose your man card. Unless she's high on painkillers. And that's exactly the bucket of ice water I need splashed over my head as a reminder.

The elevator dings and the doors swish open to the parking level where I check to make sure there's no paparazzi lurking about. We stumble to the limo and I let her in the back, making sure she doesn't bump her head, and I click her seatbelt for her.

When we're back on the road she won't shut up, and has too much fun with the partition controls. I have to lock it in the down position after she rolls it up and down four million times.

She's like a child, and everything she sees out the window is a wonder to her.

"What are those white things?"

"Those are clouds."

"Are we flying?"

"*You* sure are."

She gasps. "Weeeeeee. Can you put on some music?"

That's something I never thought I'd hear her say. I put on my Beatles playlist and "Strawberry Fields" comes on.

"I love this song," she says, all dreamily.

"I love it, too."

She starts to sob. "I love it so much. Why did John have to die?"

I have to get some food in her. It's after 2 PM and with

nothing in her belly to soak up the drugs they gave her... well, it just makes me worry.

"I'm just going to make a quick phone call, okay? Keep watching the clouds."

I raise the partition window and use the voice command to call Ignacio. The lunch rush is over so he's probably available. I'm relieved he answers on the second ring.

"What's up?" He sounds stressed so I make it quick.

"Hey, Nacho. I need a favor."

"If you want to borrow my leather jacket, the answer is no."

"Noted. But I just need a couple of smoothies."

"Then come over and get some, sonso."

"I can't get out of the car. I have my client with me. She's high as a kite and I'm worried she'll stumble out to follow me. I can't go into detail right now."

He's quiet for a second before he responds.

"I'll have Bernadette take them out for you. But you're gonna have to explain the next time we talk."

"Fine. Oh, and can you add a couple orders of barbacoa? And some guac?"

I don't know what January can handle after having dental work, but I want to be prepared. Besides, I'm starving.

Ignacio sighs. "Okay. How soon?"

"Fifteen minutes?"

"Call me when you get here."

He hangs up before I can ask for extra salsa.

When I get to the restaurant, my cousin, Bernadette, comes out immediately. It's like she was watching from the front window.

"I threw in extra chips and salsa," she says, peeking in the car. She can't see January from outside, but that doesn't stop January from blurting out a greeting.

"Hey! Who are you? I'm Madison."

"Sounds like you have your hands full," says Bernadette, straining to get a peek. "Nacho said it was an emergency. What's going on?"

"It's not an emergency. My client hasn't eaten in a while, that's all."

"Who's your client? Anyone I know?"

"I'm Madison!" January shouts from the back seat.

"Don't mind her," I say "The dentist gave her something and now she's loopy. Thanks for the extra salsa."

"I know what you like, primo. I gotta go back to work." She waves to January through the tinted backseat windows. "Bye, Madison. Nice to meet you. Sorta."

She runs off and I pull back onto the street.

"What's that smell?"

"Avocado toast," I say.

"I think it's Mexican food. Am I Mexican?"

"No, *princesa*."

She gasps. "I understood that. How can I understand that? Do I speak Spanish? Where are we going?"

I thought about taking her back to the hotel, but I don't want all those people seeing her like this. Her house is the best option, and she'll be more comfortable there.

"We're going home."

"Oh." Realization dawns on her features. "Do we live together? Are we married? Can we get a dog?"

"No."

"Why not? I love dogs." I think she's about to cry again

so I try to deflect.

"What kind of dog do you want?"

She thinks for a few moments, her head lolling to the side. I wonder if she's fallen asleep, but then she says, "A Yorkie. I love the ears."

Figures she'd want a purse dog.

I'm treated to more nonsensical conversation all the way to her house. Once there, I help her out of the car enough for her to unlock the front door with a code. It takes her a few tries but we finally get in. With the door shut behind me, I scoop her in my arms and carry her to the living room couch where she has an entertainment system to die for. I gently place her on the sofa, find a blanket from a basket by the fireplace, and go back to the limo for the food. I'll have to air out the entire car to get rid of the smell.

When I return to January, she's smashing her fingers on the remote buttons.

"Do you want to watch something?" I say, trading the remote for her smoothie. "Drink up."

She slurps on her straw, spilling smoothie down her chin. I sweep in and catch the dribble with my finger before it gets on her designer clothes. Her blouse alone is probably worth more than my house.

"Here." I position the straw against her lips and gently tip her chin back. "You need something in your stomach so you can get well again."

And once that happens, she can go back to being rude to me again.

"Am I dying?"

"No. Just a few more sips and then you can take a nap."

She slurps again, this time getting it all in her mouth.

Hooray for small victories. I want to cheer for her.

She squints at me. "Why are you being so nice? You hate me."

"I don't hate you."

"I don't believe you."

"You don't have to believe me. You have to drink your smoothie. And when you're up to it, you can have some meat."

She slurps again, getting better at using a straw with each sip. After she finishes about half the smoothie, she burrows drowsily under the blanket.

"Can you put on the sleepy channel?"

I set the smoothie on the side table and point the remote to the TV. "The sleepy channel?"

"Yeah. There's a puppet and he's sleeping and there's twinkly music. That's all there is. Hours and hours of the puppet sleeping. Where's my puppet? Did they cancel his show? Ricky?"

"Okay, okay. I'll find your puppet. Close your eyes and I'll find him."

I stroke her hair with one hand while surfing channels with the other. She has ten-million-and-one channels. Surprisingly, I find the sleeping puppet fairly quickly. Just as she described, there's a purple puppet wearing a sleep cap. He's tucked in a bed under a window showing the backdrop of a deep blue sky with a yellow crescent moon. He's breathing in and out. In and out. His chest rises and falls with each breath. And there's soft music with an underscore of chirping crickets. It's actually rather soothing. I cast my eyes down on January. The audio from the TV seems to calm her. There's a soft smile on her face. How peaceful she looks. I continue to stroke her hair until my arm gets tired. Maybe a half hour, I'm not sure. I'd stay for as long as it takes when she's as sweet as she is right now and not giving me a death stare.

Just to make sure she's okay, I remain at her house for the next few hours, bringing down a pillow and the comforter from her bed. I eat alone in the kitchen, and once the sun dips behind the trees in her backyard, I write a note to let her know there's food from the restaurant in her fridge.

Right before I go, I check on her once more, tucking the covers in the sofa cushions so they—and she—don't fall on the floor. I pause for only a second, but in that second, her hand wraps around my wrist and she snuggles my arm like a teddy bear—like I used to hold onto my toy cars as a kid. It's an awkward position but I don't pull away. Instead, I kneel down on the rug until she lets go.

But she doesn't let go for a long while. She's got my arm in a sleepy vise. To reduce the discomfort, I settle on the floor, dipping my head on the small space of couch she's not occupying. The fatigue of the day sets in and I doze off. When I wake up, January's in a new position, snoring in the softest way imaginable, and my arm is finally free of her grip. Her snoring almost sounds like music.

I'm tempted to stay until she wakes. She'll be hungry and she might need help. But I know she's a capable woman, and if I'm still here when she's in her right mind, she might cut my head off. So I quietly gather my food trash, my jacket, and the guacamole that has turned brown by now, and let myself out the front door.

With any luck, she'll forget everything in the morning.

Chapter Eight

JANUARY

We're told by magazines and social media that if you're wealthy, famous, and beautiful, you'll be happy. But that's not entirely true. People seem to think I sleep on a bed of one-hundred-dollar bills and take baths in diamonds. How glamorous it is to be me. The truth is, being famous is like living in a luxurious prison. Especially when I'm here in Dad's tower. I don't have to use the word lonely for Nancy, my therapist, to know how I feel. But I am. I'm in a bubble.

Nancy sits in the armchair across from me in the penthouse study. I'm fortunate she makes house calls. I'm not ashamed to attend my sessions—every celebrity does. But I'm glad I don't need to rely on Enrique to take me. It's just highly personal, that's all. I guess I just don't want to seem vulnerable around him. Maybe I should tell this to Nancy—another time.

"I'd like to give you permission to say no to things you don't agree with," she says.

"Like staying here at my dad's place?"

She nods. "If that's how you feel, then yes. Do you still feel unsafe at your house?"

I snort. "I never did. But Dad is a control freak, so here I am, humoring him. Picking my battles. I only stay here two or three nights a week, now that things have settled."

Nancy tilts her head, studying me empathetically. "Do you think he still sees you as a child?"

I think back to my last birthday when I turned twenty-six. He was in New York. No phone call, no happy birthday text. Just a check. A physical check for ten-thousand dollars sent via his personal accountant. It's little actions like that which assert his power over me. Drip-feeding me money here and there to keep me on his chain. He's not interested in giving me a role in the hotel business other than making sure I show up at press events. He gives me just enough responsibility to keep me under his thumb and dangles my allowance—and ultimately my inheritance—over my head like a carrot. Keeping me to stay a couple nights a week at his penthouse is just another one of those control tactics.

The only reason I agreed to the reality show was so I could make my own money. And also one of the reasons why I'm trying to get my skincare business off the ground.

"I think that's part of it," I say. "We don't exactly have the best relationship."

"And you don't speak to your mom?"

I shake my head. She knows this already, but I sense she's using that as a springboard to take this conversation somewhere else.

"January, I want you to think back. Can you remember your longest relationship with anyone? Friends? Lovers?"

I want to laugh. Lovers? Who says that? And why does my stupid brain conjure up images of Enrique carrying boxes around, parading in front of me with those wondrous muscles rippling along his back. Or when he extends his hand to help me out of the limo. The time he drove me to the SAG Awards, how dapper he looked as he guided me onto the red carpet with a glimmer in his eyes. Eyes black as sin pouring over me in my Gucci gown. I didn't want him to let go of my hand. I would have taken him with me down the red carpet if I could.

Ugh!

I shake out of it. "Friends? I don't know if I'd call Shauna a friend, per se."

Is it totally sad that Shauna is my most stable relationship? Yeah, I think so, too.

"And you know I don't like to keep guys around longer than a week or two," I add.

"Why is that?"

I think Nancy should be the one telling me why I do things, being a professional after all. But I know this is her trying to get me to work it out. That's what these sessions are for, I guess.

I sigh dramatically. "I have a hard time connecting."

She smiles and I chuckle. It's an ongoing joke with me. I repeat it like a mantra and she tries to break me of it every time.

"Tell me about what you've been doing to remedy that since the last time we spoke."

Other than throwing myself at my driver under the influence of dental surgery drugs? I don't recall much from that day, but flashes of an elevator ride fly through my memory. I seem to remember feeling extra frisky. And then there's the way I react to his presence every time he gets my name wrong on purpose. There's an electric charge between us, even though we're sparring to the death. I can't stand the guy. Right? But there's something about our animosity that makes me feel more alive than I have in years. A quickening awoke in me. Fighting with him is… fun.

The corner of my mouth twists upward as I stare into the middle distance. Nancy hooks onto that and lassos me in.

"Ah. Who is he?"

"He?" I feign ignorance. "Who said anything about a he?"

She shrugs. "Or she."

It's not a she. Enrique is most definitely a he in every sense of the word. I smile again, thinking about all the ways he is a definitive male. All male.

"Nobody," I lie.

"Mmm-hmm." Nancy swings her leg over her knee, bobbing it like a pendulum. She's wearing a slick patent leather pair of So Kate pumps. The ones with the red soles. Business must be rockin' for her.

"What?" I say defensively. "It's nothing."

"January, I'm not going to make you talk about anything you're not ready to talk about. We'll circle back another day."

"Well, there really isn't anything to say on the subject. I was just thinking about my travel plans."

"To Palm Springs?"

"Yup. It's still a few weeks away, but I have to arrange some meetings and stuff."

"And your limo service is taking you there? In lieu of a helicopter?"

Sure, it makes more sense to zoom over to Palm Springs by air instead of driving through the desert for three or four hours, but I'm always up for finding new ways to piss Dad off. So driving we shall go.

"I prefer the limo," I say.

"Okay. The last time we spoke you were at odds with the driver. Is that still the case?"

Yes, Nancy. Oh yes.

"I don't remember telling you that."

Nancy folds her hands on her lap. "It was the subject of almost the entire session."

"Oh." I scratch my chin. "Well, I can handle Enrique."

She grins. "I'm sure you can."

Nancy always knows what to say. The easy way she teases makes me feel more like we're painting our toenails at a slumber party rather than working out my problems in a counseling session. If I wasn't paying her so much, I'd count her as my most stable relationship.

"Shall we move on to affirmations?" she says. That's also so Nancy, sensing the end of the hour without looking at a clock.

"Sure. Where should I start?"

She waves a hand in a fluid gesture. "Anywhere you'd like."

Anywhere I'd like, huh? I don't always recite all the affirmations, but I'm feeling extra aware today. Darn errant thoughts about a young, hot chauffeur.

"I am unique and also the same as everyone," I begin.

"Good."

"Love, joy, health, and happiness are available to me."

Nancy nods silently. I think she's proud of how far I've come with these cheesy affirmations. I used to scoff at them, inwardly rolling my eyes while a *Saturday Night Live* skit played in my head. But after I really thought about it, the words started to make sense. Now I find myself chanting them in the shower.

"If it exists in the universe, it exists for me."

"Yes. And that's because..." she prompts.

"I'm enough. I matter. I'm significant. I'm loveable."

Nancy grins proudly. "You most certainly are."

I watch her in silence while she gathers her purse and her sweater. Session's over. Nancy's done here. I'm enough. Gawd, I need a donut.

"Venmo? Same as last time?" I ask, already feeling the isolation.

"That would be perfect." She heads over to the elevator, clicking across the shiny floor in those red-soled pumps. Just before the doors open for her, she says, "Oh, just a reminder about my vacation."

"Yes, of course. Have fun in Hawaii."

The doors to the elevator open and she sashays inside, practically doing the hula. "See you in six weeks."

I wave as she disappears into the elevator and I'm thinking to myself, I'm enough. I'm loveable. Oh crap.

Chapter Nine
ENRIQUE

If there's one thing my brothers and I can agree on, it's soccer. None of us are amazing players. None of us ever want to join a league. We don't even really like to watch it on TV. But we all love to play against the old guys on Sunday mornings so we can cream the ever-loving daylights out of them. With our busy schedules, we're lucky if we can kick the ball around once a month. But today, we're almost all in attendance.

Out of my six brothers, only Sebastian is missing but he's away at college so he gets a pass. Even Memo is here having carpooled with Nate from Orange County. He fulfilled his responsibilities with an early morning Mass so he could join us today, which is the only reason Mom's here. She'd rather be anywhere than a soccer field.

Currently, my dad and his brothers Enrique, Pedro, and Borris, along with two of Dad's *compadres* are taking a breather after only fifteen minutes in the game. It's a beautiful, sunny day. Not tremendously hot, but Dad's sweating like a sumo wrestler in a sauna.

Ignacio's our goalie, and even though he's blocking the ball, he seems off today. I can tell something's weighing on his mind. Earlier, when he kicked the ball back into the game, he smashed it so hard with his foot, it landed smack dab in the middle of a Little League baseball game in the next field over. Dad ran over for the ball. Hence the water break. Obviously that's too much running for him.

"Don't tell me the old guys are making you work hard," I say to Ignacio while we both grab a sip of water. I know it's not that, but he's not the type to say what's bothering him. I might as well lighten the mood. He chugs half the bottle of water and splashes the rest over his head, grunting like an ox.

"I'm going to need another week to transfer the money, brother."

"I don't care about the money. I should be paying *you* to run the restaurants. It wasn't fair of Dad to put that on you."

"It's my idea. I know you guys have other things going on. Trust me. This can work. But not this week."

"Okay. Whatever you say."

"Or maybe this month."

He blows out a hefty breath and I know it's not from the exercise. Seriously, playing with my dad and uncles is like a sad game of hopscotch. But it brings the family together. I look over at Mom. She's happier than a clam, making sure Memo is hydrated.

"I can't pay any of you," Ignacio continues.

Okay, now I'm worried. I really don't care about the money and I know my siblings feel the same way. But if the restaurants are struggling, I'm afraid this will put Ignacio in a bad place and this is his dream. I can't help it. I have to ask. If there's anything I can do, I'll do it. I might as well make use of my business degree somehow.

"Business a little slow?" I ask, treading lightly.

He shakes his head, dripping water all over his shirt. "Nope. Business is rockin', actually."

"Okaaay." I hope he didn't get himself into some other kind of financial trouble. I can't imagine what. He doesn't gamble that I know of.

"You aren't going to ask for details, *chismoso*?"

"No way. Last time I pried, you bit my head off."

Did I mention my brother has a hot temper?

"That's because your head was in my kitchen. Heads roll in my kitchen."

"In my defense, raisins in rice? Come on."

"It was a Persian dish. And you liked it at Lola's wedding."

Oh yes. If my stomach had lips to lick, they'd be doing it right now. "I still have dreams about that koobideh."

"Maybe I'll make it at your wedding."

"No way. First of all, I'm never getting married."

"Never?"

"And second, I wouldn't ever ask you to cater it. You're a chef-zilla."

I'm not even kidding. The man grows scales and breathes fire when he's stressed. Between the restaurant and Ignacio's catering company, I'm sure he doesn't sleep. His body is fueled by ambition and those green juices he drinks.

"Well, I'm about to get full-on prehistoric."

"Okay, I'll ask, only because I'm curious now. But keep your knives away from my neck."

"I actually might need some of your business savvy to get me out of this mess."

"I'm listening. I don't trust your confidence in me, but I'm listening."

"Pancho Two left the country."

"What?"

"He said he wanted to cash out on his investment and get married."

"Wow. So he's out of the picture. That's great news." Dad has been wanting to keep the Dos Panchos Restaurant chain all in the Precio family for years, but Pancho Two wouldn't take his greasy fingers out of the cochinita pibil. "That must have been a pretty big payout."

"It was. But Dad's been putting money aside for a long time. We got it covered. That's not the problem."

"What is it?"

"Before Pancho Two left, he racked up hundreds of thousands of dollars in debt with Southland Wine and Spirits. More booze than we could use in a year."

"Maybe it was a mistake. Can't you return it?"

"I could if I knew where it was. The sales rep told me they delivered the cases to a party hall in Compton. He thought it was for a big party so he didn't think twice about it."

"Oh snap. But aren't you in charge of purchasing?"

"Exactly. I chewed the guy out so hard for not confirming with me."

"I would *not* want to be in his shoes."

"So Dad and I went down to the place the booze was delivered. Nothing. We asked the venue manager for confirmation and he told me that they were closed that day."

"I don't get it. What would Pancho Two do with all that booze?"

"Sell it on the black market, *sonso*."

Oh. Yeah, that makes sense.

"He even used the company credit card to rent a truck to move it. By the time we figured all this out, he was in Costa Rica with his new wife."

I whistle. "I take it he left no forwarding address."

"Exactly."

"Okay, listen. File a police report. I'll call Southland Wine and Spirits to try and iron this out. I'll do everything I can to—"

"*Que tranza, animal?*" Tío Pedro slaps me on the back. I'm not sure how much of this conversation he overheard, but I'm guessing it would go over his tiny head. He's only five foot four, has selective hearing, and all he cares about are three things: beer, women, and leftovers. Only two of those things are within his reach.

"Hey, Pedo," says Ignacio with a chin nod. "Are you ready to get thrashed?"

"Thrashed? What is thrashed?" Pedro may have a hard time with English slang, but at least he always has a smile plastered across his face.

"It means we're going to kick your old butts," says Ignacio.

"*No manches*. I been practicing, you know? I going to score… five goals. No. Six goals."

"Dream on, David Beckham," I say.

He laughs. "Yes. Beckham. That's me."

Tío Enrique shouts from the middle of the field where he's doing some weird stretches. "*Venganse, flojos*."

Pedro runs out into the field singing the song they chant at stadiums. Mateo, Dante, and Nate gather around Ignacio and me like it's a freaking pow wow or something. Mateo's all about strategy and the most competitive out of all of us.

"Enrique, I need you to switch to midfield," says Mateo.

"What for?"

"Because you suck at center back."

Nate snickers. "He's got a point there."

I'm not going to argue because I really am terrible as center, but I'm even worse as midfield. And truth be told, I only like center (which is closest to the goalie) so I can joke around with Ignacio.

"Leave him alone." Dante scowls at Nate and Mateo. He's a no-nonsense kind of guy. "Can we just play already?"

"We'll be there in a minute," says Ignacio with a death glare at all three of them. "Nate, you didn't even warm up yet. Go stretch your girl legs."

"Aye-aye, *Capitán*." Nate salutes Ignacio and jogs onto the field followed by Mateo. Dante stomps, rather than jogs like the other two, but that's just the way he walks. Like he's a tree with legs.

Once he's sure the others are out of earshot, Ignacio says, "The sales rep comes on Wednesday. Maybe instead of just calling, we can set up a quick meeting, too."

"I'll be there."

"Great. I wouldn't ask except for how well you did with the books before."

"No worries. I got you. It'll be a good distraction from… oh, freakin' A."

"What? What's wrong?"

"I just remembered I have to take Veruca Salt to Palm Springs. We leave first thing Thursday, but she has me taking her shopping on Wednesday. I'll try to make it but I can't promise."

Igancio laughs. "Veruca Salt? She's that bad, huh?"

"I don't know. I guess. Mostly. One day she's all business, going to some swanky public appearance, acting elegant and reserved, and the next day she's biting my head off if I take surface streets instead of the freeway."

I don't mention how I secretly love the biting of my head.

Back when I first started," I go on, "she had me move stuff out of her house to take to her dad's penthouse. Heavy boxes she just *had* to take right away."

"What was in the boxes?"

"I dunno. Gold bars? And sometimes she has me doing asinine things like check her light bulbs or move a piece of furniture. She has other people on her payroll to do those things."

"What's the inside of her house look like?"

"You're missing the point here, *Nacho*. The woman drives me nuts."

"You like her. Holy—"

"I don't like her." Even as I deny it, my body warms at the thought. "She's hot. I'm not blind. But I do *not* like the woman."

"Okay, sure. But what I don't get is why do you have to take her shopping? Events and appearances, fine. But shopping?"

"I take her e-ver-y-where. I've never met anyone so incredibly spoiled. Sometimes she just wants a ride from her dad's hotel to her house and vice versa."

"Hmm. Maybe she got a DUI and got her license taken away."

"Nope. I googled it."

Boy, did I google the heck out of her. I'm not proud of it, but after almost falling for her sweet beauty while I watched her sleep, I went down a very long, very dark Google rabbit hole in January Madison Land. It was not a pretty place. Picture after picture of her party lifestyle, a different man at each nightclub, bikini modeling (okay, those weren't so bad), a straight-to-DVD horror film, a tediously pointless reality show, and a raid at a Hollywood party. She wasn't arrested or even found in possession of drugs, but she was there, and that's enough to tarnish a reputation for a hot minute. With as much info online about January, a DUI would have shown in the search results.

Anyway, I'm glad I saw the things I saw; now I won't take her for anything other than who she really is. Her endearing temperament after the dentist was an anomaly. That's it.

Speak of the devil, my phone rings with Mr. Madison's assistant's ringtone. I still don't know what V stands for, so I named the contact Venus. Watch it actually be Venus and I'll have to choke laughing.

"Sorry, I have to get this."

"No problem. See you out there." Ignacio runs to the goal post and I answer the call.

"Miss Madison requires your services in thirty minutes."

"Well, hello to you… Veronica. I'm fine, thanks for asking."

She breathes a grunt-like snarl into the phone. "You'll be taking Miss Madison to the address I'll text you now."

"Why doesn't she just call me?"

"All correspondence goes through me as was established in your contract."

Yeah. The contract that I believed was for the hotel executives. That'll teach me to read the fine print.

"Well, *Victoria*, I was told I'd have today off."

"Need I remind you, Mr. Precio, that you agreed to the terms of arrangement with Madison Industries. Is the compensation not satisfactory?"

"The compensation is just fine."

"Good. I'll text you the address."

"Thirty minutes won't cut it. I'm not dressed. I mean, I'm exercising. I'm in shorts."

She says something I don't catch as it's muffled, like

she's having a conversation with someone else. Then she returns to me. "Come as you are. It's casual."

Before I can reply, or ask any more details, she hangs up.

I'm completely irritated, but there's a small part of me excited and curious to drive January to whatever emergency excursion she's been called to.

I hug Mom goodbye, ask Memo to explain my departure to my other brothers, and drive straight to the Madison Towers.

When January descends from the elevator, she's wearing flannel pajama bottoms, an army green jacket, combat boots, and a baseball hat. I hardly recognize her except that I'm starting to know her form well enough to identify in silhouette.

Ever since the dentist a few weeks ago, there's been an awkwardness between us. But today, there's a spark in her, like she's ready to give me a hard time again, waiting for me to react. Once I put the car in gear, she barks at me from the back seat.

"Take me to the Santa Monica Pier."

Hang on. That is not the address I was given.

"The what?"

"You heard me. Drive, please."

Okey-dokey. I guess asking questions is above my pay grade.

In Sunday traffic, it takes a while to get there, and once we arrive, I'm not exactly sure where she wants me to drop her off.

"Park here," she orders.

Obviously, she doesn't understand us mere mortals

need a parking space. Double parking on the street won't cut it.

"There's no place to—"

"Right there." She leans through the partition window, pointing at a space behind the last car in a line of parked cars on the street.

"That's a no-parking zone."

"All those other cars are parked here."

For heaven's sake. Do I really have to explain about loading zones?

"I can't park here, *September*, because this is for taxis and Ubers. I can drop you off but then I'll have to circle back around. Is that okay?"

"No, I need you to go in and buy something for me. Don't worry. I'll wait here."

"Are you going to ward off the parking tickets for me?"

She regards me thoughtfully, still with her head poking through the partition window.

"Yes."

I slide the limo along the curb and put the hazards on. I suppose a parking ticket would be pocket change for her, so I decide not to worry.

She passes a one-hundred-dollar bill through the window and shoves it in my face.

"Go into The Scoop Deck, get me a toasted almond gelato in a waffle cone."

I'm sitting here with a Benjamin in my hand, still sweaty from the soccer game, gobsmacked at what I just heard. Gelato. She tore me away from my family because she was craving gelato.

"Please tell me we're taking it to a sick child in the

hospital, or are here for an important meeting with the president of CBS and just passing time."

"Why would there be an important meeting on a Sunday?"

I crane my neck around to face her just to be sure she's serious. "It's my day off. I was at the park with my family. I thought this was an emergency."

"It is an emergency. A sugar emergency."

I take a deep breath. Then another. I will not blow up right now. "What's wrong with the gelato at the hotel?"

"Nothing compares to The Scoop Deck."

Keep it together, man. Do not scream at the heiress. "Have you heard of a thing called DoorDash? There's this app, see? It's groundbreaking, really."

"It's not the same. Besides," she continues, "I never said it was an emergency. You assumed it."

She's right. I did assume.

"Do you have anything smaller? They might not have change."

"Eww. Do you have any idea how dirty money is? I never take my change back. Tell them to keep it."

"That's a crazy generous tip."

She shrugs her shoulders like it's nothing. I guess it is nothing to her—a ninety-dollar tip.

"And get one for yourself."

I leave her there, hoping I can be quick enough to not get a ticket. The line at The Scoop Deck is a little long, but it goes by fast. The selection of flavors is amazing. I order her toasted almond and choose key lime for myself. When I return to the limo, there's no ticket on my windshield. I hand January her cone and a napkin through the partition window.

"Back to the tower, Rapunzel?"

She sniffles. If she didn't appear perfectly composed, I'd have thought she was crying. "Can we just walk around somewhere?"

Walk around somewhere. In Los Angeles.

I let out an over-exaggerated sigh. "We can see if there's parking down PCH a bit."

She squeaks with delight and holds out her hand. "Here. I'll hold your ice cream while you drive."

Never a dull moment in Januaryland.

A few blocks down the road, I find a metered parking lot. After I pay at the machine, I open the car door for January to find her with sunglasses on and her hair tucked under the jacket.

"Nice disguise," I say.

"Really? I hope it works."

I look at the limo, back to her, and back again to the limo. "Nope. We're not drawing attention at all."

This stretch of beach is less crowded than up the street, and although there are families and skaters around, it's relatively peaceful. We stroll down the boardwalk, eating gelato like ordinary people. Correction: I am an ordinary person. January is extra-ordinary. Even in her disguise.

"I have a confession to make," she says. "I tasted your gelato."

"Hmm. I think it's only fair if I get a taste of yours."

"But I already licked it," she protests.

"And you licked mine. It's a little late to avoid your cooties now."

We pause our stride so I can get a proper angle to try her gelato. To make sure she doesn't get a wild idea to shove it up my nose, I take hold of her wrist, also wrapping my hand around part of her hand. Looking straight into her eyes, I lower my lips over her treat, grin, and take a massive bite.

"Hey!" She jerks her hand away.

I'm laughing despite the brain freeze. "You can't finish the whole thing. I'm only helping."

Seriously, they're gigantic servings. I'm definitely coming back here again.

"You don't know that. I happen to love gelato."

"I've never seen you eat more than a few bites of something. You're telling me you weren't going to throw half of this out?"

"Yes." She seems really offended now. "It's a waffle cone. You need to let me have some of yours now."

"No way, June. One lick is all you get."

"Well, I want more than one lick and you're going to give it to me."

A young family passes us just as January shouts at me, the mom covering her child's ears while shooting us a dirty look.

I smile innocently and wait for them to pass before crowding January's personal space, dragging my tongue in one fat sweep around my gelato. Her eyes go wide as they track the movement of my lips slurping up the excess drippings. Her gelato is better.

"You want this?" I tease. She barely nods. "Then come and get it."

I take off down the boardwalk, not running, just speed

walking. I'm used to January in heels, not January in combat boots. It's like she's someone else entirely as she chases me. I have to speed up. I weave past slow-walking couples and children, avoiding skaters and joggers. January's on my tail, holding up her cone like the Olympic torch. I only catch a glimpse or two when I glance back to make sure I have a good lead. I don't. Up ahead there's a crowd. The boardwalk is blocked with all sorts of people watching a performer. It must be pretty good for people to gather. I'll have to stop and let January catch up to me. Unless…

Just before I reach the crowd, I veer off into the sand with the intention of skirting around them before finding the boardwalk again. But I feel a tug on my t-shirt, and before I know it, one combat boot hooks around my ankle, causing me to tumble down face forward on the sand. January's body crashes over me in a spectacular tackle worthy of the NFL. My gelato flies from my fingers, landing in the sand. January's gelato is partially in my hair and partially dripping down the back of my neck.

She's laughing, splayed on my back, the rhythmic movements of her body rocking against my spine. I rather like her here, but the sand is sticking to my lips and cheek, and I'm just a little disappointed at losing the best gelato I've ever tasted. I flip my body over, and with one swift motion, I pin her down by the arms, letting her body sink into the soft, cool sand as I hover over her. Her eyes dance over my face, and that stubborn pout of hers makes an appearance. She lost her sunglasses and hat somewhere between the boardwalk and here, and strands of her golden hair flutter across her face. I'm struck with the desire to kiss her, to press my sandy lips all over hers and rub my sandy cheek in her hair. Her chest heaves from running, her breath shallow and fresh. This is not an appropriate position for a Sunday, and my body is not reacting decently. I should move. I know it. I really should. But there's a challenge in her eyes that seems to say, "I won. Now what are you going to do about it?"

Call it my competitive spirit, even though I can't be bothered with competition on the soccer field. There's just something about this woman that ignites friction within me. Okay, maybe friction isn't the best word under the circumstances. Rivalry. That's what this is. So I lower my lips to the shell of her ear and I whisper, "Do you still want a lick?"

Chapter Ten

ENRIQUE

"**W**ow, what a freaking mess. How did he get away with this?"

I'm going through the vendor accounts for Dos Panchos in Ignacio's office, and with every discovery, I'm more and more floored by the audacity that is Pancho Two. He racked up charges with several vendors at at least four locations. The financial setback for the restaurant chain is devastating.

I don't know whether to be impressed or to fly to Costa Rica and get all Scar Face up his *culo*.

It's clear to me he wanted to do anything in his power to bring down the business after he got his share. But Ignacio's not so sure about my hypothesis.

"I spoke to Dad about it," he says. "Apparently, Pancho Two had been griping about his cut for some time. He got in a pretty ugly argument with Dad about it last summer when they started the legal stuff. He thinks he's entitled to more money, and now Dad's convinced that's why Pancho Two did this."

I run my fingers over my scalp, trying to squeeze out the headache that's coming on. "So basically stealing from the restaurant and fleeing to Costa Rica is his way of giving Dad the middle finger."

"Not only Dad, but us, too. If the restaurants fold because of his stunt, hundreds of people will be out of a job. Rosa's been working here for over thirty years. Armando for fifteen. Hernan sends half his paycheck to his elderly mom. What am I going to tell them?"

Ignacio's veins are popping out of his neck so fiercely, I'm worried he'll punch a hole in the computer.

"We'll figure this out," I say. "You're good with numbers, and I have some marketing ideas. Starting with happy hour."

"Oh, heck no. Do you know how long it took me to recondition our customers to expect a quality product from us? Not just tacos and burritos, but high-end Mexican cuisine?"

"Oh, I remember World War III when you fought with Dad over his bargain menu and dollar margaritas." I say.

"And who was right about that? Our margins increased tenfold when we started pushing top-shelf tequila. Sorry. I'm putting my foot down here. If people want a dollar menu, they can go to Taco Smell."

"Whoa whoa, whoa. Let's reel that in real quick."

That's one thing about Ignacio we all tease him about. He's a good guy, a hard worker, runs his restaurant like a well-oiled machine (most of the time), and is a fair employer. But he's a hothead and a curmudgeon.

"Have you ever heard of botana? It's a concept I came across in a bar when I visited Abuela in Mexico. I thought it was a genius idea, mostly for the free food, but by the time I left, I'd sucked up five drinks."

"You want me to give away free food? Are you nuts?"

"Just hear me out. A customer comes in for happy hour and orders a drink, right? The server not only brings the drink, but a small appetizer. I'm talking really small. If they want more, they'll either have to order food from the menu, or another drink."

Ignacio runs his hand over his chin. "Go on."

"Drinks can be full price or reduced by a dollar or whatever. You'll need to crunch some numbers there. But the point is to push the high-profit items in exchange for low-cost appetizers. What's your profit margin on, let's say carne asada?"

"Something like a hundred percent."

"Okay. What's your profit margin on a top-shelf margarita?"

I can tell the second a light bulb shines above Ignacio's head. His eyes light up and the corner of his mouth curls up. "Four-hundred percent."

"Ding-ding-ding. He wins a prize." I do a spin in my chair, then slap my palm down on Ignacio's knee. "Now think about menu items that you can serve in small bites but won't cost an arm and a leg to produce. Nachos, mini quesadillas..."

"Tortilla soup. Molletes. Oh! I can create a special menu not offered outside of happy hour times." He's rubbing his hands together like an evil genius. "Dos Panchos Secret Botana Menu."

"Now we're talking. I also have an idea for a rewards app. Customers can rack up points and even pre-order packages for a discounted cost...you know, like a hundred dollars of food for only eighty bucks. Exclude tax and tip and booze. I don't know, just spitballing, here."

"And do away with Dad's paper gift certificates. We're still getting those, you know."

"Do they expire?" I ask.

"Unfortunately, no. We have to honor them. But I finally put the last unsold certificates through the shredder about a year and a half ago. Dad threw a fit."

Apple doesn't fall far from the tree.

"Ugh, I've got such a headache," he says, rubbing his temple.

"Me too."

"Kevin will be here in about twenty," he says. Kevin is the sales rep for Southland Wine and Spirits. We're hoping we can work out a plan with him so we still get deliveries while we pay off Pancho Two's debt. "I haven't eaten. Can you stay after to have a bite?"

I shake my head. "I'm starved, but no. January has me running errands all day."

"Dude. Is she your wife or your client? You need to draw that line."

"I'm not running the errands *for* her. I'm driving. That's kinda my job."

He grunts. "She's got you trained like those dolphins that do tricks at Marine World. She blows a whistle and you jump and do a flip and balance a beach ball on your nose."

"I do not."

"Mmm-hmm." He crosses his arms and throws me a hard stare. "What was so important that had you leaving the soccer game on Sunday?"

I really don't want to admit this to my brother, but I'm a terrible liar and he'll get it out of me eventually. I raise my eyes to the ceiling for a brief moment to avoid eye contact. "She wanted ice cream."

Ignacio blinks, processing what I said, and slowly, his lips curl up and his eyes shine with amusement until all at once, he busts up laughing. Roaring, boisterous laughing at my expense.

"You are the most pathetic human being I have ever known. Ice cream?"

"Well, it was more like gourmet gelato," I say defensively.

"Did she make you spoon feed it to her, too?"

The picture of January dragging her tongue around her gelato springs to mind unbidden. The way she licked the excess off her dainty pink lips, and how her eyes sparkled when I took a bite. And then, when she chased after me, tackling me on the sand... how she looked when I tossed her onto her back, hair shimmering in the sunlight. Her skin, dewy and flushed. Everything about her body language broadcasting that she was ready to be thoroughly and extensively kissed. What is this game she's playing? Calling me out of the blue to take a stroll along the beach with ice cream cones like we're living in a frickin' Hallmark movie. Did I inadvertently sign a clause in my contract to take part in a twisted reality show?

I, the undersigned contractor, agree to be available to drive the client to and from any desired locations and consent to being filmed while aforementioned client bats her eyelashes and puckers her lips.

No, thanks.

How did I get caught up in her web of... whatever this web is? Ignacio's right. I'm wrapped around her little finger and she's so good at it, I willingly let her. How many men does she have on her string? And what does she seek to gain by entrapping me? I'm a nobody to her. The help. I'll bet she gets off on flicking her pretty little wrist to get people to heed her beck and call. She's so used to men tripping over themselves to please her every whim. *Take me here, get me that. Carry my heavy boxes.* I took a peek in those boxes she made me take to her dad's penthouse. None of it was essential.

And here I am like a dork, doing as she bids, falling at her feet, almost kissing her. Freaking A... I *am* her trained dolphin. Worse. I'm being paid to be her trained dolphin. What a loser.

Ignacio snaps his fingers in my face.

"Hey! Duncemonkey."

I'm jolted back to the present, blinking rapidly at my brother. "Oh, sorry."

He pulls a face. "Your eyes went glassy there for a second. Did you hear anything I said?"

"Uh, something about Kevin?"

"Wow." He shakes his head like it's such a sorrowful thing to have a brother like me. "Are you sure you don't like the girl?"

"Who? January? Pshh. No way. She's basically the devil in a blue dress. I do *not* like her. Nope. Liking her would be like a mortal sin or something. That would be so wrong. *So* wrong. Hugely wrong."

Ignacio's grinning ear to ear. "Yeah. I can see the apparent wrongness there as you so eloquently stated. But come on. You've got the hots for her."

"I do not."

"You crave a seat at the buffet. Thou hath eyeth her attributes."

"Thou hadsth conjectured incorrectly. Thou art crazy."

Ignacio chuckles and narrows his eyes in my direction, inspecting me. "Let's get you something to eat so you don't faint on my floor."

I follow him out of his office into the back of the prep kitchen. There, he pulls stuff off the shelves, makes his way to the walk-in refrigerator, gathers a few items, and then tosses all the ingredients on a counter. He gets right to work, squirting mustard on a bolillo roll, adding slices of carne asada steak, cheese, lettuce, tomato, and jalapeño. All the best fixings for an authentic Mexican torta. Then he puts the sandwich on a plate, disappears into the cook's line, and comes back with steaming hot red enchilada sauce smothering the bread, and slides the plate at me. Mmmm. Torta ahogada.

"Why don't you serve this on the menu?" I ask.

He grabs a fork and knife for me. "Because nobody would order it. Hurry up and eat."

I dig in, hovering over the counter, standing up while eating. The bread is already soggy from the sauce. I'm in heaven.

"Now that your mouth is occupied," he says. "You're gonna hear me out. And I'm only going to say this once. Okay?"

I bob my head, completely enraptured by this torta.

"Good," he continues. "Brother, you know I love you, but that's why I have to say it. Get your head out of your ass."

I almost choke on a piece of shredded lettuce. "Beg pardon?"

"I can see the writing on the wall and you can't. Or in this case, lipstick on the mirror. That woman is bad news. You keep telling yourself it's just business. Just your job. Sorry but you're pretty much an idiot."

"What!?" How dare he?

"You not only drank the Kool-Aid, you're mixing another batch. Stop it. Just stop."

"I can stop whenever I want to," I say with a mouthful of saucy, bready goodness.

Ignacio slides the plate out of my reach and levels me with a hard glare. "You are a professional with a new fledgling business you built out of nothing. You are clever and savvy, and have never taken crap from anybody. Let alone a sassy, entitled socialite. Do I need to slap you?"

I swallow down a big bite. "No, you do not."

First of all, I've been slapped by Ignacio before. It's not

fun. I did deserve it, but still, I'd rather not repeat the experience. Second, I've already made up my mind to do something about my January situation. I have a friend who runs a souvenir shop on Hollywood Boulevard who owes me a favor. I could tell Ignacio that, but he doesn't subscribe to my brand of humor. In any case, now I have extra motivation to take action—to not get slapped.

He nods once. "So, what are we going to do about it?"

"We?"

He shrugs. "When I say we, I mostly mean you. But I'm here to cheer you on."

I steal the plate back, sliding it to the other end of the counter. "I have an idea," I say. "But first, I'd kill for a Coke."

Chapter Eleven

JANUARY

What was I thinking, inviting him for gelato on Sunday? I call temporary insanity. I blame the stress. I've got a lot on my plate right now, what with the future of my new business on the line, and then, every corner of the Internet is coming at me with pitchforks for breaking Jonny Z's heart. The world had moved on months ago, but no! Jonny, with his addiction to publicity, decided to go and tease some of his new songs about me on TikTok, trudging things up anew. His fans are all over it. Oh, and Dad is being his usual horrible self. First thing that Sunday morning, he barged in my room to yell at me about canceling an appearance on *The View*.

So I had to get out. I was suffocating in that tower and just wanted to get back to my own house for a night or two—after sugar therapy, that is. Enrique's joke that day about Rapunzel didn't escape my notice. It kind of made me laugh. I was beginning to warm up to him, and for a suspended moment, I wasn't an heiress or the latest victim of internet gossip. I was a woman having gelato at the beach, and my companion just so happened to be drop-dead gorgeous. Now I just want him to drop dead. How dare he tease me? Flirt with me. Almost kiss me.

I officially hate him.

Today we leave for Palm Springs, and I'm prepared with a Bose Bluetooth speaker and an angsty Taylor Swift playlist.

We're departing from the penthouse and Enrique's called up when he arrives so he can help me with my bags. I think five suitcases will do. I make him wait an extra fifteen minutes in the front room in order to execute phase one of my plan. Sometimes it works in one's favor to have the hotel staff to do your bidding. Yes, fifteen minutes should do it. Part of me wants to see the look on his face when he discovers his car covered in plastic wrap. But I know me and I won't be able to appear innocent in response to his reaction. I send him down with my bags and follow five minutes later. That should be enough time for me to catch the tail end of his rage and act shocked and surprised.

"Who could have done such a thing?" I'll say. And I'll take great pleasure in watching him struggle with the cling wrap. But I won't laugh. As the elevator doors swish open, I keep my head down to school my features. I'm not sure what to expect, or how good of a job the bellboys I paid did. I instructed them to go to town, holding nothing back. I'd commandeered an industrial-size roll from the hotel kitchen and told them to use the entire thing. I'm actually feeling a little giddy. It's like Christmas. But imagine my dismay when I come upon Enrique, standing ready and completely calm next to a pristine, shiny limo, *not* wrapped in plastic. Those bratty bellboys took my money and ran. I am going to get those little buggers when I get back from Palm Springs.

I'm frozen, scanning the limo back and forth for any trace of cling wrap.

"Are you missing something, madam?"

Yes. I'm missing four-hundred dollars. I knew that was too much to pay the bellboys.

"Uh, is my luggage in the trunk?"

"Of course. Safe and sound. Shall we be on our way?" He opens the door for me and gestures with his arm. He's being extra sweet, which is making me suspicious.

"What are you up to?"

He laughs. "Oh, March. Does somebody have trust issues?"

"Stop calling me every month of the year except January."

His eyes gleam playfully. "You love it."

As I bend over to get in the car, I cover my butt with my purse in case he's planning on kicking it, but he just shuts me in as usual. That's when I realize the interior lights are all off, and with the parking garage somewhat dark, the passenger compartment of the limo is cast in shadow.

"Are your lights broken?" I tap at the outside window. But he's already moving to the driver's side.

"Unbelievable," I grunt under my breath, digging for my phone so I can use the flashlight app. But when I glance up, an imposing silhouette of a man lurks in the seat across from me and I scream, kicking madly with my Louboutins. I throw my purse, shrieking in fear. As Enrique opens the driver's door I cry for help, shielding my face as the shadowy figure lunges at me. I brace myself for the attack, but once the figure lands on me, it's surprisingly light. And made of cardboard. My legs are tangled up around the thing, one foot in the air.

Enrique clicks the dome light on, and I find myself entangled with what seems to be a life-sized cardboard cutout... of Nicolas Cage.

"Everything okay, Miss?"

Oh that smirk on his face.

"I thought you'd like some company, but I see you're already getting cozy."

I hate this man. He rolls up the partition window and starts the car and I throw Nicolas Cage across the limo back to the rear-facing seat. My head is steaming with rage. The only thing that keeps me in check is looking forward to getting Enrique back. I can't believe he Caged me. How long has he been planning this? That stupid thing is sitting in the seat across from me, staring me down.

When we're well on our way down the highway, I blast the songs I'd prepared on my playlist. The Bluetooth speaker arrived in a brown box this morning with a factory charge. It's on the highest volume I can stand, but Mr. Happy's singing along in the most obnoxious way imaginable. It's like he's doing everything in his power to disarm me. I've never met anyone so ridiculous.

Maybe Taylor Swift isn't the best choice for the task, so somewhere past Redlands, I switch to gangsta rap. That only gets the man to tap his thumbs on the steering wheel, and I definitely do *not* notice how large and strong his fingers are. I mean, they're the hanging-off-the-side-of-a-building-in-an-action-movie kind of strong. I never thought those scenes were believable but I do now. Enrique would survive by the sheer strength of two fingers.

I switch the music to the worst version of "YMCA" I can find on YouTube. The composer modulated the song to a minor key. It's worse than nails on a chalkboard.

Enrique twitches. Eureka. But halfway through the song, the freaking speaker battery dies. I'll have to wait until the next stop to get the charger from the trunk. Just as well. My ears are bleeding at this point.

I brace myself for him to retaliate with mariachis or Def Leppard or something, but he doesn't take the opportunity. Instead, there's silence other than the hum of the engine. We're in the middle of the desert now, so there's no traffic or any outside noises. I'd say it's peaceful, but being with Enrique is anything but peaceful. Even if I were to close the glass partition between us, I'd still be acutely aware of his presence.

At length, he clears his throat, like it's a huge effort to say what he says next.

"Are you comfortable back there?"

Wow, where did that come from?

"Uh... I'm fine. Thanks."

"Perfect. Well, just let me know if you need anything, August."

Aaaand…there it is. There's no point in trying to correct him. He's such a tool.

"I'll do just that... Babaloo." I have no idea how that escaped my lips but it's out there now. So I decide to own it with a haughty glower in his direction.

He is nothing but amused, but I don't care. I don't care one bit.

"You should really shave better," I say after a period of uncomfortable silence. "All that scruff isn't very professional."

And if I'm being honest with myself, it should be illegal how well it looks on the sharp edges of his jaw—dusting over that dimple. This is ridiculous. Thomas was more like a fatherly figure from the front seat. Not sex on wheels like this guy.

"Duly noted, December."

"You should address me as Miss Madison," I say with my nose in the air just a little bit. His eyes should be on the road, but a part of me wants him to look in the rearview mirror so he can see the strength I'm projecting. I'm in charge here, dude.

He chuckles unapologetically. "Oh, should I? And you should address me as Mister Hot Bod."

"I certainly shall not."

"I certainly shall not," he repeats in a whiny, mocking tone.

"What are you, five? I don't sound like that," I say.

He throws his hands up. "Hey, all I'm sayin'—"

"Put your hands back on the wheel," I cry. "You're gonna get us killed."

He places his hands back at two o'clock and ten o'clock. "My brother's a mechanic. The alignment's perfect on this beauty." He's stroking the wheel now. I scoff. Guys and their cars.

"So," he continues, "all I'm saying is, since we're establishing how to *address* one another..." He does air quotes on the word *address* and I shout.

"Wheel!"

"Okay, okay." He's shaking his head like a mom at a teenager. "I'll call you Miss Madison and you can call me Mister Hot Bod."

"I'm not going to call you..." I can hardly get the words out, "Mister Hot Bod."

"Suit yourself, May."

"Fine," I spit out, searching for something to jab back at him. "Ricky Ricardo."

With that he explodes into laughter. He's bellowing so hard and so long, I wonder if he's laughing at me or if he's delighted I'm so funny. And why does my belly warm at the idea of him finding me funny? Like if I told a joke he'd laugh and look at me with admiration. It shouldn't matter. I don't care what he thinks. Not really.

"Ricky Ricardo?" He coughs between peals of laughter. "Is that why you said Babaloo earlier?"

Tears are dripping down his cheeks and he leans over to the glove box, I presume, to get a tissue. He's freaking me out with the leaning because his eyes are definitely not on the road now. An eagle or a vulture or something swoops in front of us and I scream, "Watch out!"

He jolts up, and I don't know if it's from my screaming or his shouting at me to calm down, but he swerves onto the shoulder and hits a rough spot. There's a loud pop, the Nicolas Cage cutout flies at my face, and now I'm about to have one of my anxiety attacks. My therapist has been making strides with me, but lately with my life upside down, I'm having them more.

Enrique growls a long string of curse words and pulls over as soon as it's safe to do so. He storms out to check on the damage and I hear another round of cursing. Mostly English with a few Spanish ones thrown in. I recognize one that I know is the equivalent of the S word. My Spaniard nanny taught me all the fun ones at my insistence. It was our little secret.

Enrique opens my door and slides in next to me. He's radiating so much anger, I don't say anything about him being in the back seat. I just slip across to the facing seat and put Nicolas Cage back in his spot. Enrique is punching something into his phone.

"We have a flat," he snarls. "Thanks to you."

"Me? You're the one who wasn't paying attention."

"I was doing fine until you started screeching." He smashes his thumbs on the screen as if his poor phone had anything to do with his agitation.

"You were about to hit that eagle."

He glares up from his phone and gives me a hard look. "There aren't any eagles out here. It was probably a crow."

"Well, you almost hit it."

He swishes the hat off his head and tosses it on the seat,

running a massive hand through thick hair, causing it to poke all over the place in an unruly mess. And oh my. The warmth in my belly spreads.

"You can't hit a bird. They have echolocation," he says.

"You're thinking of dolphins. Or bats. Birds don't have echolocation."

He grunts. "They have something—electromagnetic senses—I dunno, I'm not an animal expert. But I know you can't hit them."

"Um, that's not true, genius, and I just saved your windshield. And the bird."

"Do you have any idea how insurance works?"

Great. Now he's going to mansplain me.

"If my tire blows from getting hit by a flying object, or from vandalism or something—don't get any ideas—I can file a comprehensive claim and get it replaced for free. I don't pay a cent because I have a zero-dollar deductible, and it won't go against my insurance. But if I blow a tire because I *hit* something," he gestures wildly in the direction of the tire, "I have to pay for a new tire myself because if it's *my* fault, I'll lose my good driving discount."

I snort. "I'm surprised you didn't lose that a long time ago."

He taps at his phone, mumbling under his breath. "My brother's an insurance agent. He'll know what to do."

"I thought your brother's a mechanic," I say.

"That's my other brother."

Oh. I don't know why it always surprises me when people have more than one sibling. Not everyone's an only child like me, and the primary victim of my parents' constant bickering.

After a few minutes he declares roadside service is on the way. Then he goes on to say that his insurance agent brother (probably a massive nerd) texted back and advised him not to file a claim.

"You're paying for the new tire," he says, pinning his eyes on me.

"Dream on, Ricky."

"You do know Ricky is my actual name, right?"

I bristle. "I know that. Duh."

There is no way this infuriating man is going to win whatever this is. If anyone's going to be on top, it's me. My own betraying thoughts bring a flush to my cheeks. That sounds *way* worse than what I intended.

I decide to find that Bluetooth speaker charger. I know I shoved it in one of my bags. I slide over to open the door, moving Nicolas Cage out of my way.

"Where are you going?"

"To pop the trunk." I hobble out into the crisp desert air. It's colder and windier than it looks from inside the car. I'm about to open the driver's door to hit the trunk button when Enrique leaps out and swallows my wrist with his aforementioned large hand. He spins me around, pressing my back against the door. A devilish grin spreads across his features while his black opal eyes unabashedly rake over me, lingering at my chest. I'd slap him in the throat, but my other arm is pinned to my side by his very hard, very muscular frame. Why can't the man have a squishy dad bod under that chauffeur uniform?

"I can't let you do that, princess."

I take a shallow breath. "Why?"

And if I thought his body was close to me before, he

presses even closer so there's no possible way I can slip out of his hold on me. Or cause his foot damage with my stiletto heel.

"Because," he says all gruff and grumbly. His face is so close to me, I feel the roughness of his whiskers when he speaks. "I don't want you touching my stuff."

Oh heavens.

"If there's one thing you can count on, it's that I'll *never* touch your stuff," I say.

Something of a low rumble sounds in his throat and his sizzling gaze dips to my lips. If this were a guy I was into, I'd want him to kiss me right here. Right now. On the side of the road with semi-trucks rushing by and clouds of dust and sand forming on our shoes. I'd want him to kiss me hard and hot, maybe tugging at my hair a little bit. His powerful hands would roam over my back, pulling me firmly against his form. And I'd kiss him back, devouring his glorious lips, dipping my fingers under his shirt to explore the muscles I know are hiding under there. I'd show him how good it could be, how insanely and wildly attracted to him I am.

But I'm not. And he's not. And this is *so* not happening.

Chapter Twelve

ENRIQUE

January's features alight with fireworks, even as she pretends to wiggle away from me. And I'm pretty sure I've lost my freaking mind. I don't know what's come over me. Not only is January my client's daughter, but she's also the bride of Vlad the Impaler. She treats me like the farm boy in *The Princess Bride* without the lovey-dovey bits, snubbing her perky little nose at me and flipping her long, golden hair in an act of superiority. I know she looks down on me and my profession, and that makes me angrier than almost anything. But the way my body reacts when she's near—the way every cell springs to attention at the awareness of her— how this chemical reaction in me stirs my blood, it makes me want to throw reason out the window and see where this attraction takes us. Because I know she's attracted to me, too. It's why I've found myself resorting to pranks and jabs. To keep her where she belongs—in the hate zone.

But I'm only human. Actually, I'm worse than human. I'm a red-blooded man who's been good as a Boy Scout for far too long. Enter January stage left and I'm in serious trouble.

I could kiss her right now. It would be raging, heated, ferocious. Passionate. She'd pretend to fight it, but it wouldn't be long before she'd be warm and soft in my hands. I think it's her fiery nature that's such a turn on. And then I'd be completely ruined. She'd turn our kiss into a power play, and I'd be all in. She could use me and I'd willingly go.

Her heart-shaped lips part. An invitation? A dare? I have no willpower. I say a silent prayer (because Catholic guilt) *Lord, forgive me,* and let my lips lead the way. But then January brings us back with her ice cube words.

"You stink," she says with a shaky breath. "Like bad tuna."

Good girl. Smart girl. Hate zone.

I pause a hair's breadth away from her perfect pink mouth and force a playful grin as if to say, *"I'm just testing you, woman."* I picture those ice cubes in all the right places to cool my engines down because there's steam coming from this train and it's running off the tracks. And for the record, I don't even like tuna.

"Well then," I say, disengaging my fingers from her wrist, "I think we can both agree you'll keep your hands to yourself from now on."

She has that look on her face where she's about to make a show of being appalled, but I shush her with a finger to her lips as I take one step away.

"I'll pop my own trunk, thank you."

I reach into my pocket and her eyes grow three sizes—like a Grinch who can't decide if she's offended or aroused. I can only guess what she's thinking, but I find it immensely hilarious and satisfying to see relief wash over her when I come up with the car remote in my hand. I lift it to the space between our faces and tap the button, which opens the trunk with a soft click.

I'm rewarded with a swift shove to the chest as she shuffles off to get whatever she needs from her bags. I'm standing here wondering what just transpired between us —extremely uncomfortable in my own skin right now. Call me crazy, but if this were any other woman, I'd take her banter as flirting. Playful, even. *Ricky Ricardo*. Why do I find it adorable how hard she's grasping for an annoying nickname? Personally, I think Mr. Progresso is clever enough. I secretly love it.

The desert wind muffles her angry roar from behind the trunk hatch. So she found her surprise. Game point.

When I'd come down the tower with the ridiculous amount of luggage she'd packed, I found my limo completely encased in cling wrap. Whomever she got to do it did their job with zealous enthusiasm. They even individually wrapped each tire.

Well played.

But January didn't count on my years of experience with seven siblings who live for April Fool's Day. With the pocketknife I keep in my pocket, I cut the plastic neatly and used it to wrap January's luggage. I added packing tape for good measure. It's always good to be prepared with supplies.

"You think you're funny," she cries. "But you're just a big child."

I chuckle. "What gave it away? Is it the smile on my face?"

I take pity on her and plunk my pocketknife on top of her suitcase. I'm not going to cut the plastic loose. That's all for her to do.

We spend the rest of the time waiting for the Motor Club outside the car because I can't trust myself in an enclosed space with her. She must feel the same because she's been leaning on the other side of the limo scrolling through Instagram or TikTok or whatever. What could she possibly be doing on there for so long? I don't want to know and I definitely will *not* be checking later.

Finally, a tow truck appears on the horizon and January perks up. I expect her to scramble back in the limo but she struts right up next to me with her hands on her hips. If she starts a fight with the Motor Club guy, I'm throwing her phone in front of the next big rig.

"It's about time," she says.

"We're in the middle of nowhere. This isn't Starbucks."

She throws me a killer glare.

The tow truck pulls up right behind my limo, and as the

guy hops out, I can hardly believe my luck. Elvis Wilson (yes, his parents really named him Elvis—don't ask), a friend of my brother Dante, recognizes me right away and speeds up his gait to meet me.

"Heeeey, Kiki. I thought it might be you." I hate that nickname, but it's hard to outgrow these things. He only gets that from Dante who prefers to use as few syllables as possible. We slap hands and he does a double-take when he notices January. I mean, I'm sure he noticed a gorgeous woman standing here, but I can see awareness dawn on his face when he realizes who she is. I'm about to clamp his jaw shut on his tongue when January barks a laugh.

"Kinky? Ha! I need to hear the story behind this one."

"Not Kinky," I growl. "Kiki. It's short for Enrique."

She doesn't hear a word, though, because she's laughing too hard.

Yeah, real mature. Well, I guess she finally found an amusing nickname for me. I'm just going to let this one go.

"Holy sh- I mean... wow, I'm a huge fan." Elvis regained the faculties of his tongue and now he's just tripping over it. January's not fazed at all, though. She's way too amused right now, and if I'm honest, I think this is the first true smile I've seen on her face. And it's beautiful. She should definitely smile more often. She says hi to Elvis, and instead of a handshake, she goes in for a hug. A hug! And trust me, he's not at all good-looking, so that couldn't be the reason. In fact, I'd be willing to bet his coveralls are a few days ripe. His face is priceless, though, and he's still wearing a goofy grin when the hug is over.

"Oh, man. No one's going to believe this," he says. Have

you ever seen the most ridiculous people meeting celebrities? That's Elvis right now. My teeth hurt from the cringe.

"Do you want to take a selfie?' January's all sugar and rainbows now. There must be something up her sleeve. She's not this nice in real life. Is she trying to make me jealous? I hate to admit it's kind of working.

I'm not even going to bore you with how uncomfortable this makes me. They take some selfies, Elvis asking for just one more, just one more. It's when his hand slips too far that January cuts the photoshoot short. She's polite about it, but firm. She's obviously done this a thousand times, swift and professional in the distance she places between them, all the while leaving him on cloud nine. Touched by an angel with a story to tell for years to come of that time he met January Madison.

I snap in his face. "Hello?" He's still basking in the afterglow and I'm invisible. Ladies and gentlemen, Elvis has left the building.

"I guess I'll change my own tire, then."

I'm practically inside his truck when he runs up to me. "Dude, how did you get this gig?"

"Never mind that. What are you doing way out here?"

He flashes his Motor Club badge. "I got a sweet set up in Idlewild. Two days a week, a grand per."

I whistle because that's a pretty good payday. And he doesn't have to put up with bratty socialites to earn it.

"And it's worth the drive from LA?"

"Heck yeah. Easy money. Mostly schmucks who break down on the side of the road. No offense."

"None taken. It was her fault." I toss my chin in

January's direction. She's filming video with her phone. Great. Now my flat tire's going viral.

"Her fault?" Elvis snorts. "Look, I'm not judging if you're into a little rocky road surprise..."

"What? No. No way."

He laughs. "Dude, I was just joking, but your face is bright red. You're into her."

"Her? Me? No. That's ridiculous. That's... that's..."

"Okay, okay. Don't have an aneurysm. Let's get you back on the rocky road."

"Shut up." I follow Elvis to get my spare and January looks up at me just then. My face flares and her lip twitches at the corner knowingly.

I'm going to murder Elvis.

Chapter Thirteen

JANUARY

By the time we get to the hotel I feel like we've traveled across the Wild West in a covered wagon. There's dust caked inside my shoes, under my fingernails, and also where the sun don't shine. A film of roadside grime adorns my clothes, and I've picked several briars out of my hair. We pull up to the porte-cochère and I'm just glad security is tight because looking like this is not how I'd want to go viral. Kinky's whistling as he opens my door, and you'd think he was on some kind of vacation. I'm greeted with a welcoming party (my dad's doing) and I nod at every "Good afternoon, Miss Madison," as Kinky opens the trunk. I'm ready to get inside and shower all this gunk off as I head for the grand entryway, but Kinky's not behind me. I've grown so used to this horrid man's presence, I'm acutely aware of a disturbing lightness without him disrupting my space. I turn and he's just standing by the limo.

I toss him a glare. "You coming?"

"What for?"

I storm back over to him and hiss, "To bring my bags up."

"Listen, sister. That ain't in my job description."

Is it just me, or is he giving off a serious Han Solo vibe?

"Charming," I say for lack of something more clever.

He leans against his limo like it's the freaking Millennium Falcon and studies his nails. "That's what the ladies usually say."

"You are the worst driver ever."

"I got us here in one piece, didn't I?"

But can you make the Kessel Run in twelve parsecs? I don't think so.

I don't say what I'm thinking. Instead, I settle for, "Barely." Lame.

He pushes off the car and invades my air. He's totally in my face now.

"Look. I'm sure Daddy's got a whole staff of boys who'll be at your constant beck and call. They'll fall all over themselves to make you happy, and will marvel at the privilege to kiss your feet. But my work is done until you're ready for me to drive you somewhere, so if anyone asks, I'll be by the pool because the bellmen can get your bags for you."

With that, he turns on his heel, heaves my bags from the trunk with one swift stride, and plops them on a luggage cart.

"That one was free, princess," he says, taking his leave with a soldier salute.

The first thing I do when I get to my room is toss my clothes in a corner and jump in the shower. There's so much dust and grime all over me, I soap off twice. I just might burn the clothes I wore today, actually. After twenty minutes of standing under the hot running water, I'm finally relaxed. I have to be on my game tonight for the investors' dinner. This meeting is for a venture apart from my dad's reach. My own line of organic self-care products. If I can get this business off the ground, I'll be able to walk away from the hotel fortune with no worries. I still have a few hours before the meeting, but I want to respond to emails and do some busy work I've been putting off. My mind's been distracted lately with thoughts of my driver. He's ruining my life. I have to focus.

I step out of the steamy shower and wrap a towel around my hair and another around my body. Maybe I'll wait to get dressed. I feel light and airy...and clean. I go to find my phone with thoughts of sinking under the soft covers on the bed and resting for a bit when I'm confronted by Enrique unbuttoning his dress shirt. I scream (mostly because he startled me) out of instinct.

He screams back. Mockingly, I imagine.

"How did you get in here?' I cry.

"This is my room. The bellboy let me in." He's frantically re-buttoning his shirt. I get a glimpse of tan skin against white cotton and my voice cracks.

"This is my room, you idiot. Yours is next door."

His eyes dart to my luggage. "I can see that now."

It's now that I remember I'm wearing nothing but a woefully inadequate towel. "Don't look at me."

"I don't want to look at you, woman. Put some clothes on."

"You're in *my* room. Leave, LEAVE!"

I grab the closest things I can reach and throw them at him. He's dodging complimentary shampoo and soaps like he's in the Matrix. I throw a bottle of conditioner. Narrowly misses his ear. I'm running out of things to chuck at him, hoping he'll get a hint before I have to resort to the coffee pot or hair dryer, but he's laughing. I'm on the verge of having a wardrobe malfunction and this is all hilarious to him. Bright, straight teeth sparkle, and behind his scruff, the jumbo-sized dimples twinkle on either side of his smile. I'm blind now. I shouldn't have stared at the light. Must. Throw. Something. Else. Ah! Lotion. Slam. Right in his chest. My towel is slipping with each angry movement and his eyes flash.

"Out!" I point furiously to the door adjoining our suites together. Whose terrible idea was that anyhow?

He surrenders his hands in the air. "Okay, okay. I'm leaving. But I'm taking this." He swipes the chocolate mint off my pillow, unwraps it, and pops it in his mouth.

"Mmmmm," he hums, licking his lips. "So good."

"I will seriously kill you, Kinky."

He winks. "That's my name. Don't wear it out."

He makes a dramatic exit, slamming the door, but comes back two seconds later, scowling. He grabs his duffle bag and leaves for a second time, which greatly decreases the impact of his exodus.

I want to be extremely angry, but something bubbles from deep in my chest and a deluge of giggles escape me. This whole situation is so ridiculous, it's the stuff of classic black-and-white comedy movies. I can't stop, which is amazing in itself because I don't remember the last time I laughed, let alone uncontrollably. Is this what years of repressed emotions feels like? Like I've been holding every ounce of mirth in a Mason jar and Enrique comes along with a hammer, breaking the glass? I still can't stand him, but I have to admit he shakes things up inside me like no one ever has. He's a 9.0 earthquake, and I'm walking on stilts. There's no hope for me.

Chapter Fourteen

ENRIQUE

I didn't sleep last night so I'm making up for it on the poolside chaise lounge. Just knowing she was on the other side of the hotel room wall made me restless. Was she awake too? Was she planning to bludgeon me in my sleep? Did she have one of those silky, rich girl pajama sets? My mind was in perpetual motion. It didn't help that I'd spotted her having a romantic dinner with some stuffy Ivy League guy when I passed by the formal dining room. I just *had* to go wandering around, didn't I? Why didn't I just stay put and order room service? It's not as though I could have taken the limo out by myself to the casinos. I settled for an overpriced hamburger at the bar, and instantly regretted it. I guess I'm spoiled with a chef for a brother and growing up in the restaurant industry.

This morning, I was resolved to drive into town to get a reasonably priced, yet not disgusting, breakfast. Maybe eggs Florentine, or at least an omelet that doesn't come with a side of gold. But when I got to the limo, the entire car was covered in Post-it notes. The *entire* car. I don't know if January hires people to do these pranks for her, or if she gets her hands dirty herself—which is doubtful as she wouldn't want to be photographed doing something like this—but one thing's for certain. There's no way she'll get the satisfaction of a reaction from me. If she thinks I'll march up to her room with a handful of Post-its, just so she can laugh at me, she's got another thing coming. I won't even bring it up in conversation. That'll show her. I'm not going to let her know she's getting to me. And I mean that in more ways than one. She is as beautiful as she is infuriating. She will either bring me to my knees, or I will bring her to hers. Either scenario sounds intriguing to me.

It took me twenty minutes to remove all those sticky notes, and by that time I was so famished, I settled for McDrive-through. The day's agenda has January doing PR stuff on site at the hotel—something about a ribbon cutting. In other words, I'm not needed until tomorrow, so I threw on my swim trunks and headed down to the pool.

Now I'm groggy from an afternoon nap, the heat of the sun, and the effects of the cheap rum in my cocktail. There's a figure above. A vision in white—a desert mirage with a striking resemblance to January. Golden wisps of hair float in the breeze, haloed by the sun, and the face is shadowed in blue silhouette. My vision is a blur, retinas burning from the UV light, and I'm vaguely aware of the slender form towering over me.

"Get up, you lazy good for nothing."

"Welcome home, dear," I grumble with the most luxurious yawn. My eyes are slowly peeling open, taking a narrowed glimpse of loose-fitting pants flapping in the wind. My gaze travels up to find palms planted firmly on cocked hips, and a tantalizingly low collar dipping toward the waistline. Am I still dreaming? A tug of the towel under me flips me over, and because I'm still in a sleep state, I'm on the ground face down with very little difficulty. Definitely not dreaming.

"Why don't you answer your phone, Kinky? It could have been an emergency."

"Somehow I doubt I'd be your first contact in an emergency." I peel myself off the ground and try my best to emerge from this dizzy feeling.

"It could be a transportation emergency," she says smugly.

I retrieve my phone from under the chaise and shade the screen from the sun. Three missed calls from Maleficent.

"I told you yesterday I'd be at the pool. You don't have to be so needy."

She clicks her tongue, but instead of lashing back with a witty comeback, she steps on my foot. It doesn't hurt because she's in flats today, but it's the principal of the thing. So I react for her benefit only.

"Ouch."

She snubs her nose up. "Serves you right."

I'm actually starting to get weary of this whole enemy act, so I resign myself to just ask nicely, "What was it you needed, Miss?" I say the last part through clenched teeth. It's the best I can do. It catches her off guard.

"If that's your way of getting me to call you Hot Bod—"

"No, I don't need to fish for compliments. I really would like to know what you needed."

She gulps on a reply, and it's freaking adorable how one nicety clams her up. It's like she doesn't know how to function without sparring with me.

"I don't need anything *right now*," she says all pouty. "But there's been an update for tomorrow."

Couldn't that have waited, or she could've sent me a text since she obviously has my number? Why go out of her way to tell me something she could have told me later by knocking on my door even?

She crosses her arms defensively. I've come to realize this is a self-preservation technique, and I wonder what she's hiding from.

"Check your email," she says, and makes to leave, but then stops to look at my empty hurricane glass with the umbrella still perched on the rim.

"That's quite the manly drink you have there, Kinky."

It's fruitless to try and hide it. She's seen the evidence—along with a few other discarded umbrellas.

"That? Oh, my new lady friend left that behind. I had a beer." I force a burp for good measure. "See? I'm a guy." Her eyes dart to the nearby lounge chairs, but it's obvious there's no sign of recent occupancy. She gives me a lazy grin.

"Liar."

Pants on fire? Possibly.

Her eyebrows rise up in a challenge. "What's her name?"

"Hmm?"

"Her name. Fruity drink girl. What is it?" Her arms cross casually across her chest, causing the top part of that white jumper to pillow apart at the collar. There's a thin gold chain clinging to her skin, so long it disappears down to her navel. I heave like a cat dislodging a furball.

"H-h-h-h-emil… ia."

"Hemilia? Really?"

I clamp my lips together and nod. Can't say stupid stuff with my mouth closed.

"Uh-huh." She's not buying it even a tiny bit. "Where did she go? Did you scare her off with that Erik Estrada thing you've got going on there?"

She twirls her finger at me in a figure eight. Hardy-har-har. So what if I own motorcycle cop glasses? I bet she's secretly into it.

"No." I shrug one shoulder. "She's coming up to my room later."

She snorts. "Does she charge by the hour, or did you get a package deal?"

I feel the corners of my mouth curl of their own volition. This sparring. It's more than meets the eye. Why would one of the world's most influential socialites care what I was drinking, who I was with, or what I did with my spare time? She could have sent someone to fetch me. She could have sent me a message. But she didn't. She went out of her way to find me, wake me up, and now it's like she can't help herself.

"Why? Jealous?"

"Ha!" Her laugh is incredibly fake. "Hardly. I'll just lock the door to our adjoining suites so she doesn't steal anything."

"Mmm-hmm," I hum.

She mumbles something incoherent under her breath and struts away. Her white jumpsuit hugs her curves, and the fabric swishes around her ankles as she retreats. I realize (while appreciating the view because I'm a straight guy with eyeballs) that I'd been tempering my breaths—like a scuba diver conserving oxygen. I need to get a grip before I find myself with brain damage.

Chapter Fifteen

ENRIQUE

The next day January had some dog charity thing. It's just outside the main strip at a children's hospital. I have new instructions to not only drive the woman, but act as a temporary bodyguard. The email came yesterday. Apparently, the Madison Palm Springs security staff is spread too thin today, and a skeleton crew went ahead of us to the event. The email from V. Taylor *(Vivian? Valerie?)* said

January's regular bodyguard is "no longer with us." What's that supposed to mean? Did she drive him to an early grave? Sounds completely plausible.

January's quiet today. She avoided me the rest of the afternoon and came back to her room pretty late last night. I wasn't waiting up to listen for her or anything. She just brushes her hair and blinks extra loudly.

We're pulling into the parking lot of the hospital and I'm already salty about my new responsibilities as a bodyguard when January says three dreaded words.

"Use the valet."

I laugh sarcastically. "Over my dead body."

"You do realize that can be arranged," she says. Yesterday I would have taken her seriously, but right now her voice is soft and there's humor in her tone. What is this strange universe?

"Remember when I told you I don't like people touching my car?"

I steal a glance at her from the rearview mirror and her eyes flicker with awareness. Yes. I'll not soon forget that either, woman. I take that as a yes.

"There's no way some teenager is going to park my Caddy."

"As my bodyguard, you have to stay near me at all times, and you can't do that if you're off parking your car." She waves her hand around, "Wherever it is you park cars."

"In parking lots, generally. Sometimes on the street or in a driveway."

She rolls her eyes and I'm aware for the first time how incredibly blue they are. Keep your eyes on the road, dude.

I drive toward the main entrance where there's a balloon arch waiting for us and a host of women dressed like nurses flanking the entryway like the servants in those British shows my sister likes to watch. I'm slowing down, but January pounces to the seat nearest the divider and flails her hand through the window, practically smacking me in the face.

"No, no. Keep going."

"What the…"

"Just take me with you to park and we'll walk in together."

I grab hold of her hand just to annoy her. She's stuck now. I'm going to hold her arm captive just to watch her squirm. Her skin is soft. Really, really soft. I don't realize I'm stroking her wrist with my thumb until she yanks free.

I clear my throat. "What about taking you door to door, princess? It's what you wanted, remember?" I'm taking her back to that first day we met and all the vitriol between us because it's familiar. It's comfortable. This attraction I'm beginning to feel has to die a swift and bloody death.

"Just do as I say." She crawls back to her seat facing front. That's better.

I continue on past the balloon arch and the line of nurses. Their faces as I wheel right by them cracks me up. All heads turn in unison. Classic. I circle the parking lot for what seems a small eternity, but this place is packed in anticipation of January's visit. Not one open space, not to mention the two spaces I need to park this limo.

"I'll have to find a spot on the street. Are you sure—"

"Yes, for heaven's sake, just do it."

I pull down my sunglasses and wink at her in the mirror. "That's what *she* said."

Princess is not amused. I find an open spot about a block and a half away in a nearby strip mall. We exit the limo and head on down the sidewalk. January's wearing a flowy floral dress, which is equal parts conservative and flirty. Or maybe it's just me who finds it flirty. She's wearing tan heels, but at least they're not sky-high, so the walk won't be completely unbearable for her. Still, I can't help but wonder if her pampered, privileged feet will make it.

"You okay?" I ask.

"I'm capable of walking a block, if that's what you're asking."

Okaaay.

We arrive to find some of the nurses have dispersed. Our drive-by must have discouraged them. As soon as we're spotted, though, a couple of them scatter to call the others back outside. January is greeted like royalty. You'd think she was Princess Diana come back to life by the way they're fawning over her, faces beaming with admiration. There's press, but I recognize some of the hotel security have come over to keep them at bay. They won't let them get within five-hundred feet of the hospital entrance. January doesn't pose for the cameras like I thought she would. Not even a wave. Maybe a big network has an exclusive inside. The administrative director ushers us in with a huge grin.

"I'm Holly Gallagher. We're all so thrilled to have you. The children can hardly contain themselves. A lot of families drove in from miles around to be here today."

January smiles warmly and it freaks me out a little. She

seems so... so... genuine. "I'm sure their excitement is for the dogs and not me."

Holly chuckles as women do when they get together, and January shares a moment with her. In two seconds flat they're BFFs or something. I don't get females.

We're led through several corridors until we reach a courtyard nestled between the buildings. It's a child's oasis with lots of open space and a playground on one side. The event's already in progress when we arrive. There's a guy doing wildly intricate balloon sculptures and several game booths, face-painting station, and all-you-can-eat carnival food.

"The adoption kennel is right over there," Holly points out. A fenced-off area near the makeshift stage holds at least twenty dogs of varying breeds. A few kids at a time are let inside to play with them while a line of more kids wait impatiently. On the stage, a magician is finishing up his act, and Holly directs us in that direction. I'm scanning the whole courtyard because I'm supposed to be January's tough bodyguard, but there doesn't seem to be any threats —unless you count the creepy clown trying to not make the kids cry.

We pass by the adoption kennel and January slows down to greet the Kanines for Kids staff. She knows each and every one of their names, asks specific questions about their families, and checks with a couple of the girls about how the dogs are doing. One of them makes a quip and January laughs lightly, a soft, bubbling giggle that's completely contradictory to her iconic celebrity-influencer persona.

Eventually, January makes her way to the stage while I

stand by, watching the crowd like a watered-down secret service agent. Holly thanks the magician and goes into a speech about Kanines for Kids, introducing the charity's founder, January Madison. *Founder?* As in she *found* a charity to latch her name onto, or *founded*, founded it? I'm pretty sure celebrities get paid a nice kickback from charities as a spokesperson for the commercials and stuff. I wouldn't be surprised if her dad's making her do it. But at least she acts passionate about it when she takes the mic and invites about ten random kids on stage. She talks about her vision for the non-profit, how she wishes that every child and their families here today would adopt a dog if they're able to care for one. Most of the children here today are living at home with their disabilities and would greatly benefit from the companionship a pet would provide.

"Kanines for Kids is for anyone who has a need," she says. "Pets help reduce stress and anxiety for not only the children, but for their families as well. Whether a child is in remission, has a permanent physical disability, or is mentally or sociologically challenged, Kanines for Kids will afford them a chance to adopt a pet at absolutely no cost to their families."

She goes on to say how the organization also plans for therapy dogs to visit children's hospitals once a week to lift the spirits of the kids still getting treatment, and anyone willing to go through the training could register for the program.

"It's through the generosity of donations that we can continue changing lives every day," she says, and wait—are those tears in her eyes? "But you didn't come here to see me."

Yes, yes, they did.

"What's your name?" She squats down to the eye level of a little girl on tiny little crutches and tilts the microphone to her.

"A-a-allison."

"Allison. What a pretty name. How old are you?"

Allison giggles. "Five."

"Wow. So big. What do you want to be when you grow up?"

"A vet-i are-ium."

The crowd all goes awww.

I can tell January wants to laugh, but only because Allison is so darn cute it would be a crime to ignore it. With amusement in her tone, she says, "Well then, you can come work for us at Kanines for Kids when you're all grown up."

Allison beams and January gives her a hug. She interviews a couple other kids in the same manner and then takes her leave, deflecting the attention to the bluegrass band coming on next. She doesn't pose for a photo op, doesn't hog the spotlight, isn't taking selfies to post all over the Internet. She's just a lovely woman, helping dogs and kids. Beautiful, even—effervescent as the wind gently rushes over her dress, tossing her corn silk hair in wisps around her face. I don't get it, which really ticks me off because I don't like puzzles. Tía Lucy's always doing puzzles. Those really difficult ones with ten-thousand pieces. When I was in fifth grade, she lived with us for about five months after her divorce and had puzzles on every flat surface. That might have something to do with my aversion. But I digress. January is a puzzle, too. Far more complicated than Tía Lucy's. Where are the press? The TV stations? The bloggers?

We don't stay long after the short appearance. We sneak out the service entrance and get to the limo through a back alley instead of the way we came. January doesn't complain about the pungent smells of the garbage bins we pass. In fact, she's in a great mood. There's a spring in her step and a contented smile on her face. I'm wracking my brain to remember if she has a secret twin that only comes out for charity appearances. This can't be the same woman.

I must have a goofy expression because she squints at me sidelong and says, "What?"

"What?" I repeat like a fool, and now I'm grinning stupidly which seems to propel her to come over and poke me in the dimple.

"Poke," she says as her finger smashes into my face. "Poke, poke."

"Are sound effects really necessary?"

"I've been wanting to do that," she admits, owning it confidently. I'll bet she just does whatever she wants, no matter how silly, like it's the most normal thing in the world. And I don't know why I feel a rush of heat spread up my neck when she says that, but something inside me loves that she's been thinking about touching me. Even if only on the cheek with the tip of her finger. If anyone else did that, they'd be toast.

"You were really good with those kids back there," I say. "Do you make a lot of these types of appearances?"

"No. I'm usually more behind the scenes."

"Oh. So did your dad make you come out here for this?"

She snorts. "Yeah, right. My dad hates that I do this. He

thinks I'm just here for the ribbon cutting of the hotel's new spa, but I used this time away to…take care of some personal business. When the Kanines for Kids team found out I was coming out here, they set this up."

"Huh. All this time I was thinking it was your dad's charity."

"No way. The only reason he doesn't fight me on this is because he realized it's good publicity. But I showed him."

So that's why there was no press allowed inside the event. For her to stick it to her dad?

"This charity is near and dear to my heart. I started it with Rachael, a woman I met when Madison Industries dedicated a wing at the Beverly Children's Ward. She had this fantastic idea and I'm trying to help her fulfill it."

She's in full-confession mode now and I'm here for it.

"I hate the press. Don't get me wrong, they have to feed their families, too. But today was all about the kids. I didn't want cameras and paparazzi to ruin it."

Wow. That's… that's… honorable. And lovely. And absolutely not what I was expecting. We reach the limo and stand there for a moment. I don't want to break the spell of this new side of January. Or her not-evil-twin, perhaps. She's smiling at me, inching closer. Every breath of mine is faulty as she nears until we're toe to toe. I'm existing between two heartbeats. She tilts her head like she's thinking. What could she be thinking about, I wonder? She lifts her hands, smoothing her palms over her hair as her head swivels side to side, all the while her eyes remain trained on my—wait a second.

"Are you admiring yourself in my sunglasses?"

She chokes a laugh. So busted.

"The mirrors are distracting. Got me thinking—what if I go dark?"

"Dark as in... the dark side of the Force?"

"Uh, no. I was talking about my hair. Dark brown." Her tone softens and I can barely hear her when she says, "Like yours."

Chapter Sixteen

JANUARY

He opens his door, wearing low-slung sweatpants and nothing else. Is my mouth salivating? I think so. I think I feel a dribble of drool on my chin.

"I'm ordering room service," I squeak. "Might as well join me." I turn my head away from him so he doesn't see the fierce blush in my cheeks. Looking at Enrique shirtless is like staring into the sun. "And put a shirt on."

What is it with the men in my life? Must I constantly remind them to dress from the waist up?

He leans against the doorjamb, straight in my line of vision.

"Don't you want to spend your free evening with that guy?"

"What guy? There's no guy."

"The suit you had dinner with the other night. Not that it's my business. I just thought—"

"Will you shut up?"

I risk a glance up at his face. Those dark eyes are black as coffee in this lighting. He's studying my features, scanning my eyes with a furrowed brow.

"I had dinner with my investors the other night if that's what you're talking about. It's not on your itinerary because… reasons. And what were you doing spying on me anyway?"

"I don't spy on people, lady. I was walking by looking for somewhere to eat that wasn't a thousand dollars a plate. The only place for a single guy to eat affordably in this place is the bar."

I groan, giving him a hard stare.

"Do you want to have dinner with me or not?"

I swear, this man is so infuriating.

He winks playfully. "Are you asking me out on a date?"

Heaven help me.

"Bye. Enjoy your bar food." I turn and walk back to my suite, unable to close the door on his face since he's leaning on it. That would be so satisfying, though.

"I'll have the porterhouse," he calls after me. "With fries."

I wave him off behind my back. "Whatever."

"I'll be over in twenty minutes."

"I don't care."

I hear a small laugh as he shuts the door. Why am I such a sucker for a handsome face?

"It's not a date," I cry out, hoping he hears me through the thick door.

I haven't eaten since the protein shake I had for breakfast and I'm famished. I think I'll have the salmon. One thing I love about the new features the hotel is adding to the rooms is the iPad concierge. With the in-room iPad, guests can request more towels, get a wake-up call, order room service, and almost anything they need without having to call the front desk. Of course, we do still have an excellent concierge on staff, but the digital feature eliminates the wait for small requests.

I start the order process and am startled by the joint door flying open.

"Medium rare." Enrique pokes his head in and just as quickly shuts the door again.

I place the order, laughing at the situation I'm in right now. And if I'm being honest, I'm a little nervous, as if this really is a date. Which it's not.

My phone lights up with a text, and a rush of butterflies swoop in my belly at the idea it might be Enrique adding to his order, or teasing about this being a date. But the contact on my screen shows it's my dad.

Dad: Why haven't you checked in with me?

Aaand the butterflies are gone.

Me: The ribbon cutting went fine. Pix online.

Three dots appear and disappear. Then nothing comes

in. I set the phone face down, more than happy to ignore any more texts from him. I consider taking a shower, but that would appear too eager. And this is definitely not a date. I decide to just freshen up with a damp towel, change my underwear, swipe on a fresh layer of deodorant, and touch up my makeup. I would do the same for anybody. Maybe a little dab of essential oils for good measure.

Despite putting my phone on the dresser with the screen face down, it still buzzes with the next incoming text. I try to ignore it, but I have self-diagnosed nomophobia. As in No Mo Phone… ia. It's a thing.

Dad: Come straight to the penthouse on Monday after your trip. Papers to sign.

Papers to sign? I'm not feeling this. When Dad says something abstract like papers to sign, it usually means there are lawyers involved.

Me: Explain please.

Dad: Not over text.

I consider leaving it like that, then maybe turn my phone off. But he's not getting off that easy.

Me: I'll think about it.

Then, I shut off my phone. No Mo Phone Anonymous would give me a medal.

True to his word, Enrique knocks on my door twenty minutes later, but it's not the door we share. He's at the front door.

"Did you lock yourself out of your room or someth—"

I'm arrested by the eye candy before me. Enrique's dressed in a pair of stretched washed jeans and a button-down cotton shirt with a subtle pink gradient. Let me tell you. Only a handful of men can pull off pink, and Enrique and the copper hue of his skin is one of them. Also, when I say button down, I mean button *down*—as in, the top four buttons are undone revealing miles and miles of caramelized golden abs adorned with a small rectangular pendant on a delicate silver chain, and a shorter silver necklace with a turquoise cross. He looks so delicious, the food I ordered will never compare.

He reveals a single tulip he had hidden behind his back. "The gift shop was closed so I found you this."

I love tulips. This one is especially beautiful with shades of orange and red.

"When you say you *found* this, you mean you picked it from the hotel grounds?"

"Technically, yes, but it's the thought that counts."

I level him with a stern look. "That's technically stealing."

"You want me to put it back?"

No, I do not. I want a lot of things right now, but sending him off isn't one of them.

"Just get in here," I say.

The sunken lounge of my suite is about three steps down from the sleeping area and is only separated by a wrought iron railing. For practical purposes, I chose not to occupy one of the deluxe suites for this trip, but there isn't a room in this hotel that isn't fitted with luxury. I place the flower on the coffee table and find myself awkwardly standing here, not sure how to proceed.

It's not a date. It's not a date. I changed my panties. It's not a date.

Maybe if I chant it over and over in my head, my palms will stop sweating.

"Would you like something to drink?" I gesture to the mini fridge.

"Water. Thanks."

So weird. He seems just as nervous as I am.

"No beer for you?"

He looks around the room, his eyes briefly landing on the bed, then moves to sit on the sofa.

"As your bodyguard, I want to keep my wits about me." His fingers loop around his silver necklace, grazing the rectangle pendant with involuntary, habitual strokes.

"You're not my bodyguard anymore. That was just a one-time thing."

He tilts his head, studying me, then leans back casually, crossing his ankle over his knee. With new confidence, he spreads out his arms on the back cushion.

"What if a big, scary man such as myself comes in here demanding steak? I'd have to defend your honor."

I snort. "Big? Somebody is a bit overconfident."

A wry smirk creeps across his face. "You'll never find out, I'm afraid."

I feel my cheeks flare up. "That's not—" I can hardly get the words out. "I wasn't talking about… forget it."

He laughs; a bright, full sound. Open and free. "You're too easy to tease."

He rises from the sofa and approaches me, stopping inches from where I'm standing.

"May I?"

He leans in closer and I turn into a statue. What is he doing? And am I going to let him do it?

His chest brushes against my arm, sending sparks of awareness all over my body. It's almost like I'm one of those buzzing fobs they give you in restaurants to let you know your table's ready.

Bzzz, bzzz, bzzz.

His eyes lock with mine and I follow his every miniscule move, every breath. The way his midnight gaze dips to my mouth and back up to my eyes. His lashes are like black velvet, so thick and luxurious. I want to brush my lips over them. Heat pours off him in waves and I take in the tang of salty herbs embedded in his skin. His scent is clean and masculine and something else I can't put my finger on. If I could bottle it, women would be knocking down my door to buy it for their men.

Without releasing his stare, Enrique leans past me and opens the mini fridge.

"You promised me water?"

Oh. I blink the steamy haze away. I feel so foolish.

Trying to laugh it off, I say, "I never promised to get it for you."

He reaches in, gets his water, and slowly unscrewing the cap, he says, "My mistake."

His takes a long pull, almost finishing the entire contents of the bottle in one swallow.

"You must be really thirsty," I say lamely.

"Parched."

He returns to the sofa looking every inch the Adonis that he is. I might explode. Thankfully, the knock on the door announcing room service saves me from further embarrassment.

The attendant sets up the round table with a white linen tablecloth, silver flatware, cloth napkins, and a small vase of flowers. When he leaves, I add the tulip to the arrangement, which seems to please Enrique. Or maybe I'm just imagining it.

When we sit down to eat, he crosses himself and says a silent prayer. Then he practically mauls his food.

"There's this thing called chewing," I say. "Maybe you can try it sometime."

He brings his napkin to his mouth and swallows. "Sorry. With six brothers, if you don't eat fast, someone will steal food off your plate."

I drop my jaw. "Six? Oh my word, there's *seven* of you walking around this earth? Heaven help us."

He smiles. "Eight, actually. I have a sister, too."

"Wow. That sounds…"

"Noisy?"

"I was going to say amazing. But yeah. I guess it would get loud with so many people. Did you have a big house growing up?"

"Yes, actually. My parents bought the next lot over and built on it. But we did all cram in a VW bug when we went places. Like a clown car."

"Really?"

"No. You really are easy to tease."

I throw my napkin at him and he throws it back, hitting me in the face.

"I'm an only child," I say. "Sometimes I wish I had a sibling, but then there would be two children for my parents to ruin."

"I'm sorry." He leans across the table, covering my hand in his. His palm is warm and soothing. I could live in this warmth.

"Anyway." I shake my head to ward off the sting of

tears behind my eyes. "I want to hear all about these barbarian brothers of yours. What happens when they steal your food?"

He squeezes my hand and returns back to his meal. "It's knives out. Full-on war."

"Hmm. I was going to sneak a bite of your steak but I'm glad I didn't."

"Take a bite." He's already cutting me a piece. A really big piece.

"I was just kidding."

"I insist." He pokes it with his fork and offers it to me.

"I can't fit that much meat in my mouth."

"Then don't marry a Latino."

Whoa.

He starts to laugh so hard, tears form in his eyes. "I mean… yeah… we love our meat."

I'm busting up, unable to tamp down the laughter. "I'm sure you do."

We giggle for what feels like ten minutes. We're basically a couple of college frat boys. It feels so good to laugh so freely. When I finally catch my breath and gain some control, I wrap my fingers around Enrique's hand, pulling the fork toward me, and shove the entire piece of steak in my mouth.

Enrique immediately stops laughing and stares at me wide-eyed. This bite really is too big for my mouth, but I'm committed now, so I chew and chew and chew. And chew. Enrique parts his lips as he watches me. He hardly blinks, but when he does, it's like a sonic boom. Seriously… those lashes! It's not even fair.

I finally finish, and without realizing it, I swipe my

tongue over my lips to clean the excess grease and seasoning. Enrique's Adam's apple does a little dance.

"Do you want some of my fish?"

His eyes go wider. "I think I'll take you up on that beer."

"Good call." I shoot up from my chair and swiftly bolt to the mini fridge. As I open the door, the cold blast in my face jolts me back to reality.

This is not a date. He's your driver. This is not a date. Although… I did change my panties.

I'm pretty sure we have one-hundred percent gotten off track. And it's my fault. I'm the one who invited him for dinner. I need to get this night back on the normal train. Okay, we've *never* been on the normal train. We've always been on the crazy train. We're two people within close proximity to one another, eating food. I can do this.

I give him his beer and try to think of a safe subject. A conversation with Enrique is like walking through a sexy, very dangerous field of land mines.

"Tell me about these seven siblings. Are you the oldest?"

The tension in his brows slides off his features. "No, I'm the middle child."

"Oooh. So in other words, there are less photos of you, and your parents forget you exist."

"Actually, not really. There are so many of us, I think my parents forget *all* of us exist. Except Memo."

"Is he the mechanic or the insurance agent?"

"He's the priest."

"Seriously?"

"He's the oldest, so my parents made all their mistakes on him." He's laughing as he speaks so I know he's kidding, but I'm still fascinated by the family dynamic when there's so many brothers.

"Sebastian is the baby, so he gets away with everything."

"Okay, I promise to try to remember all this. Which one is the mechanic?"

"Dante. He doesn't work as a mechanic, though. It's just a hobby. He owns a towing company. That guy who came and fixed our tire? He works with Dante sometimes."

I remember that guy. "Elvis."

"Yep. Don't ask about the name."

"Okay. And then you said one of your brother sells insurance?"

"This can't be interesting to you. If you're trying to kill this wildly romantic moment, getting me to talk about my brothers is a good way to do it."

Thick liquid boils in my belly at the words 'wildly romantic', but knowing he's joking with me, I laugh it off. "I enjoy hearing about your siblings. It's like watching TLC, but considerably less hillbilly."

He chuckles and takes a pull of his beer. "Okay. Nataniel, who likes to be called Nate—is the other middle child. He's a year younger than me and he owns an insurance agency in Laguna Beach. And before you ask, yes, he's annoying. But he also has some good advice, so we don't tell him to shut up as much as we'd like to."

I feel like I should be writing this down. I'll probably never meet these brothers, but I'm learning more about Enrique when he talks about them. I don't know why I want to get to know Enrique better but I do.

"So who are we missing?" I count on my fingers. "We've got four so far?"

He counts on his fingers, too. "Yeah. I think so. I forget how many brothers I have sometimes."

"Get out." I throw a piece of parsley at him. It bounces off his rock-hard pecs. "Tell me about your sister."

"Francesca." His face softens and there's a twinkle in his eye I'd not seen before. "She's the sweetest person you'll ever meet and sings like an angel." His gaze drifts to the window. His sister is the sun and moon to him, I can tell by the way he sighs wistfully.

"I'd like to hear her sing one day."

His eyes slice back to me and he smiles. "Maybe."

"Anyway. Two brothers to go."

"No. It's your turn. I want you to tell me something about yourself."

I laugh halfheartedly. "You know, for someone who's chased by the paps all the time, my life is pretty boring."

"I don't believe that for a second. What was that dinner about? The investors. Even though I only saw one guy."

"Wow. Are you jealous?"

"Why would I be jealous? I'm your driver. Plus, who's the guy you're with now? Me."

"Okay, Casanova. I'm starting an organic skincare line. It's safe for the environment, non-toxic, hypoallergenic, and it actually works. And there were *two* investors. One of them must have been in the bathroom when you walked by."

He stares at me, by the way he leans forward with his elbows on the table, I can almost believe he's fascinated by this.

"You invented a skincare line?"

"Not all by myself. I have an old friend in Paris who's simply brilliant. She used to make creams and soaps and bring them to school. It wasn't something I'd ever come up with on my own. But sometimes I'd go to her house with ideas for fragrance combos. When we got older, we got to talking one night over too much wine and we came up with the crazy idea to start a business. It's all her. I'm just along for the ride."

He reaches to fix a lock of my hair. "You bring more to the table than you give yourself credit for."

"Well, I know how to talk people out of their money. Plus, everyone's always trying to get into business with the Madison clan in some way."

"That's a rare talent, being able to talk people out of money. Maybe you should go work for Nate."

I snort. "To sell insurance?"

"Yeah." He's joking, of course.

"Okay. I told you something. More brothers, please."

"Fine. Mateo is the third youngest. He's entirely irresponsible, and thinks he's a ladies' man, but he's really a hot mess. And Ignacio, whom we call Nacho, is a chef. And he would blow a gasket if he tasted this porterhouse."

"Like, in a good way?"

He shakes his head solemnly. "In a very bad way. You had a bite. What did you think?"

My face goes hot. I was thinking quite a lot of things when I took that bite, but not about how it tasted.

"I don't know. Maybe it was hard to chew." *Probably because I had too much of it in my mouth.*

"Exactly. It looked beautiful. It was cooked just right.

The seasoning was good. But your chef is cutting corners. The menu claims it's grass fed. A choice cut of beef should melt in your mouth, not give your jaw a workout."

How on earth did we circle back to this? I refuse to get embarrassed again. Instead, I cast my eyes to my plate and take a sip of my chardonnay.

"I'm sorry. You were enjoying your meal. I grew up watching those shows on the Food Channel. You know the one with the surprise ingredients? At the dinner table, my dad, who's also a chef, would play a game with us to see if we could guess what herbs and spices he used in his cooking. We'd pick apart the flavors and pretend we were the judges on those shows. My brother, Ignacio, had a lot of fun voting my dad off. Now I can't eat out anymore without analyzing every ingredient. And you definitely don't want to eat out with Ignacio. He'll ruin the entire experience."

I've never seen him so animated before. It's contagious and I realize there's a huge smile on my face.

"Sounds like a fun way to grow up to me. My dad was always at some business trip, and my mom at the bottom of a bottle of gin."

I don't tell that to many people, but the couple of friends I've confided in before only feigned pity. Enrique isn't looking at me like that. Not even real pity—which is refreshing. His expression is more akin to admiration. Or maybe he's falling asleep? Either way, his eyes are dreamy and heavy.

How did this happen? This shift. I woke up this morning determined to hate the man, and I'm fairly certain he felt the same way. But here we are, not only being civilized, but dare I say it? Flirting?

He sips his beer and seems to survey my face. A thunderstorm of questions behind those dark lashes. His lips hitch into a lazy smile and I feel exposed under his stare.

"If this were a date," he says, clearly changing the subject.

"It's not."

A pause. He's switching gears, here. "No. That would be wrong on several levels."

"So wrong," I agree.

"Completely inappropriate."

"Oh so, so, so astronomically… not right." I take a big swallow of wine. What was left in the glass got a little warm so it doesn't even taste good anymore.

"But if it were," he continues. "Hypothetically speaking. I'd dance with you."

He *dances*? Not a single one of my past boyfriends would dance with me. I was beginning to lose faith in the idea of ever meeting a guy who liked to dance. Apparently only the off-limits men are up to the task.

"Hypothetically, if we were to dance, what kind of music would there be?"

His voice grows deeper. Almost coaxing. "Oldies. Nat King Cole, Fred Astaire, Frank Sinatra. The golden era of romance."

Gulp.

I wiggle in my seat. "It's probably a good thing there's no music playing, then."

His dimple makes a stunning appearance. "I'm not much of a singer, but as I recall, Fred would sing to Ginger while they danced."

In a graceful maneuver, he's on his feet, extending his

hand to me. My body reacts of its own volition, letting him guide me to an open space of the floor. I'm in his arms in a fluid motion, my right hand cradled in his left, his right arm curled around my waist. He sways me, rocking side to side.

"Forgive my singing voice," he says in a whisper. "I'm not that good."

I'm a ball of nerves. Every point of contact with him is a tiny firework. His hand slides to the small of my back and he draws me closer to him. His firm body presses gently to my belly and fire alarm bells go off inside me.

One Adam-twelve, we have a situation. All units report to the scene. This is not a drill.

The scruff of Enrique's whiskers scrape against my cheek and he holds me there, still swaying.

"Heaven…" His warm breath caresses my ear, my neck, my shoulder. The man dances *and* sings. Okay, it's more of a mumbly chant than singing, but that's not the point. I'm being serenaded. His tender voice carries our dance steps. Cheek to cheek. Just like Fred and Ginger. Well, more like Ricky and Lucy. But I don't care. My inhibitions can go take a hike. It's not a date. But does having a good time need a label? His body fits mine so perfectly. As dance partners go, that is. Strictly on a professional level—let's say if we were competitive ballroom dancers. I can dance with my chauffeur if I want to. And boy do I want to. There are no fancy moves. No spins. No dips. The way he sways me is almost lulling.

When he forgets the words he hums, and the rumble of it sends my skin ablaze. I lean into him to feel more of it.

"Do you like this?" he asks into my neck.

Yowza.

"As long as I'm not expected to break out into a tap sequence."

A soft chuckle vibrates his chest. "Only during the orchestral break."

We dance for as long as possible without it getting awkward. He hums the melody long after what would be the duration of the song. For a while, we stop dancing entirely. We're just two people holding each other in silence, not willing to let go.

He's the first to break away, keeping contact until the last moment. When we're nose to nose, that crooked smile of his plays on his features.

"Thank you," he says simply.

As he takes another step away, my whole body protests.

"For what?" I ask.

He cradles my hand and brings it to his lips. "For the best not-date ever."

Chapter Seventeen

ENRIQUE

After my not-a-date with January, I'm too pent-up to go to sleep. Pacing the length of my room was only making my thirst for her worse, knowing she was probably in a cute little nightgown on the other side of the wall. So, I came out to the pool to clear my mind.

It's closed for the night and the gate is locked, but it's not difficult to find a way in. The water gleams with gentle ripples under the golden bulbs strung around the surrounding palm trees. There's a cluster of glowing blue lights surrounding the perimeter of the pool, creating an almost surreal atmosphere. It's not completely quiet yet. Muffled laughter and distant voices fade in and out, carried by the breeze. Even so, the peaceful respite gives me a chance to think about what an idiot I am.

I wanted to kiss January so freaking bad. At one point, while dancing, our noses brushed and I could have sworn she'd parted her sweet pink lips and was already undressing me with those bedroom eyes. Not to mention we were actually in a bedroom.

She was so soft under my fingers, her delicate hand swallowed in my own, her lower back, swaying in tandem with her hips. My fingers burned with want, begging me to roam the length of her spine. To explore her body like tiny conquistadors. One small nudge to bring her closer, my motive concealed under the guise of dancing, and her breath hitched—just barely. And I knew I could claim her lips if I wanted.

I was willing to throw away my job and my integrity for one night with her. And I almost think it would have been worth it. But somehow the angel on my shoulder won over the guy with the horns and pitchfork.

Besides, I can think of a handful of reasons kissing her would be wrong on so many levels.

First of all, she's my client.

Second, I'm still not sure if she likes me or just likes to hate me.

Third, if I kissed her, I would never, ever stop. Of course, we'd have to take breaks to eat, sleep and do bathroom business, but other than that, I'm pretty sure my lips would always be on her. All over her. We'd have to live in this hotel forever and have crappy room service delivered.

But those are only minor issues that can be overlooked. If I'm honest with myself, the real reason I didn't kiss her is because she is essentially another species. She lives in a world of glamour, insanely over-the-top opulence, and fame. She's always in the public eye and absolutely loves it there. The blazing spotlight she basks in is her daily dose of vitamins. Mortals like me get Vitamin D from the sun, but she thrives on the flashy glimmer of celebrity.

There's no room in her life for a regular guy.

And even if she were interested in me—which I'm sure she's not—I wouldn't want to hold her back. She flies above the clouds. It's not fair to ask her to stay on the ground.

"Kinky?"

She speaks!

January peeks her face between the wrought iron fence, looking at me bemused. "How did you get in there?"

I wave. "But, soft! what light through yonder window breaks?"

She laughs, tilting her head. "Ah, he quotes Shakespeare now."

I shrug, marveling at how the lights bounce off the water and dance across her face.

"Seriously, how did you get in there?" She's looking around for a secret breach in the hotel pool's defenses. "Let me in."

I take my time making my way around the pool to meet her where she is. Did she come out here looking for me? Or was she wandering the hotel grounds coincidentally?

"Before I let you in," I say, drawing close. "Tell me. Were you missing me?"

She snorts. "What? No."

"Then why come looking for me?"

Her jaw drops open and she stutters her answer. "I... I wasn't looking for you."

I reach her but keep walking along the fence with her following from her side. My finger bounces from one iron rod to the next as we make a slow pace toward the gate. All the while, I keep my eyes on her and she doesn't take hers off me.

"So... you didn't come out here to say 'wherefore art thou' and all that?"

She grins. "Did you scale the fence? Is that it, Romeo?"

"A magician never reveals his tricks."

She extends her pointer, running it across the fence in concert with mine. "If they do see thee, they will murder thee."

We stop in front of the gate and I wink at her.

"No, they won't. I'm with you." I push on the bar and swing open the door.

She comes in, wagging her finger. "Don't be so sure about that."

She brushes by me, close enough where I catch a hint of her jasmine scent. I inhale, hoping she doesn't notice. I watch her walk around the pool to where I was standing before. From that spot, there's a spectacular view of the mountains, even under the cloak of night.

She kicks off her sandals and sits on the edge, dipping her toes in.

"Come on. The water's fine."

Not one to back down from a challenge, I toss off my shoes and socks, rolling up my jeans as far as they will go. I sit next to her and plunge my feet in the water.

"I couldn't sleep," she says.

"Me neither," I admit, although I'm not about to tell her why. She's looking up at the stars, but I can't take my eyes off of her. There's magic in the small space between us, and I don't want to miss a thing.

She sighs, tilting her head back even farther. I'm mesmerized by the line of her perfect jaw. How I want to graze my mouth there, sliding my lips down her neck to her collarbone. Shrapnel explodes deep in my belly like shards of glass piercing through a marshmallow. It's achingly delicious.

"I never thanked you for what you did for me," she says finally. "After my dentist appointment."

"Oh. It's nothing, really."

She lobs her head my way, giving me a sidelong glare. "This is me, displaying gratitude, buddy. Take it, because it might not be repeated."

Ha. She really does love to hate me. Or at least pretends to.

"Okay. Was that so difficult to do?" I tease. "Maybe we'll work our way up to little compliments next."

"Don't push your luck, Kinky."

She smiles at me, eyes shimmering like blue glitter. I mirror her expression, holding her gaze for a long while. The air is thick between us.

"Whoever blinks first loses," I say, widening my grin.

She busts up, scrunching her cute little nose, doubling over right in my space. Her hands fall on my leg. She's just leaning into me, cracking up, like we're such good friends. We're BFFs. Next, we'll braid each other's hair and rate the hotness of the Avengers.

Her laughter settles into a happy sigh, and now my chest swells knowing I did that. I put that smile on her face. I'm already scheming ways I can do that again.

She scoots flush against my hip and nudges my leg with hers. I don't even care that my jeans are getting wet at this point.

And when she tilts her head and rests it on my shoulder, my heart sputters to a stop.

It's a dangerous game we're playing here. This morning we weren't even friends. And now all I want to do is coil my arms around her and gather her onto my lap. Okay, that's not all I want to do, but I'll spare the details.

I'm afraid to move. What if she's been suffering from amnesia the whole night and suddenly remembers she hates me? I don't want to do anything that would break this alchemy.

A flash goes off just outside the fence followed by a rustle from the bushes. Someone curses under their breath and we see a figure run away down the path toward the golf course.

I jump up to follow but January stops me.

"It's probably just a fan. Leave it."

"Are you sure?" I say, all serious and grave. "It might be a guy like me."

With a twinkle in her eyes, she glides up close to me. "Well, then," she says on a sultry whisper. "I better watch out."

With a witchy grin, she slides her palms up my chest, and pushes me into the pool.

———

Later at night I'm lying in bed, barely able to sleep. I'm living in the Twilight Zone, here thinking about the past few hours. I didn't even bother to dry off. I just peeled my clothes off and crawled under the sheets. My mind buzzes with too much energy.

But remembering the way January rested her head on my shoulder sends a warmth through me, letting my body relax in a strange glow I've never experienced before. I let it take over, lulling me to sleep—to where I can dream of a life that can never be. I'm in a half state of dreaming when I hear a crash followed by shouting—a man's voice coming from January's suite. And then she screams. I jump into action, stumbling out of bed, throwing on sweatpants, and flying to our shared door. It's locked. She'd locked it from her side? I mean, I don't blame her. What if I was a naughty sleepwalker?

I ram into the door with my shoulder. I kick it barefoot. It's not budging. I need a big log. Or a stick of dynamite. I find the fire extinguisher and slam it into the door handle until I finally break the lock. Adrenaline is coursing through me. I'm the Hulk and Black Widow is in distress. She's standing on top of her bed using a hair dryer as a weapon. She's holding it two-handed, pointing it at him like a gun. What's she trying to do, blow him out the door?

"What the hell is going on in here?" I cry, and they just *now* turn their heads to me as if I hadn't made a heckavalotta noise banging in the door a minute ago. My eyes are on the guy. He's huge and it's now I recognize him. The giant from the parking garage. Tight jeans guy. He's got to have six inches and a hundred pounds of muscle on me, but I have righteous fury (and a fire extinguisher) on my side. I charge at him, and the last thing I see is a fist flying at my face before the world fades to black.

Chapter Eighteen

JANUARY

What am I supposed to do now? Even with a bruise forming on his brow, Enrique is a stunning specimen of a man. Thick, inky lashes fan across his cheekbone, curving in an arch of male beauty toward a long, Romanesque nose. And nestled like two pieces of bubble gum amidst a forest of sandpaper scruff are a pair of generous, kissable lips.

He's on my bed wearing nothing but a pair of gray

sweatpants, and I'm thinking I should have let the hotel security keep him on the floor. He looks waaayyyy too good tangled in my sheets, and the sight is doing things to my girl parts. I'm hovering over him with an ice pack in my hand, feeling like it would be a shame to break the crystals inside when I could just let him sleep. He's so passed out he wouldn't even notice if I brush my lips over his, maybe a little nibble.

But the head of security warned me to watch for signs of concussion right before they hauled Ugo away. Plus, I expect the police to come knocking any minute now. I snap the ice pack and feel the rush of cold move through the bag, placing it on his eye. He wakes with a jolt, and I have to apply gentle pressure to his shoulders to keep him from sitting up. I keep my hands there (because muscles) and am tempted to let my palms drop just a little bit down his biceps, or maybe to those abs where a dusting of charcoal hair trails to his belly button.

He sucks in a breath, remembering the danger as he wakes, but I shush him.

"It's okay. He's gone now."

"I'm sorry," he says. "I'm a crappy bodyguard."

I breathe a half-formed laugh. "That was my ex-bodyguard and he's built like a tank, so you didn't stand much of a chance."

"If he hurt you, I swear—"

"He wouldn't hurt me. He's a little too clingy, yeah. Dad fired him because he said he was in love with me, but it's only a mild obsession."

"A mild obsession had you standing on your bed wielding a dangerous hair blower?"

"I guess."

"Where is he?" There's action in his tone, and I inwardly laugh at his eagerness to play the hero even with an ice pack on his face.

"Security came in right after you got knocked out. Don't worry about that. How's your eye?"

He pulls the ice pack off and tosses it to the side table. "Fine. How did that giant get up here?"

"He's a crafty son of a gun. Ooh, that's going to leave a nasty bruise." Instinctively, I run my fingertips over his brow. A tint of yellow, blue, and pink rise to the surface of his skin. "But you'll live."

We're suspended in this moment—his eyes fixed on mine as I gently stroke the hairs of his brow into place. They'd gone askew from Ugo's fist and then the ice pack. Enrique flutters his eyes closed like a tamed beast while my nails do their work, righting the hairs in the correct direction, then finding another task of combing back his unruly locks behind his ear, twisting stray curls around my index finger. I find my other hand moving of its own volition, sliding over the mound of his strong chest and across his rib cage. His lips part, a shaky breath escaping them, and I want to capture it with my mouth. This desire. I've never known anything so compelling.

"Thanks for being my knight in shining armor," I quip, palming his six-pack. But I shouldn't have spoken. His hands fly to cover each of mine where they touch him and he holds me there, squeezing gently. His brow furrows and he winces. Am I hurting him? His eyes are still shut, and with a rumbly, painful murmur he says my name softly. "January."

The sound of it sends a thrill of bottle rockets down my center.

Then his eyes flash open and his lip twitches. "February. March."

I wrench my hands free and throw a pillow at him. "Kinky."

The bedside phone rings and I hesitate to answer.

"You should get that," he says thickly.

I acquiesce, knowing he's right. It's the head of security telling me I can make a formal police report in the morning. Meanwhile, Enrique finds his way off my bed and to our shared door. What's left of it.

"Sorry about the damages," he says. "I promise to keep an ear open for any more intruders."

And just like that, he walks through the rubble of the door wreckage and crawls into his own bed leaving me with the lady blues.

"Don't worry," I want to say. But I do want him to worry.

Chapter Nineteen

ENRIQUE

I'm in my bed with January. Her hands are planted on my chest, the tips of her long hair brushing against my skin. She's a take-charge kind of girl, pushing me down, rocking me on the mattress. She's crying out my name.

"Ricky..."

Her voice seems far away.

"Enrique..."

I reach out but my fingers can't find purchase.

"Mmmm," I hum.

"Kinky..."

Why does she sound so far away?

"Wake up."

I'm only vaguely aware of my surroundings. My body feels weighted down.

"Kinky!" Her hands are on me again and she's jostling me around now. I force my eyes open, short of breath, and still feel a weight on my chest.

"Huh? What? I'm up, I'm up."

"Freaking A, Kinky you sleep like a rock."

Now I'm in panic mode. "Is there something wrong? What time is it?"

"Three thirty."

"In the afternoon?" Nothing is making sense. I still might be dreaming.

"In the morning. Get up. We have to go."

It occurs to me now that there might be more danger. I shoot out of bed, definitely awake now.

"Are you okay? Is he back?"

"No. I'll explain later. Let's just go before the paps get here."

I don't know what's going down, but that doesn't matter. If she's got a tip the paparazzi are coming for her, it's my job to sneak her out. I'm dressed, teeth brushed, and out the door in three minutes flat. With my duffel bag in hand, I go get the limo, pulling it around to the service entrance. There won't be a show today, folks. When I get back up to the rooms, I find January ready to go. One of the security guards is with her, helping her with her suitcases.

We're stealthy as we go down, not saying a word. A covert operation on the service elevator.

I want to comfort her somehow, reach over and touch my fingers to hers, wrap her in my arms… anything to let her know she's not alone in this. Unless, of course, she needs someone to beat the burly guy up. Then I'd be useless. She'd said security detained him, but I have very little faith in the Madison hotel security team. I'm not convinced he won't be waiting outside for us.

I watch January's profile. She's incredibly brave, taking this in stride. Anyone else I know would be freaking out in the face of danger. But not January Madison. My heart swells with something akin to pride even though it's not my place. I'm just her driver. Still, I will do anything in my power to keep her safe. Even though I don't have a stitch of power. I'm less like a guard dog and more like that purse dog she wants to get. I wonder if she even remembers telling me she wants a Yorkie?

The elevator reaches the lowest floor and we're moving again, down a long corridor, past rooms with industrial washing machines, massive supply closets, storage areas full of carts of all shapes and sizes that are bulky and plastic for transporting things out of the view of hotel guests, and some shiny and ornate like the one used to bring our dinner to January's suite last night. For our non-date. A sweet ache spreads behind my ribs at the memory. A heavenly moment suspended in time, and now the harsh reality of our different lives punches me in the stomach. There are so many ways last night could have gone. I could have kissed her. The way her face shone, the longing in her eyes, the desire in her lips.

She wanted it. And even though I missed out on the most incredible experience in my life, I would have regretted it. I would have loved every minute of it, but cursed every damn second of my life thereafter. Nothing would ever compare.

The guard bids us to wait just inside the loading dock while he checks to see if the coast is clear. This part of the hotel is enclosed inside a twenty-foot gate, and he says he doesn't expect a breach, but stranger things have happened.

As he peeks out, I brush the back of my knuckles along January's arm. A feather-light touch to show compassion, but not enough to make claim on her affection.

"Are you okay?" I ask softly.

She rolls her eyes. "It's just the paps. I eat guys like that for breakfast."

"A little early for breakfast. Think they're serving coffee?"

"Forget the coffee. It's a bloody Mary kind of breakfast."

Dang! This girl's got fangs. I am here for it.

"What's taking him so long?" she says. "It's colder than an old lady's feet."

That's probably not how I'd describe the early morning air, but I wrap my arm around her anyway.

The guard scurries back inside with a troubled expression. "There's a handful of reporters outside the gate. We can't do much since it's off the hotel property. Would you like to wait it out, Miss Madison? Maybe if we call the police…"

"No. If we wait, it will only get worse."

He concurs with a stern nod. "Very well."

He leads us out the roll-up door and down the ramp to where I'd parked the limo. I pop the trunk, and as he loads

January's luggage, I escort her to the car, shielding her with my jacket. But just as she's tucking her head in the car, we hear a shout.

"Over there!" A flash goes off. They're far enough away and didn't get anything but a car door shutting, but I gotta get her out of here. Making sure the guard is done loading the suitcases, I hop in and start the engine.

"I'm sorry," I say through the partition window. "I have to drive through."

The paps are practically blocking the gate. More flashes go off. The guard runs ahead of us, joined by a couple of his coworkers. They're shooing the paparazzi, clearing a way for us to drive through.

"They came here for a show," she says, rolling down one of her windows. "Let's give them a show."

Has she lost her mind?

She crouches down as I approach the gate. I see January move around in the rearview mirror, but it's so dark I don't realize what she's doing until we're rolling through the gate right past the paparazzi. January's sitting on the floor of the limo, holding up the cardboard Nicolas Cage cutout at the open window, dancing it around. Flashes go off, and I even hear one of the photographers shout, "Nicolas, Nicolas."

That stupid piece of cardboard is bouncing up and down, floating from one side of the window to the other. More cameras go off rapidly, triggering their flash bulbs like strobe lights in a nightclub. The paparazzi are shouting things like, "Mr. Cage, over here." And, "Nick, are you dating January Madison?"

What a bunch of dimwits.

A minute later, we're driving down the road, home free.

"I can't believe that worked," she says, getting back up into her seat and rolling up the window. We make brief eye contact in the rearview mirror and burst out laughing.

"Oh my gosh, how ridiculous was that?" she says.

"Wow, what a bunch of idiots."

"Right?"

She's laughing so hard, she's practically in tears and neither of us can stop.

"Who knew Nick Cage could come in so handy?"

"I know," I agree. "I'm never throwing that thing away."

"Thank you for your help, Mr. Cage," she says and kisses it on the face.

"I can see what you mean about the photographers. Your ex-bodyguard busting in isn't even that exciting of a story."

"That's not the story," she admits, sobering up some. "It's something else. I'll fill you in when we get out of town. But can we grab that coffee?"

I pull into a gas station, making sure there aren't any other curious people around, and run in for the coffee. At this hour, the attached market, is closed so the best I can do is buy a canned frappachino from the guy at the window.

When I get back, January's in the front passenger seat.

"What are you doing up front?" I ask. "You'll get recognized."

"It gets lonely back there."

"What about your new boyfriend?" I point my thumb over my shoulder toward Nicolas Cage.

"Conversation's a little flat," she says with a silly grin. How can I even resist that adorable sense of humor? "Do you mind if I stay here?"

Do I mind? Not in the least.

"Meh," I say, shrugging my shoulder. "If you insist."

She socks me in the arm.

"All they had was this," I say, giving her the canned coffee. "It's an off brand, so who knows how it tastes."

She scans the nutrition information on the back of the can.

"High fructose corn syrup, maltodextrin, xanthum gum, taurine, caramel color… this would make a good weapon against the paps."

"You can stow it in your purse just in case."

I drive onto the interstate and we let the darkness of the night cover us in a serene quiet. It's strangely familiar and feels nice. After a while she sighs dramatically.

"If you must know, I'll tell you, I guess."

"Pardon?"

"You're dying to know why we had to flee in the middle of the night, and I suppose I'll tell you if you insist."

"Nah, I'm good."

She turns her body to face me. "It's my ex-boyfriend."

"Really not interested."

"He's been trying to sue for defamation of character, but he doesn't have any grounds whatsoever. That's why my dad had me cooped up in his penthouse."

"You really don't have to tell me—"

"After our lawyer pretty much laughed in his face, we thought it was all over. But he's a slime ball and will do anything for money. And vanity."

"Uh-huh." Sounds like she just wants to vent, so I nod and keep my eyes on the road, only half listening. I really need a coffee.

"Late last night he leaked some nude photos of me."

Whoa there. And now I'm wide awake.

"Hold up. N-n-nude, nude, or just ya know... nudes?"

She's giving the death glare, I can feel her lasers on the side of my face. "Uh, I mean... what a scum bucket."

"They're not me. He must have hired someone who's great at Photoshop."

"So just to be clear, are they nudes of you photoshopped in compromising places, or is your head transposed on someone else's body?"

She socks me again. That's going to bruise.

"You're a pig."

"I'm just trying to be helpful, that's all."

She laughs despite the gravity of the situation. See? I made her laugh. Helpful.

"They're really bad. It could hurt my charities, my endorsements, my environmental work... I need to get away for a few days to figure it out."

"Alright. Just name the place. I'll take you there."

She has a smile in her voice. "Thanks."

She yawns, watching the vast nothingness out the window. It doesn't take long for her to drift off to sleep. This is a dangerous road at night if you don't pay extra attention to the lines, but I can't help stealing a glance her way when the moonlight hits her face just so, casting a silver lining around her profile. Somehow over the next several minutes her body slides across the bench seat and she nuzzles up to me, resting her head against my leg.

Eyes on the road, dude.

I venture one hand off the wheel to stroke her hair. I tell myself it's because it's falling over her face, restricting her breathing. But it's silky and soft, and my gentle touches seem to give her some comfort. After a while my arm rests across her back and we stay that way for a long while.

The promise of dawn glows on the horizon. Hues of orange and purple peek out over the mountains, feathering across a dark blue sky. It's peaceful out here, cutting through the stillness of nature before the rest of the world wakes up. I feel like an outlaw running from a band of vigilantes. Or maybe a man stealing away with his love in the night.

January stirs just outside of Beaumont and I'm a little sad to lose the warmth of her body pressed against mine.

"I'm starved," she says, all groggy.

I point out it might not be the best idea to stop in a café for breakfast, but I find a Denny's that delivers curbside, so I stop to order from by phone.

Once we get our order, I find a quiet spot and park by a tree. I don't generally approve of eating in the limo, but I make an exception just this once. We both sit in the backseat, where there's more room, and shovel pancakes, eggs, and bacon in our faces. And coffee. Mediocre coffee, but adequate enough.

For a brief reprieve, we forget about who we are and all the stupid drama in our lives and just eat, just talk, just be. In a couple hours, we'll be back in LA, and this moment will be a memory, but for now I'm a man and she's a woman and that's all that matters. She seems so vulnerable right now, like everything hangs in the balance. She pokes the Styrofoam container with a plastic fork, deep in thought.

"He broke down crying, you know," she says out of the blue.

"Your ex?"

"No. Ugo. After he knocked you out."

"Ugo's your bodyguard?" She hadn't told me his name, but I don't get knocked out very often, so I'm making an educated guess.

She nods. "I almost feel sorry for the guy. Unrequited love and all that."

"It's not love when you have to break into someone's room to get their attention."

"I know. It's just… you should have seen him. Sobbing on the floor, blubbering about how I sent him the wrong signals. That he was sure I loved him back. I only wanted to show kindness."

She meets my eyes with a pleading look. "Do I give off the wrong vibe? Did I lead him on by mistake?"

Ouch. Her words, although not referring directly to me, are like a knife straight in the gut. She only wanted to show kindness. In what way? Inviting him to dine with her in her hotel room? Resting her head on his lap? Sharing titillating, flirty banter over a steak dinner?

I'm such a freaking idiot.

All I can do to keep from slapping myself is to force a smile and gather the trash into the take-out bag.

"I don't know," I reply. "Did you wrap his car with cling wrap? Nothing says *I want to have your babies* more than a plastic shroud."

Estúpido, idiota, tonto.

Leaving January in the rear of the limo, I toss the trash in a nearby bin and reclaim my position in the driver's seat.

That is my role and I won't be another Ugo in January's life.

Once we're about an hour from home, January pokes her head in the partition window.

"Velma texted me," she says. "Paps are all over the hotel and in front of my house."

Velma. So *that's* her name.

"Okay, then. Do you have another place? A safe house, maybe?"

She shakes her head. "Every known place is inundated with press. And my ex would happily tip them off to all my favorite spots. I can't even trust Shauna."

"You're toastless avocado toast lunch friend?"

"I'm never going to live that down, am I?"

"Nope."

She sniffles, wiping her cheeks. If she's been crying, I'm about to feel like the biggest jerk on the planet. I hadn't answered her question about Ugo. I didn't say anything at all—just got in the cockpit and drove.

Even though January gives her kindness out a little too freely to gullible men like me, I can at least be a decent human.

"What happened with Shauna?"

"She tweeted support for Jonny—that's my ex—and blatantly lied about me taking the nudes."

Sniff...

"How I bragged about it to her and she begged me to delete them. I would never do such a thing. You believe me, don't you?"

"Of course I believe you."

She heaves a deep sigh and rests her head on her arms,

still in the partition window. I wish she'd sit back and put on her seatbelt.

With a measure of resignation, I ask, "Where to, then?"

"I dunno. Could we hang low for a while? I need a few hours to figure this out."

I groan. "It's Sunday. My mom will kill me if she finds out I'm in town and don't go to Mass with the family."

"I'll go with you."

"To church? Are you trying to stir up *more* gossip?"

"I can wait at your house."

Seriously, I'm in major trouble with this woman. What would she do alone at my house? Go through my stuff? Touch my personal things? Sit where I sit? Lounge where I lounge? No way. My January problem is getting out of hand. She's already living in my mind, I don't need her in my personal space.

I inhale her scent—jasmine shampoo mingled with pancake syrup. This is a bad, bad idea, I know. But what's a guy to do when there's a woman hanging over your shoulder who tugs at your heartstrings? And other unmentionable strings, too.

"You'll be safe at my parents' house. We have dinner together every Sunday, and Mom will be over the moon I'm back a day early. My family is a bit terrifying, so consider yourself warned."

January claps her hands together. "How bad could they possibly be?"

"Last week my mom sprayed my uncle head to toe with bathroom cleaner. And she didn't hold back. His clothes were soaked."

"Whatever for?"

"I guess he blows his nose in the shower. Don't ask me how this came about. He doesn't even live there."

"I like your mom already."

Calm down, racing heart. This is not a meet the parents' situation. Keep it together.

"Then, there's the rivalry between my dad and brother over anything food related. That's always a fun argument to witness. And don't even get me started on my Tia Lucy. One time, she toilet-papered the living room because she couldn't find party streamers."

She chuckles. "Gotta give her points for creativity."

"That's what Mom said. All I remember is Dad getting so angry, and then making my brothers and me take it down. We had to use crumpled-up toilet paper for weeks."

"But what about the party? Did someone at least put out balloons?"

"There was no party. It wasn't anyone's birthday or anniversary. Not even a national holiday."

"Well, national holidays would call for red white and blue toilet paper."

"That's what I always say."

I catch her smile in the rearview mirror. She's watching me like no woman has ever watched me before. And I hate how much it sets my heart on fire.

She reaches through the window and strokes the curls behind my ear. She's killing me right now.

"I can't wait to meet your family," she says in a breathy tone.

Ay caray!

Chapter Twenty

JANUARY

Enrique grumbles under his breath as we pull into the driveway of his house.

"The only reason we're here is so I can switch cars. And get a change of clothes. And shower. But don't touch anything."

"Yes, you've told me several times now. I promise I'll keep my hands to myself."

He glances briefly at me, then cuts the engine. "Good."

We're parked next to a shiny orange muscle car, and as I climb out of the limo, I find him transferring my luggage from one trunk to the other.

"I might need those. Shouldn't we…"

I incline my head to the house.

"Not here you won't. This is just a pit stop."

"Aye-aye, Captain Crunch."

He pauses to glare at me. Amusement passes over his features. "Did you just quote *Veggie Tales*?"

"What if I did?"

He shakes his head and closes the trunk of the orange car. "I never met anyone outside of my family who's seen that show."

I shrug. "Nice car."

"You like her?" He beams. "She's my baby."

"Sure is… orange. Is this a Mustang?"

"A Mustang!? What? No." He strokes his palm over the rear fender as if I just offended *her* as he calls it. "She's a '68 Camaro 582 CI Coupe. And it's *burnt* orange."

"Oooh, my bad. I didn't study my crayons as I ought."

"Clearly." He sees a spot that bothers him and buffs it with his shirt.

I raise a brow. "Wow. You really love your cars."

I knew he was obsessed with his limo but didn't realize he was such a gearhead. All he needs is a mullet.

"Cars are easy to understand. Unlike women."

He goes up the walkway to the house, expecting me to follow.

"You're unbelievable," I say, chasing after him. "It's like you're afraid of being a nice guy so you go and say something incredibly sexist."

He unlocks the front door and turns to me before opening it.

"I just admitted I don't understand women, and you claim to understand me based on what? My backstory? You want the truth? I don't understand women. Most men don't."

"Well then, I appreciate your honesty."

"Fine."

"Fine."

He storms in the house, tossing the keys on a table. I pass over the threshold and—well, I'm not sure what I expected, but it wasn't this. His house is really nice. Not your typical bachelor pad. It's an older house, typical for this part of LA, and the yard is well maintained. The lawn is small but a beautiful shade of green, and the perimeter is adorned with jolt pink dianthas, lavender, and sunflowers.

Inside, the décor has a bright, farmhouse vibe—white shiplap walls, splashes of color in the throw pillows, and large canvas paintings without frames. They look like original pieces judging by the texture.

"You made a promise," he says, almost in a teasing tone, stopping me from touching the painting. He's waving a finger back and forth.

"Don't touch anything. I remember. Can I sit down, or is my butt not allowed to touch the couch cushions?"

His brows lurch down and he grunts. "I prefer not. But I guess it's okay for a few minutes."

"How gracious of you."

He finds a throw blanket in a basket and spreads it out over one of the couches.

"There you go."

I stare at it and back at him. Is he some kind of germophobe?

"I can assure you, I'm clean."

His eyes are wide, like he's scared of me or something.

"Well, I'm not. I'm just going to go take a quick shower."

"Okay, go. I'll behave."

He disappears down the hall and I'm left standing in the front room trying to decide if I even want to bother sitting. A few seconds later, he returns, stomps past me, and goes into the kitchen. Maybe he's one of those people who can't take a bath without a dram of whiskey. I once found a Facebook page dedicated to just photos of people in the shower with a lowball glass. It's like those *'cover your mess with a coffee mug'* posts on Instagram, but for hardcore drinkers.

I follow him into the kitchen just to be sure because he's going to be driving soon. If he's in no shape to drive, I'm definitely sprawling all over every surface of his house. Well… within reason.

When I enter the kitchen, I see him squeezing a lemon wedge in a glass, then stirring the beverage with a straw. It might be whiskey, but that's an awful lot of ice. And there's something green in the glass. Maybe mint.

He picks up the glass, turns, and, startled to see me there, gasps. "Don't sneak up on me like that."

"Sorry about that." Sorta. His reaction was golden.

"Here." He shoves the glass at me. "I thought you might get thirsty."

I take the offered glass. It's not whiskey. It's iced tea with basil leaves and lemon.

"How… how did you know this is my favorite?"

He looks at me sternly. "Instagram. The whole world knows it's your favorite."

I stand there stunned.

"You follow me on Instagram?"

He laughs. "No. I was just doing research."

He skirts around me and takes off again. I shout after his back, "Keep telling yourself that, Kinky."

I decide to sit at the kitchen table to drink my tea. It's clean in here, but not the way kitchens are clean in mansions. Those are never used. His kitchen is lived in. Containers of coffee and sugar are lined up neatly on the counter next to an espresso machine, a Nutribullet, and a toaster oven. The rustic hardwood floor is spotless, a remodeled upgrade from what was here previously, I imagine.

I'm not alone for long before my phone buzzes in my skirt pocket. I'm obsessed with pockets these days. I check if it's news about the scandal and find a text from my dad.

Dad: What is going on, January?

He attaches a photo of me and Enrique by the hotel pool, my head resting on Enrique's shoulder. I'd want to cherish this if it wasn't such a breach of privacy.

Dad: You need to fix this now.

Fake nude photos of me are circulating around the Internet and he's concerned about a harmless photo with Enrique?

Dad: Get here as soon as you can.

Me: Too many paps.

Dad: Dunn and Dunn coming in the morning. Need you here.

Dunn and Dunn are two of his lawyers. He has lawyers

for everything under the sun. These guys have their greasy paws in Dad's legal dealings with my mom. I don't want to get involved in that dumpster fire.

Me: Sorry. No can do. I'll call you in a few days.

I shut off my phone—something I'm getting used to—and finish my tea. After a while, I leave my glass in the sink and venture into the living room to take a closer look at the artwork. There are several pieces of different sizes. Probably from the same artist. As I look around, I find many art pieces. It's like a gallery in here. In the corner of the room stands a tall sculpture made of what looks like junk metal. It's a hodge podge of car scraps, kitchen utensils, and old video game parts—all painted to look like the figure of a person.

"That's supposed to be Don Quixote." Enrique's standing at the edge of the hallway, dripping wet, wearing nothing but a towel.

"What is with you and walking around half naked?" I should cover my eyes. I really should. But I'm fixated on his scrumptious abs, how the muscles seem to wink at me, how his belly button summons my eyeballs like a siren call, inviting me to follow the happy trail down to where he holds onto the barely there towel. And now I'm second-guessing my lofty TED Talk.

"I thought I heard you getting into stuff," he says in a not come-hither way. He really doesn't trust me.

"You are making it harder and harder by the minute. The more you say no touchie, the more I wanna touchie."

I lift my pointer finger and swirl it around in the air, inching closer and closer to the junk metal sculpture. My eyes are locked on his to gauge his reaction, and I am not disappointed in the least. His left eye twitches and his lips tremble. Just to see what he'll do, I let my finger come within a fraction of an inch from the sculpture. He's paralyzed in the hallway, unable to do anything about it unless he wants to risk his modesty. This is fun.

I wonder for a moment if it's just this strange Don Quixote he's psycho about or if he freaks out about other objects. I move around the room playfully, my finger poised to land on some other beloved item.

"Hmm. There are so many interesting things. And I'm a curious girl."

His face is a stern rock, but I can see him squirm under that stony façade. I glide next to a lamp. Surely that wouldn't excite the same reaction. It's just a lamp. Probably purchased at IKEA. But as my finger draws close, his Adam's apple twitches.

I wonder what he'd do if I did something horrific like go through his medicine cabinets or spice pantry. I move on, circling the room, looking for the most benign object—something a normal person wouldn't care about at all. Something like junk mail or... I spot a library book on a side table. This doesn't even belong to him. This has been touched by countless individuals and taken to unquestionable places, like bathrooms and stranger's beds.

"*All the Light We Cannot See*. I've been meaning to read this one."

I bend down, watching him from the corner of my eye. His chest heaves (and a glorious chest it is) and he almost takes a step.

"Maybe I'll skim through the first chapter while you get dressed."

His free hand flies up to tug on his necklace. The turquoise cross is gone. This one—the one with the rectangle pendant, is like some kind of security blanket for him. I wonder if someone special gifted it to him? Maybe a girlfriend? He strokes it whenever he seems out of sorts. I don't even think he realizes he does that.

"Did you like your iced tea?"

I stand up straight, bringing my hand back to my side. "I did, thank you. But I might have to use the restroom soon. Iced tea moves right through me."

"We'll be at my parents' house soon. You can use the bathroom there."

"Then you better skedaddle in that room of yours and get ready. Unless you want me to go in there with you to help you pick something to wear."

"That room's off limits."

What's with him all of a sudden? It's not like I'd barge in while he's changing. Who does he take me for?

I shrug. "Whatever. I'm happy right here. Shoo, shoo."

Flicking my hand, I take a couple of steps to the sofa— the one where he did *not* put the blanket down for me. *This* sofa is his special place. The spot where he watches TV and eats snacks and reads library books. I want to feel how the cushion sinks, how the cream fabric hits the skin of my legs. I shoot him a teasing glance and lift the rear of my skirt, careful not to let him see the lace panties I'm wearing. I slowly lower my butt, my skirt fanned out to shield my goods, when a blur of tanned skin and muscle and white towel streaks across the room. Strong, capable hands take hold of my shoulders, stopping me inches from rubbing my derriere where his derrière often lives.

I'm hoisted up squarely on my feet, and standing before me is a very hot, very naked man with a white towel pooled at his feet.

"Don't you dare look down."

I squeeze my eyes shut, already feeling woozy from the heat of his body, which is still steaming from the shower. He's wet and in the buff and my hands are inches…*inches* from his yummy muscles. If I were to bend my wrist just so, this would turn into the hottest game of Marco Polo ever.

"I didn't see anything," I squeak. "I promise."

When he's sure I'm balanced on my own, he releases me.

"Keep your eyes shut."

Not only do I keep my eyes shut, I squeeze them tighter and press my lips together for good measure. And, because I don't trust myself, I ball my fists at my sides.

The warmth of his nearness fades away as I stand for what seems like five minutes with my eyes shut. I don't move an inch. A cool breeze hits my exposed legs and shoulders, and only after I softly call out his name and am met with an empty room, do I open my eyes and walk out the front door to wait for him outside. And just because I'm feeling extra ornery, I rub my fingers all over his sunflowers.

Chapter Twenty-one

ENRIQUE

"How can you not hear *Lord of the Rings* in that chord progression?" Mateo hums the same seven notes he's been humming since we left the church.

"The only thing I heard was my stomach rumbling," Nate says.

We're walking home from church, just a block away from my parents' house. Mateo's been trying to convince everyone that the sending song had some major *Hobbit* theme song vibes. Apparently nobody caught it but him. Since Francesca is the only other musically inclined person in our family, he turns to her for support.

"I know you heard it," he says, hopeful.

She twists her lips. "I didn't. Sorry. But if it's any consolation, I hear hints of '*Evita*' every time we play '*Christ in Me Arise*' but Edmund thinks I'm crazy."

We all moan. Edmund. When will she ever move on from that childhood crush?

"Of course you would," says Mateo. Most of us siblings nod in agreement because Francesca is infamous for spontaneously breaking out into show tunes. Everything's a show tune. Even church songs, apparently.

Sebastian and Memo are the only ones not present tonight. Sebastian, because he's away at school, and Memo, because he has vespers or whatever Norbertines do on Sunday nights. Oh, and Dad's at home cooking what he calls a special dinner. We're all skeptical.

January stayed behind with Dad and Tía Lucy, while the rest of us fulfilled our weekly check-in at church. When I'd first brought her over this afternoon, Nate and Mateo were starstruck and stumbled all over themselves to make sure she was comfortable. Dad, not impressed with celebrities, greeted her politely, but then went on to criticize her dress because surely she must be cold, and demanded somebody bring her a blanket. Dante found one of Francesca's old bathrobes in the linen closet, and now January is sporting hot pink terry cloth with peeling Barbie appliqués.

Mom and everyone else tried to act casual, overcompensating aloofness, like we have celebrities visit every day. But Tía Lucy didn't hold back at all...her reaction was, "*Quien es esta flaca gueda*?" all while dragging her eyes over January from head to toe with a disapproving glower. January wasn't offended by the blatant once-over, nor did she understand she'd been called a skinny white girl right in her face, but I was embarrassed just the same.

I can't wait to get back to her, but everyone is walking excruciatingly slow.

Ignacio wraps his arm around Mom, kissing her temple. "Another for your collection?" He nods at the bulletin in her hand. Mom always takes a bulletin, partly because she feels bad turning the usher down when we exit—and she never reads them. She calls them her receipts for attending Mass.

"You never know when you might need to look something up," she says, fanning herself with the bulletin.

"Or," says Nate. "Use the church website. Just a crazy idea."

"Then what do I have to show for it?" she says.

Mateo chimes in. "Mom, you don't need physical proof you went to church."

"But I *like* taking something home in my hands."

"If we went in the morning," says Francesca with a little pout, "We could get donuts and sad coffee."

Ignacio bursts out laughing. "If you can get up before noon, you mean."

Francesca huffs. "I get up when I'm scheduled to sing."

"I personally love donuts and sad coffee," I say. There's just something about expired Folgers brewed in bulk by the Knights of Columbus.

Mom beams at Francesca, hooking her arm through hers

as they lead the way up to the house. "We'll go out for donuts tomorrow without the boys."

As soon as we enter the front door, Dad barks at us to wash our hands.

"*No saben que manos sucias metieron al agua bendita,*" he barks.

Mom rolls her eyes. "It's holy water," she argues. "You don't have to worry about germs."

"*No discutas conmigo. Que laven las manos,*" he retorts. Dad has become quite the germophobe in his old age.

I go find January in the garden, still wearing the Barbie bathrobe, where she's scrolling on her phone while sitting in the patio swing, completely alone, while Dad and Lucy work in the kitchen. I gingerly lower myself next to her, careful not to disturb the balance. She tucks her phone away and smiles at me.

"Staying out of the line of fire, I see."

"To put it mildly," she replies. "There was talk about a contest? Your dad said something to the effect of, 'Suck on it, Nacho.' I thought I'd be safer out here."

I groan. "Dad and Ignacio have this food feud going. When my brother cooks, he gets all creative with his fusion crap. It drives my dad bonkers. He's probably trying to one-up him right now."

"Whatever it is, he's about to grow devil horns. If he had a mustache, he'd be twirling it right about now."

"He can be quite wily and dastardly."

She snorts. "I mean, this is better than watching *Top Chef Battles.*"

I'm glad she's entertained, at least.

"Just so you know, my dad gets super offended if you

turn down his food. But he also complains when we polish everything off. Don't let it get to you. He's just a little intense. If it's gross, don't feel obligated to eat it."

"Didn't you say your dad is a good cook?"

"Eh. He's sort of lost his touch in his old age. Mom says all those chili peppers he eats ruined his taste buds."

"Can't wait."

———

"No me jodas, guey." Tío Enrique is arguing with Dad at a decibel only appropriate at concerts, mouth stuffed with his dinner, and sloshing wine all over himself—wine he shouldn't be drinking after he got a D.U.I. a couple months back. Food particles are spraying forth like a hose sprinkler. And that's not the worst of it. Apparently today was bring a friend day, and guess who's Francesca's new BFF? Barf Girl.

Thank goodness she's nice and not a psycho like some of the other weirdos Francesca knows. Theatre people! But Beth (that's Barf Girl's name) seems normal enough despite my first impression of her in the backseat of my Cadillac.

"I'm glad to see you're feeling better," I say.

She looks at me funny. Maybe she doesn't recognize me?

"I drove you to the Darcy mansion in my limo. You were... indisposed?"

Awareness lights up her features. "Oh, right. That was just nerves. Thanks for asking, though."

She grins at January in a warm, friendly way. "I love your bathrobe."

"Oh, this old thing?" January swishes her hand around

and Francesca laughs brightly. Now they're all best friends. I'll never understand women.

Francesca goes on to say she met Beth that night when they performed at the same fancy Hollywood gala. Makes sense. Francesca makes friends everywhere she goes.

I don't get a chance to chat much because there are five conversations going on at the same time. That's typical for the Precio Sunday dinner, but for some reason it's aggravating me more than usual. Maybe I'm over-sensitive because of what January must be thinking—that my family is a bunch of kooks.

Dad's other brother, Pedro, is also here. He only comes for the food.

"Five bucks says Pedo brought Tupperware," I whisper to Ignacio.

He shakes his head. "Too late. I already saw him come in with a whole shopping bag of them," he says. "He can have all the leftovers he wants. Nobody's gonna want to eat this again."

He's referring to the *bratchurro* my dad invented. A bratwurst dipped in churro batter, then deep-fried. This is his groundbreaking, moustache-twirling answer to Ignacio's trendy fusion dishes? It's...oddly not terrible. But it's also not good, either—and no one dares burst his bubble. Thanks to Mom's aversion to sausage, he also heated up leftover chicken, which I'm sticking to, thank you very much. But January's a trooper, working her way through an entire *bratchurro*. She's even pretending to like it, which to me earns her all the gold stars.

Most of my other brothers are here, too; Nate's chewing on his bratchurro blissfully while Memo and Sebastian are missing out on all the fun. Currently, Mom is laying the guilt trip on Dante and Mateo.

"Someone needs to go with Ignacio to help set up." She points with her fork at both of them. "And neither of you have much going on."

"I have to practice with the band," Mateo says. "The earliest I can be there is Friday.

Dante follows suit. "I'm busy. Francesca can go. She's not working."

"I have an audition on Thursday," she says, taking a bite of what looks like some kind of disgusting vegan fake meat.

This piques January's interest. "What kind of audition?"

Francesca hides behind her hair, a little embarrassed to answer, so Beth answers for her. "She's going for a role in the national tour of *West Side Story*. I'm helping her pick out her best sixteen bars."

"I love that show," chirps January. "Are you hoping for Maria?"

"Oh, no. Just ensemble. I probably won't even get past the first cut. But my friend Edmund is a shoo-in for Tony."

"Oh *him*!" Nate pulls a face. Another jab at that Edmund guy. We're still not sure what his intentions are. We get a kick out of giving him a hard time, though.

"Well, I think you'd make a great Maria," says January and takes a bite of her *bratchurro*, forgetting how horrible it is. She's trying really hard to hide a grimace as she chews.

"Good, right?" Dad prods. January's eyebrows hit her hairline as she nods slowly and exaggeratedly. "What about you?" he says to Beth. "You like my bratchurro?"

"It certainly is…unique," she replies pragmatically.

Dad tosses a proud look at Ignacio and flexes his biceps. "Thank you, my public."

Ignacio just rolls his eyes.

"Sorry, Mateo," says Mom. "You'll have to go."

January whispers across the table to me. "Where are they going?"

"Mexico. Ignacio is catering our cousin's quinceañera. But he can't take his regular crew with him for that long."

Who knew destination birthday parties would be all the rage with fifteen-year-old girls?

"Sounds like fun," she says, smiling brightly.

"It's really not," I say. And when did January's smile start to melt my butter like this?

Nate, who is in absolutely no danger of being roped in to going to Mexico five days early, mainly because of his swanky insurance job, decides to put in his two cents.

"Kiki. Why don't you go?"

"Yeah, *Kinky*." January winks at me. I'm officially dead.

"No." Also, I'm killing Nate after dinner.

"Why not?" He's egging me on, and I'm thinking I won't wait until after dinner. I'm sure I have some dirt on him. I just can't think straight with the way January's grinning at me.

I grit my teeth. "I have to work." I incline my chin toward January, and all heads turn to look at her.

She just shrugs. "I'm up for it."

Is she serious? Yes. She totally is.

Tío Enrique laughs heartily. His mouth is full of baguette now. Mom claps her hands together. "That's settled. At least *somebody* doesn't mind helping their brother."

Ignacio slaps me on the back. "Thanks, bro."

"Uh-huh," I grunt.

"*No pasa nada,*" Tío Enrique slurs. "What happen to you to me?"

Chunks of baguette fly from his teeth, the trajectory sending them to land right on January's plate. I'm mortified —and that's not an easy thing to accomplish. January's eyes bulge out, and I'm half expecting her to join Beth's barf club when Tía Lucy appears by her side, shoving a serving plate in her face.

"More *bratchurro?*"

Chapter Twenty-two
ENRIQUE

There's nothing like springtime in Valle de Guadalupe. It's not too hot, not too cold. The vines are beginning to sprout their green leaves, and it's peaceful. I don't know why it feels natural to have brought January along with me. She's not a fish out of water like you'd think a Hollywood socialite would be. We're together most of the time, except when I have to go to the local farms with Ignacio for fresh ingredients.

Today we're setting up the tables and deciding on the décor for the party. My Uncle Anslo (who's actually not my uncle but a second cousin once removed) owns a winery here. His rustic tasting rooms and the grand patio overlooking the vineyard is the venue. It's already almost perfect with string lights overhead and potted roses, but Ignacio wanted to make sure the buffet was in the ideal location so the line wouldn't spill onto the dance floor or clog the walkways.

Anslo's wife, Simone, is acting as our guide and facilities manager, offering to get us whatever we need for a perfect event. January has taken to her and already they're making grand plans for the space.

"What if we drape sheer chiffon over the string lights?" suggests January.

"Oooh, I like your thinking. I think we have some leftover from a wedding we hosted way back. What should we do for the head table?"

"Can we do a flower wall?"

"Yes! Love it."

I'm watching this exchange between the two women struck in wonderment. January has jumped right in as the party planner queen, and Simone is here for it. I'm mesmerized at the way January lights up with a task to do. The way she whisks about the space, spitballing her ideas off Simone, voicing her creative inspiration with the energy of an artist painting a mural—I can't take my eyes off her.

"You got it bad." Ignacio gives me a hard stare while shaking his head. "Think you might peel your eyes off Blondie and help me move this table?"

"Huh? Oh, yeah. I was just looking at the… counting the chairs."

Ignacio raises one brow and waits on the other end of a buffet table. I take up the other end and we scoot it over to the opposite side of the patio.

"Does she know?" he asks.

I stare at him blankly.

"That you like her. I'm guessing yes. You're one big fat heart eye emoji."

"What? No, I'm not."

He grins like a cat. "Oh yes, brother. It's pathetic."

"Are you serious? I mean… do I look that bad?"

His head bobs slowly and dramatically. Up and down. Cheshire grin. Eyebrow wag.

He ushers me far enough away from the ladies to make sure they don't hear.

"Listen, I'm not saying don't go for her. You'd be an idiot not to. Just be careful. You know… because of who she is."

"What's that supposed to mean?"

"She lives in a different world than us. She was born with a silver spoon in her mouth. You were born with your toe in your mouth."

He's kind of right.

"What should I do? What would *you* do?"

I can't believe I'm asking my brother for advice. I must be desperate.

"Me? Nothing."

"Nothing?"

"Absolutely nothing. Nada. Zip."

"Why?"

I already know the answer to that question. Ignacio is married to his work.

"Why? I mean, just look at you." He waves his hand up and down. "I don't want to look that stupid."

"Ha ha. Someday, brother, you'll meet a girl you can't keep out of your thoughts, and when that happens I'm going to take a picture of your stupid, lovesick face and post it everywhere."

"Then it's a good thing I don't go anywhere to meet girls," he says confidently.

January waves at us from across the patio. She wants us to come over. As we make our way to her, I say to Ignacio through clenched teeth, "Don't you dare say anything."

"I wouldn't dream of it."

It's a couple days before the party. Ignacio and Simone went into Ensenada to find local wait staff to work the event. Simone has some connections in town and is confident she'll be able to help Ignacio find the best available. With them gone and my cousin Anslo working the tasting rooms, I have the entire day with January. No schedules, no agenda, just us.

We're lounging by the pool after a refreshing swim. She's wearing the sexiest bikini I've ever seen, but I can, in all honestly, tell you that it's not the design or fabric (or lack thereof), that has my head in a spin. It's the woman herself. She has broken me, and I'm like her dog that will follow her willingly. I realize as I watch her swirl the water with her toes, I'm not even looking at her body. I see inside of her, and it's a thousand times more beautiful than her surface beauty. She is an angel. Even though she's not mine, I'm grateful for this moment and all the fractions of seconds I'm awarded this week. I hold each one in an imaginary bottle for my memories. We're in a fantastical bubble. It's almost magic.

"What are you thinking about?" she asks, kicking the water at me. I'm on a lounge chair, so it barely hits me, but I want her to do it again and again just to say I was touched by her.

What are you thinking? I'm too afraid to tell her the truth. I don't want to break the spell.

"I'm thinking how you must find this place incredibly boring," I say. "Not even Instagram worthy?"

I haven't seen her post on Instagram all week. She takes pictures, but there hasn't been one post. Yes, I stalk her profile. Sue me.

"Not at all," she replies. "I love it here. I just don't want anyone to know where I am."

"Ah. That makes sense after…"

I don't want to remind her of the paps or her ex or the bodyguard, so I stop myself. When I scrolled through every single one of her Instagram pictures (yes, every one) she seemed so happy. It's sad how fans only want to see the beautiful part of her life, and don't even realize how much pain she goes through. I admit I thought she was a poor little rich girl who was out of touch with the real world.

How hard could her life be? I know now I was wrong. I mean, she still is somewhat out of touch with the real world. She's sheltered, and by no fault of her own, was thrust in the glitz and glamour of the Hollywood elite. I only hope I can be the one to show her all the wonderful things the real world has to offer.

"You never told me how you got into your line of work," she says. "What makes Enrique Precio tick?"

"I love cars," I say matter-of-factly. "I have a bachelor's degree in business and helped Ignacio with his restaurant for a while, but then an opportunity arose to buy a limo and I took it."

"Did you have clients before me? Any other women who can't get over you that I should be worried about?"

I laugh. I know she's joking, but my chest swells with the manliest of manliness.

"Do you know Stella Gardiner?" I ask.

"Yes! I've never met her, but everyone knows who she is. Did you, um… drive her crazy?"

"I reserved that distinction for you."

She bites her lip bashfully, and if that isn't the hottest thing I've ever seen, I don't know what is.

"My sister was in her acting program back in high school. Stella has always been a good friend and mentor. She even awarded Francesca with a scholarship to NYU. One day she mentioned to Francesca how she had tickets to a play, and didn't want to drive and find parking in LA, you know how that is, so my sister volunteered me. I used Stella's car that night, and after that, I'd get calls for other things she wanted to go to. She'd sit in the front seat, though. Eventually I bought my own limo and got a swanky contract with a hotel mogul. But I fell victim to the old bait and switch and got stuck with his daughter, who was a real pain in my ass."

"I really was terrible to you that first day, wasn't I?"

"I was just as terrible. We're made for each other."

Her eyes lock onto mine.

"I mean… we both deserved it."

She falls silent for a moment, watching her own feet swirl in a circular motion in the water.

"I'm sorry about the cling wrap. And the sticky notes. I know you don't like people to touch your things."

"It's fine. You can touch my things all you want."

Her face burns red like the lights on a Christmas tree. Ignacio was right about me being born with my toe in my mouth.

"I mean, my personal car. You can touch it. As long as you're gentle. You can borrow it if you want to go shopping or something. It's no Rodeo Drive, but you might find a farmer selling cheese."

"I can't," she says, still looking into the water.

"I get it. It's not like you'd want to go shopping around here anyway. I'm just extending the invitation in case you get stir crazy and want to take a spin."

"I mean, I really can't." She takes a breath and lifts her eyes to mine. "I can't drive."

I stammer all over my reply. "Wh-wh-what… I don't understand. Is it a medical condition or…"

"No. I just never learned."

"Thank God. I mean, I'm sorry you never learned, but I'm glad you don't have a glass eye or fall asleep behind the wheel or something."

She laughs. "Nope. Just lazy."

"Don't ever say that about yourself. You're anything but lazy. Maybe you haven't had the right teacher."

"Yeah. Or no teacher. There's that."

"I'll teach you."

She bounces her eyes back and forth like that monkey meme.

"No, really. I'm a good teacher. I taught Francesca and Sebastian how to drive. Scratch that. Sebastian drives like a maniac. But I have a fifty percent success rate." I stand up and extend a hand. "Come on."

"Wait. Right now? I don't have a permit."

I snort. "This is Mexico. Okay, scratch that, too. There are Federales in Mexico. But not around here. This is private property for miles."

"You're really serious."

"As serious as a speeding ticket. Just kidding. It'll be fun. I promise."

I don't know what the magic word was, but she takes my hand and dries off her feet. She throws on a pair of cut-off jean shorts, and minutes later she's sitting in the driver's seat of my '68 Camaro looking better than Megan Fox could ever hope. I'm ninety-eight percent certain I've had this dream before.

I go over the basics, explaining the gears and the clutch —where to put her feet. She tosses her shoes in the back seat saying she wants to feel the machine in her toes. She's making it harder and harder for me to concentrate.

She starts the ignition as instructed, and all is good until she revs the engine so hard, she screams.

"Good," I say. "Rev it a little more. Get to know the car. Let her sing."

"I'm scared."

"That's okay. Put her in first." I cover her hand, guiding it into gear. Now ease off the clutch while pressing the throttle."

She revs the engine again.

"Foot off the clutch," I say.

"Okay."

She revs it again and the car blubbers to a stall.

"What just happened?"

"You took your foot off the clutch too soon. Go back to neutral and try again."

She goes through the same motions as before and the engine purrs to life.

"I think I just want to roar the engine all day," she says.

"You got this. Remember to ease your foot from the clutch *slowly at the same time as you accelerate.*"

Her little tongue juts out while she concentrates. I almost forget I'm supposed to be instructing her.

"Now what?" she says in a panic.

"First gear, first gear!"

Whew. She almost stalled it again. She steps on the gas too hard and the car jerks forward. And stalls again.

"Why is this so hard?"

"You're doing great. That was better. Next time, keep going."

She smiles with a sideways glance and starts the engine again. "I can understand why you don't want anyone to drive your car."

"Only hotel heiresses."

She laughs and blows out a breath. "Okay, let's do this." She flips a handle by accident and the windshield wipers engage, sweeping back and forth. It's so rural out here, they're smudging dirt all over the window.

"Oops. How do I mist it?"

"There's no mist." I reach over to switch off the wipers. "First gear."

"Aggghh."

"Foot on the gas. Ease off the clutch."

She closes her eyes as she moves her feet.

"Open your eyes, for goodness sake."

"Okay, okay."

"Now go!"

I'm surprised when the car moves.

"You're doing it. January, you're driving!"

"I'm driving! Eeeee."

"Okay, okay, as quick as you can, punch the clutch and shift into second gear. Can you do that?"

She squeals. "I don't know."

We're puttering along but she's gaining speed. If she doesn't shift again, she'll burn the engine.

"I have faith in you. Just like before, but quicker this time. Release the right foot, punch the clutch with the left, shift, then switch to the gas." I demonstrate with my hands. "Like this. Switch, switch."

"Like dancing."

"Yeah. Like dancing. I'll even count it for you. One… two… three."

She's still puttering along.

"Uh… hello. Three."

"Oh! It's a waltz? I was thinking more like a cha-cha."

I sigh. "Sure. Let's make it a cha-cha."

"Will you count it again? But this time, say the words."

"You're serious?"

"As serious as a speeding ticket," she quips.

My heart ricochets off my ribs, kicking around in my chest like a soccer ball. Ignacio may be right about January coming from a different world, but she gets me. If she wants to dance the cha-cha, I'll play along.

"Alright. Clutch, shift, cha cha cha. Gas, clutch, cha cha cha. More gas, cha cha cha. Freaking A, you did it!"

I hoot and holler like the good ol' boys from the 2005 star-studded movie classic, *The Dukes of Hazzard* (yes, I'm *that* much of a car geek), because she actually did it. I'm so proud right now.

She's screaming and squealing and probably crying for joy. I'm pumping my fists.

"Third gear! Let's do this, cha cha cha," I say in my excitement. "Same process, cha cha cha."

"Which one's third?"

"Middle front, cha cha cha."

Before I call out more dance moves, she's already done it. She's a natural. I'm so thrilled, I don't even notice when she shifts into fourth.

"This is so fun," she says. "Can I make some turns?"

She's doing so well going in a straight line down the road, I don't want to make it too hard for her on her first try. But there's an empty dirt lot up ahead, and I'm feeling pretty good about this.

"Turn in here."

January takes the turn a little too fast and skids in.

"Shift down," I say.

She shifts, but not down. She's in fifth gear, still skidding, and there's a cloud of dust surrounding us.

"I can't stop!" she screams. "Heeeeelp."

"Shift down."

"I don't know how."

"Brake, brake," I cry.

"I'm going to pee my pants."

"Not in my car you don't."

In a panic, she lifts the handbrake and that sends us into a spin. We're going around in circles while dirt forms on all the windows, rendering it almost impossible to see. January's screaming her head off while I'm laughing uncontrollably. "You're doing a donut! I can't believe it. A donut."

"Is that a bad thing?" she screams.

It took me hours and hours of practice to learn how to spin a donut, and this woman stumbles into it by accident.

"Let go of the wheel."

Her hands fly up and the steering wheel snaps into place. I lean over and hold on so we don't veer into a ditch. Through the dirt on the windshield, I barely make out a tree in our direct path.

"Brake, brake, brake!"

January screams. I scream. My life flashes before my eyes. And right when I think we're toast, January slams on the pedal, throwing us forward in our seatbelts as the car slides sideways to a dramatic stop just inches from the tree and sputters off. It's a stunt worthy of all those car chase movies I've seen.

I look over at January. Her fists are clenched on the steering wheel, face frozen solid. I'm in awe. My jaw hangs open, barely hinged on my head. That was the most thrilling, most heart attack-inducing moment of my life thanks to the alluring woman behind the wheel. She can definitely touch my things any day of the week.

The words 'Will you marry me?' are hanging on the edge of my tongue. If I had any oxygen, they'd be already out there where I couldn't take them back.

"That was… better than…"

"Ice cream?" she supplies.

I unsnap my seatbelt, forcing myself to keep my hands in place. I want her so bad it physically hurts. Ice cream is certainly not what I have in mind.

"I guess that depends on the ice cream," I say.

"Toasted almond gelato."

Her gaze drifts to my lips, and all I can think about is that moment on the sand when I was inches away from kissing her. I wonder if she would have kneed me anyway if I'd taken her lips then and there instead of saying the first stupid thing that came into my head out of fear. "Not bad for a girl." I want to take it back.

"Hmm. That was really good gelato. Even though it ended up in my hair."

"I have no regrets," she says.

"I do."

She stares at me, waiting for more, maybe? What else is there to say? That was a million years ago. This thing we have here, it's all pretend. Soon, she'll go back to her life and I'll be the guy driving her around. Nothing will have changed.

Nothing but the breeze and occasional bird call remains. I can't open my door with the tree so close, and there's no way she's driving us back to the house.

"Would you mind getting out so I can climb over?" I say. "Unless you want me to sit on your lap."

"Oh, of course." She snaps off her seatbelt and opens her door, but before she's out completely, I stop her with a gentle hold on her hand.

"Hey. Good job."

She smiles back at me. "Really?"

"We're alive. I call that a win."

Her smile grows wider and she wiggles her shoulders. "Thanks for the lesson… cha cha cha."

Oh yeah. Definitely better than ice cream.

Chapter Twenty-three

JANUARY

I could disappear here. Not in a *"search party for January's body"* sort of way. But in an *"escape to paradise for the rest of my life"* sort of way.

I've had my phone off almost the whole time I've been here. I know I should be fixing this Jonny Z situation, but I really don't want to. Maybe if I ignore the Internet, it will all go away. I only power on my phone to take pictures of the beautiful landscape—and Enrique when he's not looking. These pictures are not for Instagram. They're for me and only me. I'm snapping a few shots of the vineyards when my ringer goes crazy. If it's my dad again, I'm changing my number. But it's an unknown number. From France.

Curiosity gets the better of me and I lift the phone to my ear but I don't say anything. Whoever it is needs to speak first.

"January? January, are you there?"

Mom? How can it be my mother? It's been years.

I pull the phone away from my ear and just stare at it. I don't even have words.

"Hello? Sweetie?"

Even though it's not set to speakerphone, I can hear her voice loud and clear. A heavy lump forms in my chest, like I swallowed a whole ice block. After years of radio silence from my mother, she decides to contact me now? While I'm hidden away in Mexico, during the small window of time that my phone is on.

"I've been trying to call for days," she says. "January, please."

I swallow, trying to dislodge the lump that's not really there. I'm finding it hard to breathe. Why call me now after all this time? In the midst of the hot mess I'm in and fresh off my dad's desperate texts about the lawyers. I don't want this. I don't want to be a pawn in their marital wars.

But I'm not a teenager anymore. Nothing they can say or do now will have an impact on me. If there's one thing I've learned recently is that I need to put me first. No more living in my parents' shadows.

Taking a deep breath, I bring the phone to my ear. "You have one minute," I say, stern and determined not to crack.

"Thank goodness. How are you, sweetheart?"

"Fine." I'm not so rude as to tell her it's none of her business. "What's this call for?"

"I was worried about you."

"Well, that's not necess—"

"I know you can take care of yourself," she says quickly. "But when your dad calls me, practically foaming at the mouth I might add, I started to get concerned."

Dad called her? Himself? Dad never calls her. If he does have a need to reach her by phone, he gets someone to do it for him.

"Does this have to do with Dunn and Dunn?" I question. Maybe they're finally getting a divorce.

She sighs. "No. But I do have people in your dad's circle still. I know what he's up to with those lawyers."

I'll regret asking, but I'm way too curious for my own good. "Which is?"

There's a beat of silence where I think she's not going to tell me, but then she sighs again. She's a sigher, apparently. "They found some kind of sneaky loophole, I guess—redirecting money to an offshore bank. It squeezes me out almost completely."

Part of me wants to shrug and tell her that it's her problem, so tough luck. She's the one who chose men and liquor over family. But I don't. I don't have the words in me.

"The allowances for you and me are filtered through the company. He set that up for tax reasons. Since you're legally a shareholder, he'll need your signature to cut me out of my share."

So this is all about money. I should have known. At this point, I should be fuming. But I feel nothing.

"Not that I care about your share or anything, but he won't get my signature. You don't have to worry about it. You can go back to your men and vodka."

"I'm sober, January. Six years. And I don't know what your father told you, but I'm willing to bet only half of it's true."

"Half is enough, Mom."

She doesn't reply right away, but when she does, her voice is wobbly and thick. "You were young, January. And I wasn't in a good place. And then it never seemed the right time to tell you the truth."

"Truth? What truth? Yours?"

She sniffles and blows out an audible breath. "This isn't why I called. Maybe if you'd like to come to Paris, I can tell you everything. Or I can meet you in New York…"

She sounds so sincere. But I don't think I'm ready for this. As if she senses my hesitation, she says, "It's not about the money. I promise. You come from old money on both sides, not just your dad's. I'm more than fine."

I realize here that maybe I've been jaded my whole adult life, even since I was a teenager. It really sucks being jaded. And perhaps it took Enrique and his crazy enormous family to help me see it. I don't want to be that person anymore—the one who builds walls and blocks out true feeling. I told my therapist I have a hard time connecting. If she would have asked me why last week, I would have easily blamed it on my parents. But I'm beginning to understand that it's my choice to live in that reality or not. All I know in this moment is that I've never experienced true happiness until now. Until Enrique.

"Why now?" I ask. "Why call me now after all this time?" I'm not accusing her. I'm not even angry. I'm just tired. Tired of this strange world my parents have built for me.

"I read about the scandal, but I don't care about all that. You've pulled through the poop-end of the tabloids before and came out shiny. But I'm afraid your dad might use it to his advantage. To manipulate you. And I don't want him to hurt you like he hurt me."

I don't know what to say to that. According to my dad, she's the one who caused all the hurt. Now I don't know who to believe.

"Well, I have your number now," I say.

"That you do," she says. "I hope you'll use it."

The ice block in my chest shifts a little, as though it's melting or someone is chipping away at it with a toothpick. It's still lodged in there, but at least I can swallow my tears down.

We hang up without an official goodbye. I'm too raw to dwell on it.

This week has been perfect. Even if I'm too terrified to ever get behind the wheel of a car again. I don't want anything to ruin my time here. I suppose I'll have to face my problems soon enough. But for now, I'm in paradise. The phone is going in the luggage for the rest of the trip.

Being here is like stepping into a dream. Valle de Guadalupe is Mexico's Napa, just East of Ensenada Beach. Rows and rows of grapevines stretch out for miles on soft, rolling hills cradled by the desert mountains.

The trendy tasting rooms at Viñedas Marquez are a hot spot for tourism among the fifty other wineries in the valley. It's an oasis at the end of a long, dirt road—with rustic charm that would make California wineries jealous. I feel like I stepped into that Keanu Reeves movie, *A Walk in the Clouds*. The winery itself is beautiful and impressive, but Anslo's house has my heart. The distressed wood façade is adorned with Mediterranean tiles and sturdy stone masonry. It sits atop a hill with spectacular views of the valley, and I'm told the ocean can be seen when the air is clear, but I think they're pulling my leg.

Anslo's wife, Simone, is simply lovely. She gives tours of the winery a few days a week and homeschools her kids the rest of the time. She speaks five languages, including French, and since I spent my youth in France, we hit it off like old friends.

She's back from town now, and we're cutting vegetables for dinner. I can't remember the last time I cut vegetables, other than to press them in my juicer. I feel so domestic. At the very least, it's keeping my mind off my driving lesson today. My skin is still buzzing, and it's not from the rumbling engine or the pulsating steering wheel. I'm all jittery because of the way Enrique's eyes fell over me, quickening my pulse with just a look. Gah! Why do his dark eyes have to be so beautiful? Why does *all* of Enrique have to be so beautiful? Move over Doctor McDreamy. Here comes Señor El Dream-o. El Dream-o isn't just smiles and nice suits. El Dream-o likes to rev his engine.

"I heard you had a driving lesson today," says Simone. I'm careened from my daydream.

"Hmm? Oh yes. It was terrifying."

"It's always a little scary the first time. Don't give up."

She wags her brows at me. Why do I get the feeling we're talking about more than driving? Nah. Can't be. It's just the echo of my heart beating all over the place.

"Enrique… he is an *attentive* instructor?"

Okay, we are definitely not talking about driving.

"He is patient and gentle?" Yep, definitely different.

"Yes, he was very obliging." All that and more, to be honest.

"Good. *Porque sí no?*" She swings her knife down with a whack, beheading a poor carrot. "*Il peut dire adieu à son boîte de vitesses.*"

I watch the head of the carrot bounce on the cutting board and roll off the counter, landing at my feet. My mouth hangs as I follow the path to the sad carrot's death. Simone stands holding her knife, pointing it up, and her other hand perched on her hip. Then she blows on the tip of the knife like it's a smoking gun.

I bust up laughing. "Oh my. He'll have to switch to a manual transmission. *Il devra passer à une boîte de vitesses manuelle.*"

Simone cracks up, dropping her knife on the counter. We both double over, holding our stomachs. She blows a raspberry. "Pthhh. Flat tire!"

Laughter erupts anew. Tears are streaming down my face.

"Engine failure," I snicker.

"Oh, oh!" Simone holds out her palms like *hold the phone.* "Bad spark plugs." She's cracking herself up, and it's the cutest.

I hold up a finger. "Faulty fuel pump."

"Who has a faulty fuel pump?" Enrique's standing in the doorway. The look on his face is pure gold. Simone and I stare at him, turn to look at each other, and bust up again. I don't know why we're laughing so hard. It's not even that funny. Eventually, we decide to abandon the vegetables and let Ignacio finish dinner prep. I get the feeling he prefers his cooking over anyone else's anyway.

The following day, Anslo takes Enrique and me around the vineyard on horseback, explaining the varietals and basically nerding-out over viticulture. He speaks with such passion, that even though most of it goes right over our heads, Enrique and I are enthralled—but mostly we're doing our best to tamp down the live wire of electricity sparking between us. It's been a constant thing since the driving lesson. Stolen glances, excuses to 'accidentally' touch, more hot glances. Actually, a whole lotta glances. I feel like I'm in one of those English shows on PBS where the characters internally combust with painful longing and burning tension. I've had an irritating, stabbing sensation in my belly all week. Okay, it's more of a sweet, delicious ache, but I'm trying to keep this PG-13 here.

Anslo gallops back to the tasting room to join Simone for the sunset crowd, leaving Enrique and me wandering the fields with our Azteca horses. We're walking amidst the lush vines to take a break from saddle butt (it's a thing), just talking and losing track of time. The sun is starting to hang large and low on the horizon, casting a golden glow on the grape leaves and across Enrique's bronzed face. I've never felt so serene, and I'm thinking maybe I just might hide away from the press forever here and live a simple, domestic life with someone special.

Enrique gazes into the orange sky. "I could easily settle down here."

Did he just read my mind? Is this a sign? "Me too!" I say without way too much gusto. It seems so natural, though. His eyes cut to me, unencumbered by those mirrored sunglasses which usually hide his expression. They're equal parts wishful and incredulous. The sun is at his back, which leaves his face partially shrouded in shadow, but I can still see the frown spread across his features.

"Don't say things you don't mean," he says. His voice is soft and low, almost lost on a gust of wind. But my ears are trained to his timbre. This new discovery sends a flutter of goosebumps across my skin. When did I become so hyper-aware of him? Oh yeah. Since forever ago. Even his slightest movements. His softest sounds.

"I do… mean it."

The words hang there between us, like there's an invisible string and somebody clipped them on there with a clothespin to flitter around in the breeze. *I do.*

Enrique is frozen solid. Maybe he's thinking if he moves he might lose some kind of game or disrupt whatever magic this is. But that's the thing about magic. It moves with you. At length he turns toward the sunset, taking in a deep breath.

"Why?" His shoulders droop toward the earth, head hanging to his chest.

"Because I—"

"No. Why are you so..."

What? Shallow? Entitled? Spoiled? I've heard it all.

He scrubs a hand over his face and blinks at the sky. "Surprising."

Oh.

"Unpredictable. Aggravating. Breathtaking." He shifts his gaze at me sidelong. "Perfect."

He takes a step away, resting his arm on the saddle as he exhales deep, you know, because making a confession like that is a lot of exercise. What now, though? Does he expect me to answer a question like that? Will he ride off into the sunset now, leaving me to pine for him as the wind sweeps my hair and skirt wildly? (I'm looking at you, PBS.)

But just as I think he's going to make his epic exit, he spins, and almost like he has no control where his feet carry him, he takes me fiercely. Passionately. His massive, strong hands are tangled in my hair, tugging at my scalp. His mouth covers mine, consuming me with raging intensity. The kiss is hard and desperate. Hungry and demanding— and I'm here for it. I let out a breathy sigh and he takes that as a green flag on the racetrack. *Vaaaroooom.* I feel his arms slide around my back to press me into his body, fusing me against him. It's not close enough. I want more. I return the kiss, stroke for stroke, grabbing fistfuls of his shirt in a vain attempt to draw him closer. Heat rolls through me, my heart hammering in my chest. A growl hums in the back of his throat. It vibrates on my lips and just drives me absolutely wild with desire. The more we kiss, the more insatiable the want. I feel alive and awake and am dying a beautiful death.

He moves his hands to the delicate skin of my neck, softly brushing his fingertips from my jaw to my collarbone. A shiver runs through me at his touch. The kiss turns to sweet, reverent caresses, playful nips to my bottom lip, and tender butterfly pecks on every inch of my face. He kisses the apple of my left cheek, then my right. Then my nose. Then the crease between my eyebrows. With every pass from one spot of my face to another, I catch a glimpse of his dark eyes skating over me lovingly. He's adoring me with his lips and treasuring me with his eyes. I'm cherishing him with my heart. This man, who crashed into my life with his disarming smile and brazen cockiness, has proven to be all virtue and goodness, making it extremely hard not to fall for him. Also, he's a HOT kisser.

And I know right here and now, that even if he walks away, mounts his steed and says *"adios, pilgrim"*—nothing in my ridiculously privileged life will ever compare to this perfect moment.

Chapter Twenty-four
ENRIQUE

Her. I close my eyes and all I see is her. I open my eyes, and even in the dark room, I see her in the shadows cast from the moonlight, and in the shape formed by clothes I threw on a chair. I used to imagine monsters in my room when I was a kid. Now I imagine a woman. There has got to be a treatment for that.

Unable to sleep, I pick up my phone. Yes, the bluelight won't help. Maybe I'll google my symptoms.

'*Seeing woman in the dark*' pulls up all sorts of questionable results.

'*Imagining woman in the dark*'

Hard pass.

'*Hallucinations in the dark*'

Forget it. I pull up Instagram, and naturally the algorithms bring January's posts up first since that's where I spend all my time. My thumb hovers over the follow button. Why does this feel like I'm making a commitment? Crazy.

My phone buzzes, and I almost drop it on my face. January's calling. It's like I conjured her up from my thoughts.

"Are you okay? What's wrong?" I go straight to worry. Not, "*Hey, baby, were you lying in bed thinking about me, too?*"

Turns out, my first instinct was more accurate.

"There are chickens in my room. *Chickens*, Ricky."

I hear clucking in the background.

"How many chickens are we talking about here?"

"I don't know. A baker's dozen? Twenty? What do I do?"

Chickens. *Ay que la fregada.*

"I'll be right there."

I rush to the other wing of the hacienda, barefoot on the Spanish tiles. January's room is all the way at the end of the hallway. Anslo and Simone couldn't have put more distance between our sleeping quarters if they tried.

When I arrive, the bedroom door is open, and January's kneeling on her bed brandishing her slipper at a flock of chickens. There aren't quite twenty—she's exaggerating—but there are plenty to keep someone awake.

"What are the odds of me coming to your rescue twice in one week with you on top of a bed?" I ask, trying my hardest not to laugh. "Please try to explain this scenario."

"I don't know how this happened. I fell asleep reading in the living room. I came back to a dark room, and when I turned on the lights, all these hens woke up and started a chicken rave."

"So they were in here already? Sleeping? And woke up when you turned on the light?"

"I don't know," she cries. "Why aren't they in the coop? Won't a coyote get them if they just wander around all willy nilly?"

I don't know what's funnier. January fighting off chickens with her slipper, or that she says things like willy nilly. I tiptoe into the room, careful to avoid any chicken droppings.

"There must be a brooding hen," I say, even as a chicken pecks at my toes.

"What do you mean, brooding hen? As in… sullenly thoughtful?"

"It just means there's a hen in the coop driving all the other hens crazy. Sitting on all the eggs. So they must have ditched her feathery ass while there was still light enough for them to see." I shuffle over to the wall, checking behind the bed. "This room used to be attached to the chicken run. I thought they closed off the entrance, though."

"Can you help me get them out of here?"

"I'm not herding a flock of chickens at two in the morning, and I'm not waking up Anslo. We're going to have to lock them in here and shut off the lights so they know it's night time."

"Eww, with me in here? Isn't there another room I can sleep? Please don't leave me."

Now I have to laugh. I'm busting up as the chickens cluck all around me.

"Mateo and his band mates are taking up half the guest rooms, and the birthday girl and her parents are taking up the rest."

"I'll sleep in the car then."

"Come on." I scoop my arms under her and gather her to my chest. The chickens flutter around, poking my feet with their vicious beaks. Swinging my foot to ward them off, I click off the light switch and swiftly shut the bedroom door.

Once we're safely in the hallway, I set January down on her own feet. "It's going to stink in there tomorrow."

"No! All my stuff's in there."

Taking her by the hand, I lead her down the hallway. "You might want to buy new stuff."

We pass to the other side of the house, and before entering my room, I say, "Will this be okay with you? I promise to be a perfect gentleman."

January steps into the room, surveys the surroundings, and narrows her eyes on me.

"Of *course* there's only one bed. I'm beginning to think you planned this, Kinky Ricky."

"Yes. I devised an elaborate plan involving chickens just to get you into my bed. Chickens are good for that, you know. Where do you think the term wingman came from?"

I shut the door, and throw a pillow in the center of the bed.

"I'll stay on my side," I say. "Unless you'd rather I sleep on the hard, bumpy, tile floor."

"Are those my only two options?"

"It's me or the chickens, baby."

She grins. "How do you know the chickens weren't *my* elaborate plan?"

My heart pounds in my chest as she struts over and slides under the covers. I am in serious danger here.

Lifting my eyes to heaven with a prayer for strength, I climb onto the other side of the bed, adjusting the pillow between us to stand up long ways. It's not easy to do without propping it between our bodies, snuggling up close so it doesn't fall over. This is a terrible idea.

"My virtue won't be sullied if you remove that pillow," she says. "I trust you."

I'm so relieved because that was the pillow reserved for my use. I scoot all the way to the edge of the bed and tuck the pillow under my head. I lie there, eyes as wide open as before. Wider even. If I couldn't sleep with imaginary January in my room, I certainly can't now. Real January is warm and radiant and smells of jasmine.

After a long while she whispers, "Are you sleeping?"

"No."

I hear her rustle next to me, and when I turn my head, she's lying on her side, smiling softly.

"Thank you for rescuing me," she says. Her voice is sweet. It pierces to the depths of my soul.

"Don't be so quick to thank me. The night's not over yet."

"Are you going to kiss me goodnight?"

"Nope."

She sighs. I've upset her. Or hurt her feelings. I turn over to my side, mirroring her position.

"If I kiss you right now," I say. "I won't know where to stop. And then, my dear, you'll have something else to say about your virtue."

She laughs and tucks the covers under my hip.

"Watch out there."

She's not playing nice.

"Oops. Sorry. I was just trying to wrap you up like a mummy. To keep your business on your side of the bed.

I smile at her, my face partly covered by the pillow. She's so incredibly beautiful, an angel under the glow of moonlight. Her hand peeks out from beneath the covers and finds the bare skin of my chest. Every cell in my body springs to attention, even the hair on my toes.

"What's this?" she asks, taking my silver scapular in her fingers. "It's the only piece of jewelry you always seem to have on."

I still her fingers with the palm of my hand and hold them to my heart. "It's a reminder to keep my hands off you, that's what it is."

A reminder that would do me well right about now.

"Is that why you fiddle with it all the time?"

"I fiddle with it?"

"Yes. You tug on the chain, turning the square thingie over in your fingers, rubbing it between your thumb and forefinger."

I'm taken aback how she noticed such a small thing when I didn't even realize I was doing that.

"The 'square thingie' is a scapular. I never take it off."

"Is it for luck or something?"

I take a deep breath and let it out in thought. "I suppose it's more of a promise. A consecration to… holiness. I dunno. To be an honest, God-fearing man, I guess."

Holiness? Super. I sound just like my brother Memo. And I guarantee he'd rather sleep in the chicken room.

January snorts. "You? Holy?" Then she buries her face in the pillow. "I'm sorry."

"No, it's okay. You're right. I'm a filthy, rotten sinner. But I'm also a work in progress, or at least that's what I tell my mom." I let out a half-laugh. "I'd like to think there's still hope for me yet. That's what the mystery's about, don't you think?"

She peeks her face back out of the pillow and grins. "I like the sound of that."

We remain like this, me holding her hand to my heart, studying the soft curves of her cheek, the way her eyes sparkle as she watches me watching her. It's perfect. And I think I could stay here, gazing into her glorious face forever.

At length, she says, "Can I ask you a question?"

"I'm a captive audience. Go right ahead."

"When we went to your house. Why didn't you want me to touch anything? I thought you might be a germophobe, but if that were the case, you wouldn't have stolen little touches or danced with me. Or shared your steak with me."

"I was afraid," I admit. "You were already living rent-free in my head. Having you in my home, where I sleep, where I eat, and watch TV—somehow I reasoned you'd be a permanent fixture if you left your touch behind."

"And now?"

"Now… well, I think it's pretty clear. Now, you can touch anything you want."

A witchy grin spreads over her face. "Anything except… you know."

Her brows wag suggestively.

"Yes." I squeeze her hand closer to my chest. "Anything except that."

Chapter Twenty-five

ENRIQUE

What is it about lazy Saturday mornings that make me want to... oh. That's right. It must be the woman in my bed. The beautiful creature whose bare legs are entwined with my own. Whose skin is warm and soft, and pressed as close to my body as another human can get. She is a sleeping slice of heaven, a vision of sunshine on this bright, spring morning. Filtered light shines through the window onto her angelic golden hair. I could wake up to this for the rest of my life and never tire of it.

Also, I am all man, especially when caught in such a compromising position. In the morning. When testosterone levels are so high, they're in outer space.

January stirs, and my brain runs out the door with what's left of my good judgment.

"Good morning," she coos.

Yeah. I could definitely get used to this.

"Good morning, gorgeous."

Her little fingers brush on my skin, tickling my chest, down my ribs, and slide around to my side. She presses a light kiss on my pec where her head rests. She's nuzzled under my arm, and those fingers at my side are tracing little circles, driving me to madness.

"You are testing my fortitude, *mujer*."

"Is that a bad thing? What does *mujer* mean?"

"Woman. And it's only a bad thing if you want it to be."

"Being a woman or testing your *fortitude*?"

"Is there any difference?" My hand finds hers and I use my strength to flip her onto her back, holding her arm above her head. Our fingers lace together and I stare down at her beautiful blue eyes. They dance in the bright, morning glow, meeting my gaze. As I hover over her, my pulse drums erratically.

"Whatever happened to the saint from last night?" she teases.

"Like I said. I'm a work in progress."

I let my weight fall over her body, my lips crashing into her neck, her shoulder, her collarbone. My willpower is a crumbled ball of dust somewhere in the corner of the room.

I devour her skin inch by inch with hot, open-mouthed kisses. She wiggles under me, raking the fingertips of her free hand down my back. I squeeze our entwined hand, pressing down, devouring her with hungry strokes of my mouth along the sweet curves of her neck. She lets out a breathy sigh, squeezing my hand in return, clinging to me with groping hands and legs. I have never wanted to give more to a woman than I do in this moment. To make her delight in my handiwork, enraptured by the sensation of slow, determined artistry. To fill her with bliss.

My lips explore the line of her jaw, suckling her chin, the corner of her mouth.

She turns her head abruptly. "I have morning breath."

"Right now, woman, I don't give a fig about morning breath."

Her eyes shine on mine with approval, and that is all the encouragement I need. My mouth ravages hers, raging, consuming, greedy. Her kisses meet mine stroke for stroke, so responsive to me in every part of her body. She moans into my mouth, reaching with her left hand to grab a fist full of my hair.

"I want you so frickin' bad," I say into the kiss, trailing my mouth down the delicious column of her neck.

"Me too," she replies, hot and breathy. "I mean, I don't want *me*. I want you… so *frickin'* bad."

"We shouldn't be doing this," I say, even as my hand finds the skin behind her knee.

"I know. It's probably a bad idea."

I growl into her neck. "Definitely."

"Enrique?"

"Mmmm?"

"Talk to me in Spanish."

"Only if you talk to me in French, mademoiselle."

"Dis-moi que tu m'aimes."

"I don't know what that means, but yes. Yes to anything you say."

"Spanish," she warns.

I like this side of January. So bossy.

"*Me vuelves loco en la forma en que me besas. Mujer. Cariño. Mi razón para vivir.*"

She groans, arching her back. "More."

"*Quiero mas que tu cuerpo. Quiero ser dueño de tu corazón.*"

"Yes," she cries. "I mean, *oui, oui, ouah!*"

As I plant kiss after kiss down her neck I wonder if she understands me. From my deep dive into Google, I learned that she grew up in a country adjacent to Spain, surely she knows *some* Spanish. My desire is to say the deepest feelings of my heart. To tell her things I'm too fearful to say in English. If I could only test the waters.

I could maybe say… I'd like to take a bath in a tub of peas.

"*Me gustaría bañarme en una tina de guisantes.*"

She hums in response. "*Je veux être avec toi pour toujours.*"

Wow. It occurs to me she could be telling me I'm a yahoo and it would still turn me on. January telling me off in English sends my heart racing. January telling me off in French is just plain hot.

How would she react if I say…

We built this city on sausage rolls.

"*Construimos esta ciudad sobre rollos de salchicha.*"

I make sure to accentuate the word *rollos* with an exaggerated 'R' and a handful of her buns.

She squeals, and in a throaty whisper responds, *"Je te veux tout de suite."*

Oooh. If we play this game much longer, I'm gonna have to see her in a French maid costume. So far, I don't think she understands my Spanish. I certainly don't catch anything she's saying in French. Then again, all the blood has left my brain, so even English isn't registering right now. I decide to try one more, and if she doesn't laugh or react oddly, I'm going to tell her what I really feel.

You look like the type of person who'd wear duck shoes.

"Pareces el tipo de persona que usaría zapatos de pato."

I'm rewarded with a mind-blowing, intoxicating kiss. Breaking the bond of our interlacing fingers, I cup both my hands around her cheeks (the ones on her face) and gaze tenderly in her eyes. Between sweet, tender kisses on her perfect lips, I pour my heart out before her.

From the very first moment I laid eyes on you…

"Desde el primer momento que te vi…"

I knew you were the woman I wanted.

"Sabía que eras la mujer que quería."

I knew I had found everything I needed in a partner, even if I was too stubborn to let you in.

"Sabía que había encontrado todo lo que necesitaba en una pareja, incluso si era demasiado terco para dejarte entrar."

But now I never want to part from you.

"Pero ahora nunca quiero separarme de ti."

You are the love of my life.

"Eres el amor de mi vida."

Her eyes glisten with a gentle affection I'd not seen

before, and for a single heartbeat, we forget about bootyli-cious time. It's all about cloud nine time.

Until… a pounding thrump shakes my door, killing the moment.

"Hey, Sasquatch. Wake up."

I am going to strangle Mateo. January wants Spanish? I can think of a few choice words right now.

The pounding continues. "Are you up, brother? Nobody can find the rich girl, and we heard chickens in her room."

"Shut up, you wombat. I'm awake."

"Good, because we have to set up, and I don't have time to—" The door swings open and Mateo's jaw drops when he sees January. "Oh. Never mind. Carry on."

He tiptoes backward, gingerly creaking the door closed by inches. Before it's completely shut, he peeks his head in the crack. "You might want to lock this." Then, with a click and jiggle of the handle, he shouts down the hallway, "I found her."

Whatever this thing is between January and me, it won't be a secret for long. My little brother can't be trusted with secrets. He's the kind of guy who'll spill all the spoilers for movies the day after they release in theaters.

"I'm so sorry." I'm prepared to apologize profusely to January, but she's giggling her face off.

"The look on his face," she says, hardly able to breathe. "Carry on."

"Right? Who says that?"

"The British?" She cracks herself up again. I love to see her laugh.

"I suppose it's a good thing he stopped us from going too far," I say.

"Yeah. We got carried away there, didn't we?"

"Yup. Whoo boy. Crisis averted."

She holds my gaze for a moment, blinking at me. Did I stick my foot in my mouth again?

"Not that it would have been a crisis. Not for me. I'm only thinking about you…"

"I get it." She kisses me sweetly. "We should go see about those chickens."

I frown like a New York street mime, tracing a tear down my cheek. "Fine. But I'd like to circle back to that smoking hot conversation another time."

"Boop." She bops me on the nose. "You got yourself a deal. By the way, what was that you were saying about ducks?"

Chapter Twenty-six

JANUARY

That was an interesting experience. I've heard of sweet sixteen parties, but that church service was more like a mini wedding. A wedding with no groom—thank goodness because the girl is only fifteen.

We're walking back from the church to the reception when Enrique wraps his massive hands around my wrist to tug me into the shadows.

And all I can think about is I just want to go somewhere

with him and be alone—to blow this taco stand as they say, even though tacos are not being served from what I understand. But I digress. He pulls me into a discreet little alcove in the winery that I hadn't noticed before, taking both my hands in his, and slides up to me very intimately. The warmth is just right. There's actual steam rising from his skin. My body is just trembling, wanting him. I think that he's going to kiss me. Maybe he'll press me up against this wall and do things to me. Things that might be a little bit inappropriate. What can I say? A girl wants what she wants.

His expression is gentle. And his eyes soften. Staring really deep down into me. It's a strange thing, really. I feel at the same time naked and exposed. Yet honored and excited. It's really hard to describe. My heart's beating fast.

And then his brows furrow.

He says, "I want to apologize. I was not right. I didn't treat you right this morning. I took advantage of the situation. And if it wasn't for my brother barging in, I would have taken it too far and that wasn't my intention. I don't want to be that kind of guy. You mean more to me than that."

Wow.

What do you say to a guy who says this to you? When all I'm thinking is, "Take me, ravish me. I'm yours." I want him to do whatever pirates do to women in books. Or not. Pirates do the wrong kinds of things. What about those rakes in old-fashioned stories where they just take a woman in a gazebo, ripping her bodice? Yeah. That is what I want right now, but Enrique is being… a perfect gentleman? And yes, we just got out of church. So there's that, not to mention his family is everywhere. His mom is here, possibly around the corner. And I kind of think that maybe I'm a bad influence on him. I don't know.

He lifts his hands to my cheeks and cups my face with his massive palms.

"Please forgive me," he says. "We shouldn't ever share a bed again."

My heart swells. And then it sinks. Because really? His words are so beautiful—nobody has ever been so considerate before. But at the same time, I do want to share a bed with him again. And again. And again. I want to share a bed with him for the rest of my life. And I'm not scared. I should be scared. All this should scare me.

I want to share it with him. Right this second tonight… tomorrow. I want to tell him that. I want to grab him by the hips and thrust him toward me and say, "Take me now, you rake."

But I understand where he's coming from. And I respect that. I'm thinking maybe the reason I want him so bad is precisely because he's so respectful.

Maybe if he had taken advantage of me, I wouldn't want anything to do with him and his delicious lips. Maybe the sole purpose of him being a work in progress, and trying to be good is what's so attractive about him. I mean, hey, there's the dimples and the deep black eyes and the chiseled jaw and the miles and miles of muscles. And the corded neck. Also, his backside is perky.

I want him pressed against me. I want him more right this second than I have ever wanted any other man. More than I have ever wanted anything. And here he is, talking about how bad he feels for what almost happened this morning.

"Enrique, stop talking and kiss me."

He grins. "If that's the kind of apology you want."

His mouth falls over mine, cradling my lips with his lips, and my tummy does a flip, squealing, "Weee, weee."

He truly is an amazing kisser, I'm just gonna claim that right now. Nothing will ever compare. His kisses are ruining chocolate for me, basically. No chocolate can be this good… not even Lindt truffles, and that's saying a lot. Well, okay, truffles are pretty amazing. But seriously, his kisses are so much better. My whole body feels like it's being kissed, like every piece of me is being touched, but he's just touching my face with his hands. His long fingers go back all the way into my scalp, and his thumb gently traces against my jaw, but other than that, there's nothing of him touching me. And I already feel like my body is dancing and my lady bits are throwing a rave. Every single part of me is tingling with desire for more and yet, it's so much. It's almost too much. He has a way of capturing me with just a simple gesture. But the way his mouth moves over mine, the way he strokes me—it's like gentle waves when you're in a warm pool. For instance, the one time I was swimming in Porto Katsiki. The ocean waves were gentle, rolling me back and forth. Like those lazy rivers at waterparks—how they float you around, making you feel weightless. That's how it was swimming at Porto Katsiki with its tranquil, lulling waves and water so warm, it was like taking a bath. My whole body was surrounded by the easy rocking of the ocean. It was one of the most peaceful, serene, exhilarating moments that I can remember. Enrique's kiss is like that.

His kiss is parasailing in Cozumel. His kiss is fireworks. His kiss is the first sip of coffee in the morning. His kiss is everything comforting and beautiful. I can only imagine what it's like to do more than just kiss Enrique Precio.

As I wrap my arms around his waist, my hand travels up his back while the other reaches down to gather a handful of his glorious backside. I press myself firmly against him, wedging every bit of me into his nooks and crannies—all my squishy parts against the hard plains of his chest.

I deepen the kiss, groaning into his mouth, letting him know with simple primal signals that I want him. Things I cannot say to him. I've never known how to say tender words to someone. I've never known how to say I love you. I've never said I love you to one human being in my life. Not my mom or dad or any other distant family. I've never felt close to anyone. I don't know how to say it. And so I will say it with my body, with my kisses, with my hands because words frighten me.

He is so into it. His hands are everywhere.

As if he is reading my mind, he backs me up against the wall and I'm having an out-of-body experience.

"So good," I say while he trails his hot mouth down the column of my neck. He presses his lips along my collarbone. Freeing his hand from wherever it was on my body to trail his fingers along my shoulder and tug down the collar of my dress to expose more bare skin so he can continue along my shoulder, and that does it.

That is my E-zone. I might lose it. Right here.

I might scream.

It's a breezy spring afternoon but I'm burning up.

"Do you think they'll miss us?" I ask. "If we disappear for a little while?"

He groans into my neck, tugging at my hair.

"You are a dangerous woman," he says. "*Mujer. Mujer.*"

"Keep talking like that, Mr. Progresso, and we won't need a bed."

He curses quietly. His fingers still as he presses his forehead to mine and lets out a ragged breath.

"You're not making this very easy for me. I told you I want to respect you."

I yank at his belt loops, pulling him into me.

"My womanly needs could use a little respect right about now."

"Please," he says. "Please don't tempt me. I meant to apologize."

"Apology accepted," I say. I rise to meet his lips and give him a little nibble, teasingly running my teeth so gently over his mouth as I tug.

He growls into my mouth.

I feel the delicious pressure of his body as he backs me more firmly against the wall. The brick is cool on my back, the jagged edges scratch at my clothing.

His whole body rumbles.

"My willpower is running very low, woman."

"Willpower is for diets," I say.

"Then tell me," he grumbles. "Do I need to go on a January Madison diet?"

"I can prepare a regimen for you," I say. "But you have to stay on the plan. I'm very strict."

He laughs. "What about exercise?"

I hum. "Daily exercise is a big part of the plan."

"You're going to kill me," he says with a deep moan.

"I plan on it."

On the other side of the winery where the courtyard is, blaring horns, drums, and guitars echo against the hacienda walls to our ears. A voice on the PA system announces that the buffet is open. "Are you hungry?" Enrique asks me.

I grin. "What do you think?" I trail hot kisses along his jawline to illustrate just how hungry I am.

"I'd say you're not hungry for food," he hums.

"Like I said. I'm very strict about diet and exercise."

"The first time I make love to you," he says. "It's not going to be against a dirty wall, and it's not going to be a quickie. The first time I make love to you, I want to take my time. I want to serve you. I want to give your whole body every attention. I want to explore every single luscious inch of you, and I plan to take several days doing just that."

GAH!

My knees buckle beneath the weight of those words. I've never been one to swoon, but I am so ready for my fainting couch.

He continues, leveling his eyes deeply into me.

"I need you to know something," he says. "I need you to know that I don't do casual. I need you to know I'm the type of guy who buys the cow."

I squint one eye at him. "Am I the cow in this scenario?"

He nods slowly. "You're the cow."

"And what kind of animal are you?"

"I'm the *burro* wondering what the heck a beautiful cow like you is doing with the likes of me."

"Maybe I like *burros*. That means donkey, right?"

"January." He gathers my face in his gloriously large

hands and regards me tenderly. "I can't be one of your country club guys or rockstars. I'm not famous. I'm not in the public eye. Is that good enough for you? Am *I* enough for you?"

"Of course you are." I think about my therapist's affirmations. *I'm enough. I'm loveable. I am unique and also the same as everyone.* That last one never made sense to me until now. Feelings of unworthiness and insecurity are universal. That's part of being human, and makes me feel even closer to Enrique than ever.

"I don't want a country club guy or a rockstar."

A small voice creeps up from the back of my mind. What if he's just giving me an out? What if he has second thoughts about us? Reservations about living in the spotlight with me. What if he hates it?

"And you?" I question. "Don't you want a cow with normal... milk?"

His eyes dip to my chest and a crooked grin cracks on his face.

"Not that kind of milk, you dummy."

"Maybe we should stop talking in metaphors," he says.

"Okay. What I mean is, life with me won't be normal. I live in a fish bowl. The public thinks they know me, like they're entitled to gobble up every shred of information they can. Whether I like it or not, it's just the way things are. If you stay with me, you can pretty much kiss your privacy goodbye."

He's silent, taking long moments to study my face. His eyes wash over me, trailing my features like a map. His thumb glides over my bottom lip, stretching it down just a little. Even now, liquid heat pools deep in my belly, and I want to take every word back as if I'd just planted an idea in his head he wouldn't have come up with on his own. It's a ridiculous thought, of course. But if I'm going to lose him to Hollywood hellfire, I selfishly want to delay it as long as possible.

Enrique presses his lips on my forehead, breathing me in. My skin awakens to his touch, the delicious scrape of his jaw as he plants tiny kisses all over my face.

"I'm sorry, did you say something about kissing?"

Agghh. He's killing me. "Yes, I… oh." He kisses a trail down my neck, landing on my collarbone. "Uh… I said… kiss your privacy goodbye."

"Privacy is overrated," he mumbles, thick and heavy. I'm basically Jell-O right now.

Then he drags his lips back up my neck and devours my mouth. I match him stroke for stroke. We fall in together, panting, mashing into one jumble of lips. Gone are the feather-light pecks, the tender touches. He's a tornado of passion, feverish and masterful. My belly dips to my toes.

"Speaking of privacy," he groans into the kiss. "We need to go somewhere to talk."

"Your bedroom?" I breathe hard in a frenzy of want.

He shakes his head. "They'll look for me there."

"*My* bedroom?"

"No. Chickens, remember?"

As if on cue, the rogue chickens from my bedroom run around the corner, clucking their way toward us in a zany rush. They flock to the small walkway, blocking us in. We are stuck in this alcove with no way out.

They're fluttering their wings, joyously hopping up and down like popcorn. It's a chicken circus.

Enrique steps in front of me, stomping his feet to scare off the flock, but a few of them climb his leg, pecking at his pants.

"Shuffle your feet," he cries. "They think your toes are worms."

"Worms!? Chickens eat worms?"

I start doing some kind of dance that would make James Brown proud. Meanwhile, the psycho birds are literally playing chicken with Enrique. He barks at them, baring his teeth. My own personal guard dog. That seems to scare them long enough for him to throw me over his shoulder and kick his way out of the alcove. I cling to him as he runs, the chickens following us with their happy cluck cluck clucks.

Enrique sets me down and I stumble away from the scene as best I can with strappy heels—exposing my worm toes and all. He's making a weird crowing, growly sound from his throat and flailing his arms about. I'm not sure if he's channeling a doberman or a rooster, but it's working. The chickens sprint around in circles, bobbing their heads, doing a madcap free range thing.

"They're a little too frisky, don't you think?" I say once we're in the clear.

Enrique shrugs as he walks next to me. His pant leg is covered in dusty little chicken footprints. "Maybe they want to join the party."

"Maybe they saw the menu and are forming a revolution," I say, thinking about the creamy pasilla chicken breast Ignacio was prepping last night. I've kind of lost my appetite now.

Enrique wraps his arm around my shoulder and kisses my temple.

"That's two interruptions in one day," he says. "I think the universe is trying to tell us something."

"Oh? What do you think the universe is trying to say?"

Enrique pauses our stride to gaze over my whole face with wonder. His thumb grazes my chin and he kisses me softly and tenderly.

"Let's go to the party. Then we'll talk later tonight."

I wag my brows. "Tonight?"

"Yes, tonight," he says as one corner of his mouth curls into his glorious dimple. "With our clothes on."

Shucks.

Chapter Twenty-seven

ENRIQUE

Here I am at another quinceañera for a distant cousin I may or may not be related to by blood. Mom made her usual entrance through the double doors to the church flanked by six of her sons in our signature black suits. We all turned heads. My brother Memo, dressed in gleaming white robes, celebrated the Mass alongside the local parish priest. Francesca played guitar and sang so beautifully, Mom cried. Then again, it doesn't take much to make Mom cry. The birthday girl wore a puffy pink dress accompanied by an entourage of teen boys and girls dutifully holding court. She looked every inch the cotton candy queen.

The reception is everything it ought to be, rivaling the expense and grandeur of anyone's dream wedding. Mateo's cumbia band is providing the dance music, and Ignacio's food is divine. I saw a lady wrap two chicken breasts in a paper napkin, then shove them in her purse to take home. I hate to tell her, but I don't think the cream sauce will survive the trip. Everyone's dancing and drinking while the string lights glow against a purple sky as the afternoon turns to dusk. The guests have already danced the obligatory "Achy Breaky Heart" in Spanish, and most of the old men have had too much tequila and are getting obnoxious.

So basically the same old, same old, like the other eleventy-million birthday parties we go to as a family. Except one thing. I'm actually happy to be here. In fact, I don't think I've ever been this happy in my adult life. And it's all because of the woman in my arms, dancing to Selena songs like a true *chicana*. She hasn't stopped since the music began and, judging by the huge grin spread across her features, she's not slowing down anytime soon.

"Where did you learn to dance cumbia?" I ask after I twirl her into a tight embrace.

She giggles. I love that sound. "Believe it or not, I learned in France. I made some Colombian friends who were there on extended holidays. We're still in touch, actually."

I'm picturing these Columbian *'friends'* as she speaks. Are they guys? Why am I so jealous all of a sudden?

"Oh, really?" I clear my throat. "These, uh, *guys* taught you to dance?"

January pulls a face, totally catching on to my tone.

"Guys, yes. And all we did was dance." She steals a kiss and all is forgotten. I nuzzle my face into her neck and take in her sweet jasmine scent. I'm completely lost in her.

"And make out," she adds.

"What?" I jolt back to catch her eyes and she's laughing, an ornery expression on her face.

"Just kidding." She squeezes me closer to her body and we're not even dancing anymore. More like hugging with slight movement. Our rhythm doesn't even match the music. I capture her mouth. Her lips are so soft and responsive. I'm falling hard and fast.

"Enrique?" she softly coos and my heart cracks a little. There's only so much of this intense feeling I can take. I hold her beautiful face in my hands and tell her with my eyes *I'm yours*.

"I was thinking. When we go back to LA..." She shakes her head like she's finding the words. "I mean, once all this...all my..."

She curses under her breath and laughs at herself. "Real smooth."

"Hey." I caress her chin, lifting it up to me, and kiss her tenderly. I'm not thinking with my brain anymore. I want her. Which is bad. And good. But bad. *Ugh!* I'll just be dousing myself with holy water for the next five minutes. We really do need to have that talk.

"Wanna get out of here?" I bid. I take her hand to lead her off the dance floor, but something flying in the sky catches my attention and it's rapidly getting closer. "What the..."

Soon the whirring noise overtakes the music, the chuff-chuff of helicopter blades pulsing with a roaring intensity. As it descends too near the festivities, I feel the rumble of the machine vibrate through me.

Somebody in the crowd cries, "*La Migra!*" to which I hear my brother Nate responds, "We're already in Mexico, *sonso*. What do you think immigration will do? Send you back to San Diego?"

The whine of the engine dies down as it touches ground, the waves of wind churning up dust from the vineyard surrounding the reception area. January's hair sweeps up from the gusts of air, and although all the other ladies present struggle to keep their dresses from flying over their heads and hair flinging in their mouths, January looks like she's the subject of a high-fashion photoshoot. Even her face has that pout to it as she watches the helicopter land. I don't want to tear my eyes away from her, but there's a huge aircraft fifty feet away to draw my curiosity. From this distance I can see the writing on the side which reads Madison Industries. Not *La Migra*.

I turn to January. "What's going on here?"

"I don't know, I swear."

And although I want to believe her with all my heart, I can't help that sliver of doubt from creeping up telling me she'd called her daddy to rescue her. The door opens and out steps Velma, completely out of place in her tight pencil skirt and blazer. She hones in on January right away and makes a beeline straight toward us.

"Thank heaven we found you," she says without preamble. "Let's go."

Just like that. Let's go. Like she's picking her up from the mall or something.

January digs in her heels and takes my arm. "How did you find me?"

Velma lets out a humorless laugh. "There are what—three, four-hundred people here? You didn't notice anyone taking pictures and posting them?"

I don't know half of these guests, but whoever checked in the location on Facebook is going to answer to me and my brothers.

"You can't just swoop in here like that," says January. "I'm staying."

Velma turns her attention to me for the first time, scanning me from head to toe—and not in an appreciative sort of way.

"Oh, you." She sniffs degradingly. "Mr. Madison hasn't forgotten about your little agreement." She dips into her blazer pocket and produces a thick, bulging envelope, handing it to me. "For your troubles."

January cuts her gaze to me. "Agreement? What kind of agreement?"

I'd like to know that myself. The only agreement I know of is the job he hired me to do, but that's no secret. I peek inside the envelope to find a huge wad of cash. All hundreds. Great, now I really do look like a drug lord.

"Enrique?" she bites out. "What kind of agreement?"

"Driving, I guess."

"You can drop the pretense, Mr. Precio. You played your part well, but the performance is over now."

January's face goes white. "What performance? Velma, what are you talking about?"

"Oh, come, come, Miss Madison. Your *Latin* lover? Certainly you don't think someone like Enrique would turn down a big fat payday."

January's eyes drift to the envelope and back up to meet mine. They're glazed with a sheen of salty tears. "That's a lot of money, Kinky. Is this true?"

I shake my head adamantly. I'm no expert at counting bills by thumbing through them like a true gangster, but even I know it's more than I earned. Not to mention the advance I got pretty much covered my fee for the year.

"It's all there, Mr. Precio. We'll be in touch."

What?

January looks between me and Velma.

"I don't understand. Somebody better explain this to me right now or I'm not going anywhere."

"Fame is such a fickle thing," says Velma. "One day you're in the midst of a scandal, police raids, leaked photos, and the next, you're a woman scorned. Poor January Madison slums it with her limo driver and gets abandoned in Mexico with a broken heart." She produces a tabloid article on her phone. There's a photo of January and me in an embrace. It's from the morning we fled from the hotel. "It's just business, dear. Tomorrow, Jonny Z and those fake nudes will be all but forgotten. We have a statement prepared for you."

"Don't listen to her," I plead. "I had nothing to do with this."

Heartbreak washes over January's face. "It doesn't

matter. You played right into their hands. This is exactly what they wanted."

"And that's exactly what you're doing right now. You have to believe me. I do care for you."

Awareness dawns in her eyes, and she speaks into the middle distance, mostly to herself. "Nancy was wrong. Unique but not different. I'm so stupid."

She flashes her eyes to me. "The universe is trying to tell us something."

"That's not what I meant. We'll figure this out, January." I reach out but she recoils.

"That's not how it works." She turns, nodding to Velma. "I'll go, but not without a list of demands. Just give me a moment alone with Enrique."

Velma cracks a grin on her plastic face. That is something I won't unsee very soon.

"Wait." I extend the envelope back to Velma. "I don't want this. Take it back."

She sneers at me. "Judas also tried give back his thirty pieces of silver, Mr. Precio, but by then the deed was already done." Smugly, she turns on her heel and walks back to the helicopter.

I turn to January desperately. Hurt and indecision play on her features.

"Please. Don't do this to us," I beg.

Her eyes shift to the envelope in my hand. "There is no us. We're just puppets."

My heart sinks. "You don't believe me. Do you?"

She meets my gaze, eyes glossy wet. "I do."

"Then don't go." I reach for her, and this time she doesn't step away. I gather her in the most heartfelt embrace I can. If a hug could talk, this one would say, "I love you. I will always protect you."

She seems to melt into me, her body trembling as she sobs into my chest. I squeeze tighter, giving her every-thing—every piece of me.

"I care too much to stay," she cries.

"No," I plead, shifting so I can cup her face and dry her tears with my hands. "I can't accept that."

"It's true." Tears are streaming down her face now. "You saw the tabloid. And that's not even the only one. Remember the pool? That's out there, too. It never ends, Enrique. They will never stop coming after us. They ruin lives. And I can't let them do that to you."

I glide my thumbs over her cheeks, catching the salty droplets with gentle strokes. What have the tabloids done to her? Rage boils in my blood on her behalf.

"We'll work it out." I say. "Us against the world."

She shakes her head. "I can't give you what you want. I'm sorry. Not until I figure out who I am." She breaks down anew, sobbing a deluge of tears. "I better go."

Before January can take a step away from me, I throw myself in her path. "I'm not above begging," I cry.

Velma isn't having any of this. Impatient to go, she calls out from the helicopter. "We really must get going, Miss Madison."

January offers me a wet, warm smile and kisses me on the cheek "Thank you, Kinky. Thank you for giving me the courage to be me." Even as she speaks those brave words, she's overwrought with gut-wrenching sobs. "Goodbye."

And just like that, she runs to the helicopter and ascends with it, leaving me in a cloud of dust. I watch until the chopper is reduced to a dot in the sky and stare in vain long after it's gone, fixing my eyes to where January vanished from my life.

Somebody in the crowd of guests takes a photo of me standing there pathetically, setting off the flash on their phone. I make a mad rush to smash them to a bloody pulp, but Ignacio and Dante sweep me back by my armpits. They take me away from the party to cool me down, insisting I drink lots of water. After a while I ask to be alone, and I spend the rest of the evening in January's chicken room among her abandoned belongings.

Chapter Twenty-eight

JANUARY

There's no place more magical than Paris at Christmas. From Champs-Élysées lined with brilliant lights, to the Christmas market at Jardin des Tuileries, I make no apologies for spending a small fortune on yuletide décor and eating my weight in chocolate. The other day I went ice skating alone on the rooftop of Galerie Lafayette, and then indulged in some retail therapy because it's depressing to go ice skating alone on the rooftop of Galerie Lafayette.

I've become a regular at the Rue Montorguil for my daily trip to Fou de Pâtisserie. The ladies who work the counter know me by name, but don't care about my fame. I love to hear my name in their Parisian accents. Januarie, they call me.

I'm back at my mom's apartment on Av. d'Eylau, where I've been staying. After a long day of working on the marketing for my new organic skincare line, Jánique, I like to unwind by sitting at the bay window with a stunning view of the Eiffel Tower. This time of year, I can stare at the breathtaking light display for hours. Tonight, the display is exceptional.

"Your father made a statement about his sordid affair with Velma, so I might actually have grounds for divorce. *Finally.*"

My mother says the last word on a sigh. She's been checking Twitter ever since Velma went public with complaints of 'untoward sexual advances' by her employer. If anyone knows how to spin the press, it's her. I should know. The strategically placed leaks about my relationship with Enrique overshadowed the scandals attributed to me and Jonny Z. Then his new album flopped. Just as she predicted, news of my heartbreak satiated the public and they abandoned their pitchforks. I was no longer considered a party girl, tainting the Madison Hotel reputation. I became the poster girl for scorned women everywhere, rising up from the ashes like a couture phoenix. And I did rise from the ashes, even though the cost was too great to bear.

After my father's interference, I came to Paris to make amends with my mom, and now pass my days pretending he doesn't exist, but today is one of those rare times Mom and I made an exception, with news so juicy, how can we help it?

"Did he admit to years of cheating?" I ask.

She joins me at the window with her phone in hand. "He only states it was consensual, and is denying claims of sexual misconduct."

"He'll do anything to avoid a lawsuit. I wouldn't be surprised if he pays her a bucketload of money to drop the charges."

Mom shakes her head solemnly. "If he treats her the way he treated me, she won't go quietly. She's stronger than me, and she can drag him through the mud if she wants to. I hope she does."

Scooting over, I wrap my arm around Mom and rest my head on her shoulder. In turn, she inclines her head on mine and strokes my hair. It feels so nice to have my mom back.

"I'm so sorry I stayed away so long," I say. "I should have reached out."

Mom leans back to focus on my face, holding me still with soft eyes. "Don't you go blaming yourself. I'm not the only one he gaslighted into believing I was an unfit mother. He can be very persuasive."

"Gaslighting is a mild term for what he did to you."

Mom's addiction to pills and booze was one of Dad's devices to control Mom. He's the one who pushed her to take Valium when she caught him cheating with a random woman. Of course she'd be hysterical about it. Over time, he increased her dose, causing a dependency on the drug. When she ran out, she'd drink heavily. And that's how he was able to send her away and not grant her a divorce.

"He did put me through hell," she admits. "But I came out the other end a better person. I did get the best rehab money had to offer, and for the first time in years, I can love myself."

It warms my heart to see how changed she is. When I was a teenager, she had little to no self-esteem; a distant shadow of the bright, cheery woman I get to spend time with every day since I came to Paris.

When I first left LA, I told myself it was not only to remove myself from Dad's influence, but also put distance between me and Enrique. The reality is, when I walked away from Dad's money, his hold on me has disappeared. I hardly give him a fleeting thought. But not a day goes by that I don't think about Enrique, and not a night passes where I don't close my eyes and almost feel his presence. I live with a constant ache for him, but like my mom, I needed this time to get to know who I am. To love myself.

"You're thinking about your handsome driver again."

It's not even a question. Mom has become quite aware of my pensive looks out the window. It's like she can read my mind.

"He's not *my* anything." I don't think he ever was.

"Of course not. You made sure of it."

I slice my eyes back to her. I'm not mad at her harsh words, but that doesn't make them less true. She sets her phone face down on the seat cushion and takes both my hands. I never knew how much I missed a motherly touch until I came to live with her in this Paris apartment.

"Listen, sweetheart. Eight months is not a long time in the grand scope of things. And I'm glad you're here. So, *so* glad. But don't make the same mistakes I made."

"Your only mistake was marrying Dad."

"Maybe, maybe not. I know this sounds cliché, but if I hadn't married your father, I wouldn't have you. And I'm incredibly proud of you. You're strong and independent and smart. Your skincare line launches next month. You're a force to be reckoned with. As much as I hate to admit it, you get those traits from your father."

"And what traits did I inherit from you?"

Mom smiles warmly and points her finger on my heart. "This," she says gently. "The propensity to love and love fiercely. And when you find your one great love, you'll not easily give up."

"He hasn't tried to reach me, Mom. Not once."

"Who's the one who left the country? Who's the one who flew away in a helicopter? The ball's in your court."

"I appreciate your optimism, but I'm sure he's moved on by now."

Mom swings her feet onto the seat cushion and draws her legs into her chest. We watch the twinkling lights of the Eiffel Tower change from white to red to green and back to white again. We enjoy the quiet together for the length of several minutes before Mom speaks again.

"Before I married your father, there was this guy."

"No, no, my ears! I don't want to hear about your past love life."

"Why not?"

"You're my MOM! Please change the subject." I cup my hands over my ears.

"January, are you ten years old? You're an adult and you're going to listen."

She reaches for my wrist but I pull harder to keep my hands in place over my ears. Not that it helps at all.

"His name was Lorenzo."

"La la la. I hear nothing."

"We met while I was backpacking through Europe with some friends." She sighs wistfully. "It was a whirlwind romance. A summer I'll never forget."

"I really don't need to hear about your steamy summer fling."

"I was young and fancied myself in love. But my life was in New York. I tried to keep in touch with him but this was before cell phones and hardly anyone had email. Social media didn't even exist. With the time difference, it was hard to catch him on the phone and letters took forever to cross the Atlantic. And then I met your father at a party in the Hamptons. My parents had arranged everything. I protested and threw a fit, making plans to run away to Italy. But soon Lorenzo's letters and calls stopped. I have a feeling my parents had something to do with that, too."

She pauses to suck in a ragged breath. I realize I'd dropped my hands from my ears some time during her story. It pains me to see her cope with her memories.

"I looked up Lorenzo a few years ago. He has a son. Spitting image of the man I knew all those years ago."

"Did you try reaching out?" I ask.

"No way. I don't know if he's married or divorced or what. I couldn't tell from his social profiles. But that's not the point. I'm stuck in this life. For years, I've been under your dad's control, pinned down by his hold on me." She quickly adds, "It's not entirely bad. It comes with a lot of money, even though I have my own. And you know what I always say about that."

I chuckle. "Whoever says money doesn't buy you happiness doesn't know where to shop."

"Exactly. But I still have to live every day of my life with regret. January, honey… you don't have to."

"What if your parents hadn't intervened? What if you'd gone back to Italy only to find out you were just a good-time American tourist to Lorenzo? What if he'd moved on with another woman?"

"Then I would have felt like a fool. Maybe cried a little. But I would have at least done something."

"I'm afraid I'm too late," I admit. "If I were Enrique, I wouldn't forgive me for leaving him like that."

"Would you forgive him if the roles were reversed? If he needed to work things out to be a better man for you? Because that's exactly what you did. You're a better version of yourself now, and he'd be an idiot not to see that."

"Unfortunately, there's no way of knowing. And I'm not going to stalk him on social media. I, of all people should know that's not real life."

"Do you have a mutual friend by chance?"

"No. We might as well be from different planets." No sooner do the words fall from my mouth does a flash memory come to mind. "Except maybe… no. That's ridiculous."

Mom levels me with a cautionary look. "Don't live with regret."

Her eyes are full of sincere empathy and concern. We've had many long talks about a whole slew of things since I found her in Paris. A lot of them have been cathartic. But I never cry. It's not that I'm so jaded as to have hardened myself to the idea. I'm not unfeeling. I just haven't cried… until this moment. Now, seeing Mom look at me this way, moved by the story of her heartbreak, and talking freely about Enrique, I'm flooded with a waterfall of tears. Free-flowing, wet-faced, snotty tears.

"That's the first step," says Mom, rubbing my back.

"I'm sorry you're in the splash zone."

She runs and gets me a tissue and I use four of them just blowing my nose.

"You tell me what I can do to help and I'll do it," she says. "I can have him kidnapped and brought to Paris. I know a guy."

"Mom!"

"Just kidding. But if you do decide to invite him, my doors are always open."

"Actually…" It's a harebrained idea, so wild, I don't even think it will work. But maybe, just maybe. I have my launch next month—then a jam-packed press tour all over Europe and the States until March. But if Simone could get away from her husband and kids for a couple of weeks…

"Can we get the spare bedroom ready? I do have a friend I'd like to invite."

Chapter Twenty-nine
ENRIQUE

"Hey, sad loser. Make yourself useful and hold the pan for me." Ignacio's making a honey-baked ham for Easter Sunday dinner and if I wasn't so caught up in my thoughts, my mouth would be watering from the amazing smell. I hold the baking pan while he scrapes the drippings into a bowl. He uses them for something magical, I'm just not sure what.

"Off in La La Land again?" he teases.

I've been pretty much fine lately. I was given the *"Your services are no longer needed"* dismissal from Velma not long after that fateful day which shall not be named. Now I'm working for Barf Girl, believe it or not. Well, her husband, to be precise. She married a big shot movie star, and I'm in charge of his fleet of shiny toys when I'm not driving my limos. Yes, limos plural. I invested the restaurant money in some real estate, allowing me the capital to start a rent-a-limo service with a whole staff of drivers, but I still do jobs to keep me busy. I do a lot of quinceañeras much to Tía Lucy's delight. And I bought a Bentley—not for hire. Just for me. Nobody's ever ridden in it.

So I've been busy—and I don't pine over January as much anymore. Well, not obsessively anyway. She's been in Paris as far as I know, working on her eco-friendly products, being awesome with her charities. I'm happy for her. But something triggered a memory today—the smell of jasmine, maybe—and I've been lost in thought more than usual.

"Just hungry, that's all," I lie.

"Mmm-hmmm."

"Do you know if Dad did his exercises today?" I ask, trying to control my stray thoughts. This past year hasn't been without its challenges. Two days before Christmas, Dad gave us a scare when he was rushed to the hospital. We all thought it was a heart attack when he found out Pancho Two was in bed with the mob. But it wasn't Dad's heart—just excess gas. Imagine the jokes since then. Pancho Two is still in Costa Rica as far as we know, but now there are even bigger problems that go by nicknames such as

Billy Three Fingers and The Roach. Ignacio's trying to handle it, keeping Dad in the dark as much as possible. But I think he's in over his head. He says Dad's health comes first.

Dad's hospital visit was a blessing in disguise. The doctors discovered a whole slew of health issues like pre-diabetes, hypertension, and high blood pressure. We're all grateful they caught it early and have Dad on a strict diet and exercise plan. He's not a fan.

"Yeah," replies Ignacio. "Francesca took him for a walk, but now he's even grumpier."

I laugh. Dad is in a perpetual state of grumpiness. I wonder where Ignacio got that particular trait. "What now?"

"Francesca's trying to convince him to join her on The Dark Side."

By The Dark Side, he means vegetarianism.

"I did no such thing." Francesca sweeps into the kitchen to fill her Hydroflask. "I only suggested he eat less meat. Not *all* meat. Sheesh."

Ignacio makes a she's crazy gesture at his temple.

"I can see you," she chirps. I shrug at Ignacio like *whatta ya gonna do?* Francesca screws the lid back on her Hydroflask and tips her head at me. "Tía Lucy's looking for you, by the way."

Oh joy. Wonder what she wants now. I kiss Francesca on the head and go find Tía Lucy who's squeaking from the front living room window. "Kiki, why the limo outside?"

Limo? I know exactly where all my cars are, and my parents' house is not on the docket. I jog to the front door to find Elvis of all people walking up the path. I can hear the purr of the engine as I meet him outside. It's a nice machine. He stretches out his arms proudly. "Whaddaya think?"

"New gig, Elvis?"

He grins. "I wanted you to be the first to see. Can I take you for a spin around the block for your opinion?"

I'd rather look under the hood than go for a ride, but I agree. "Sure."

He leads me to the curb, and I'm heading to the front seat, but he opens the rear door for me. "To get the full experience," he says.

Okay. Whatever.

I slide in, and as my eyes adjust to the interior lighting, I make out the figure of a full-sized Nicolas Cage cardboard cutout in the seat across from me. In the seconds that follow, Elvis shuts my door, the car rolls away from the curb, and I see Elvis waving goodbye, all toothy smiles. Dork. The only person who would know about the Nick Cage prank is January. My heart pounds in my throat. Did she put Elvis up to this? And if Elvis isn't driving...

The silence is broken by a blast of music through the surround sound speakers. "Drive My Car" by The Beatles. It's so loud, I'm sure the neighbors will start to emerge from their houses. *Chismosos.* What is even going on, and where is this guy taking me?

I'm in such a shock I don't even notice when the driver pulls over and cuts the engine. The partition glass lowers and I get a glimpse of the driver in the rearview mirror. Long, golden hair spills out of a chauffeur hat, and a pair of aviator glasses sit on a perfect nose. January. I'm frozen solid. Is this really happening? More to the point, she's driving and I'm not dead?

"Are you just going to stare like a fish, or are you going to come over here and kiss me?"

I leap into action, tossing Nicolas Cage to the side and reaching through the partition window to cup my hands around January's beautiful face. And I kiss her. I adore her lips with every ounce of energy I possess. Half my body is jammed in the window. It's freaking uncomfortable, but I don't want to lose the few seconds it would take to meet her in the front seat. Or the back seat. Scratch that. Back seat would be a bad idea. She's trying to explain something, but I need to feel her lips on mine now. I'm a hungry dog. So hungry for her that I might even snort in a frenzied breath.

"Kiki, I'm sor—"

I capture her mouth.

"My dad was—"

I nibble her chin.

"Lying to... oooh."

I trail my lips down her neck to that sensitive spot behind her ear.

"I don't care," I say between featherlight kisses. "You're here now."

And I *don't* care. I really don't. Her father made it perfectly clear —through Velma—he wants me to stay away from his daughter. And he's gone through great lengths to make me out to be some kind of low life. Then he got into some kind of trouble, but I ignored every bit of news on the Internet concerning the Madison family. I've respected the distance January put between us, knowing she'd come back to me if she really wanted to. And now she's here, clinging to my hair, humming with delight.

"But... I left you there," she breathes. "I shouldn't have.... Oh *wow*." She's so responsive to my every touch. And I'm just kissing her through a window.

"I don't care. I don't care about what they did. The tabloids. The big wad of gangster cash. I'm just happy you're here."

"Simone taught me how to drive," she says while I plaster her with kisses. "I had to take my driver test three times. But I didn't want to come until I passed. And then I had this crazy idea to find Elvis and get his help today. Is that weird?"

I pause the kisses to look into her exquisite face. "Yes. That's weird. And perfect."

She starts laughing, really laughing hard.

"What's so funny?"

"Did you just say 'big wad of gangster cash'?" She's cracking up, hardly able to get the words out.

"Well, it sure looked like gangster cash to me. I tried to give it back," I say, kissing her again along her shoulder blade. "But they wouldn't take it. So I gave it to the dogs. *Mmmm,* you smell so good." Her jasmine oil hits me like a shower of arousing bullets through my senses. Yeah, I know bullets aren't arousing, but I'm working with no blood in my brain here.

"Dogs?" January scrunches her chin back to look at me. "You mean Kanines for Kids?"

"Mmmm-hmm," I moan, returning to her neck. I get in a couple of nibbles but she fists my collar and crashes her lips into mine. I love how she takes control over this unconventional make-out sesh.

"I love you," she says, and although it's the first time I've heard her tell me, she declares it like it's the most natural thing in the world. Like she tells me she loves me every day. "I think I started loving you when you started those ridiculous pranks. I thought I must have been out of my mind to have those feelings. But this past year has shown me it's okay to be a little bonkers sometimes."

"Is that what this is? Bonkers?"

A dazzling grin overtakes her features. "In the best way."

"Good." I plant one big, sloppy kiss all over her mouth. "Because I'm crazy in love with you, princess. And I don't ever want to be sane."

Of all the ways I could have imagined seeing January again, crammed through a partition window wasn't even on the list. And it couldn't be more perfect... except the way the edge of the glass is digging into my side. "Now, can you help me out of this hole? I think I'm stuck."

The corner of January's mouth curves into an evil smirk. She finds her sunglasses and hat and slides them on devilishly.

"I think I'll leave you there while we drive for a bit," she teases.

"I think I lost feeling in my pancreas."

"Not possible."

"January, please!" I'm desperate here.

She lowers her glasses on her nose and winks. "What's my name?"

I mumble something under my breath.

"What's that?"

"Mmmzmadnnum."

"I'm sorry, couldn't quite hear."

I grumble through my teeth. "Please… Miss Madison."

She smiles victorious, reaching around my torso to help me wiggle out of this position. And squeezes, right in the tickle spot.

"With pleasure… Mister Hot Bod."

Epilogue
part one

ENRIQUE

September

I called almost every animal shelter that works with Kanines for Kids before I found one with Yorkie puppies. The mother was found in a puppy mill, malnourished and weak. The shelter director fell in love with her while nursing her back to health and is keeping one of the puppies. The other three puppies are being boarded at a rescue center in Escondido. January has no idea we're here to adopt a dog. She thinks we came down to San Diego County to take a hot air balloon ride. When we arrive at the rescue center, she eyes me sideways.

"This doesn't look like," she checks the brochure I'd given her to throw her off my scent. "Romantic Balloon Adventures."

I shrug. "I thought it might be fun to spontaneously pop in to see all the good things Kanines for Kids has done for these animals. Since we're in the area."

"Okaaay." She scrunches her nose like she does when she's on to me. I know she suspects something. I probably shouldn't have used the word spontaneously. I'm the worst at keeping secrets from her and she can read my face like a book. But she plays along anyway. I'm pretty sure she doesn't know I called ahead and picked out the puppies already, so at least I have that surprise. I over-heard her telling her mom she thinks I'll propose in the hot air balloon today. And I already do have the ring. The diamond is bigger than my eyeball. But there will be no hot air balloon proposal today. I'm thinking maybe I'll train the dog to bring her the ring and bark, "Marry me." Or not. More realistically, I could have it spelled out in lights somewhere in Times Square, or ask Billy Idol to help me reenact the proposal in *The Wedding Singer*. January's a big Drew Barrymore fan. I'll figure it out another day.

We go inside where it's cool and air-conditioned. Escondido is blazing hot this time of year, so it feels nice. We're greeted immediately by a teenage girl tending the front desk. She's beaming, teeth aligners on full display.

"Welcome to Press Paws, Miss Madison. We've been expecting you."

She dials a landline phone and holds up her finger. Meanwhile, January stares me down.

"Spontaneously pop in, huh?"

I give her my charming smile, which is also my *I'm busted* smile and my *you are always right* smile. I have a lot of practice with the latter.

"There's no fooling you, my dear."

She harrumphs, and a moment later a woman in a Press Paws polo shirt and jeans approaches us with her hand extended.

"Mr. Precio, I'm Gemma. We spoke on the phone."

I shake her hand. "Call me Enrique."

"And Miss Madison, it's so nice to finally meet you." She offers to shake January's hand, but January has turned into a hugger—Francesca's influence.

Gemma's surprise at being pulled into a hug is short-lived. I guess she's a hugger, too.

"Nice to meet you, too, Gemma. You can call me January."

I snort. "I'm the only one whom she insists calling her Miss Madison."

January pinches me and whispers from the side of her mouth. "Watch it, Mr. HB."

That's code for Mister Hot Bod when we're in public, thank you very much.

Gemma smiles. "Okay. Why don't we go through and meet the puppies?"

"Puppies?" January squeals. There are usually a few puppies at each rescue center, but most of the dogs are fully grown. With the efforts of hundreds of volunteers, Kanines for Kids has rehomed more than eight-thousand animals over the past few years. I think it's time January takes one home today.

Gemma takes us down a hallway, passing playrooms that look more like a preschool than an animal shelter. Everything is bright and colorful. DOGTV is playing on monitors in every room while volunteers play with the animals.

"These are our lounge rooms," says Gemma. "Our residents get time to play with visitors once a day and get regular walks."

"Residents," repeats January. "I like that term."

Gemma stops in front of a door. "Yes, well, we hope they are only temporary residents."

She lets us into what can only be described as a nursery for dogs. There are small sofas and pillows on the floor, and along one side of the wall is a wooden structure resembling a child's play castle. There are turrets on each corner, an arched doorway, and where the roof would be, is an opening decorated with dentil trim. And inside that castle are three fluffy, itty bitty Yorkshire terrier pups.

"Aww." January coos with delight. "Yorkies!"

Gemma squats cheerfully at the arched doorway and unlatches the flimsy gate. Two of the puppies bumble around in circles, but one of them wobbles her way to freedom the second the gate is open. She makes a beeline to January.

"Oh baby, you're so precious." January gets down on her knees and picks up the puppy.

"We call that one Brownie," says Gemma. "But you can change the name if she's the one you choose."

January gasps. "Choose? Ricky, are we getting a dog?"

I laugh. "What did you think we were doing here? I know you don't believe my BS excuse."

"So we're not going on a hot air balloon ride?"

"I'm afraid of heights."

A shadow of disappointment flashes on her features but is quickly replaced by sheer joy.

"We're getting a dog!"

Brownie excitedly licks January's hand.

Gemma crawls into the castle to retrieve the other two puppies and hands me one. "There are two females and one male. They're current on their vaccines, of course. I'll take care of the paperwork so you can go home with one of these babies today."

"Just one?" January scoops up another puppy. "How can I choose just one?"

Oh no. With all the traveling January has to do for work, one dog is going to be trouble enough. But three? Nope. Not gonna happen.

"It's a hard choice, I know," says Gemma. "Each of them have such stand-out personalities already. Or should I say doggyalities?"

"They do have doggyalities," cries January. "I love them all."

"Um… my dear? Love of my life? I don't know if—"

"Take all the time you need," says Gemma. "I'll leave you two alone to discuss."

Once Gemma leaves us alone in the puppy throne room, January scoops up another dog and falls backward onto a pillow. All three fluff balls are crawling on her chest and face. Oh how I wish I was a puppy right now.

"I love them all," she says, giggling.

"I'm sure you do, sweetie, but we can only adopt just one, so the other two can bring joy to other families."

"Like your mom and my mom?"

"Errr."

"Kinky, you're brilliant. We'll give one to each of our mothers. That way we won't separate the siblings. They can visit each other all the time."

"Your mom lives in Italy now."

Apparently, January's mom reunited with a long-lost lover and packed her bags for the land of pasta and talking with one's hands without looking back.

"Yes! I know. And she would love a dog."

"And *my* mom?"

"She'd love a dog, too."

Actually, she's probably right about that.

My heart swells as I watch January playing with the puppies, her hair tossed in silky locks over the pillow while three squeaky, puffy things climb all over her with their tiny legs.

"If we're to do this," I say. "Who would get which dog?"

I'm actually trying to get her to make a choice. Maybe we could get all three dogs, but if she were pressed to pick just one, which would it be?

"I like the boy for my mom. She never had a son."

"And what about you?"

She sits up, crossing her legs, and piles all three puppies on her lap. Her gaze goes back and forth between Brownie and the other female. Brownie has a caramel color snout with black around the eyes, while the other one is a light tan with silver along her back. This is not an easy decision for January.

"I think… oh, I don't know. Can we choose later?"

"Nope. You have to decide now."

Her face is frowny and pouty. "This is so hard."

"I know. It's a very important decision. How about we put all the puppies in a line and see which one gravitates toward you?"

"You mean which one comes to me is the one I'll adopt?"

"Sure. Or at least it will help you make a choice."

"Okay."

"I scoop up all the pups and set them in front of the castle. Then I crawl on all fours to sit next to January. I did not do a good job planning my outfit. These chinos are comfortable enough, but when I bend a certain way, they get stretchy in very uncomfortable places. I plop myself on a pillow and wrap my arm around January's waist, stealing a quick pinch.

"What's that?" she asks.

"That's payback for pinching me earlier."

"No, what's *that*?" She's pointing at something on the floor. A small, square box. Oh no! It must have fallen out of my pocket.

"It's nothing." I lunge for it, but then I hear and feel a powerful rip in the rear seam of my chinos. January's too quick for me anyway. She holds the box in her hand incredulously, then looks back up at me. Her eyes are glossy.

Please don't cry. Please don't cry. Just give me the box and pretend you never saw a thing.

She doesn't give me the box. She opens the box.

Her whole face sparkles. "Oh, Enrique."

I realize, having attempted to grab the box before she could, I am bent before her on one knee. With ripped pants.

"I *knew* it! I knew you were going to propose today."

"I wasn't going to propose today."

"What do you mean you weren't going to propose today? You put the ring right here with the puppies and made a really big hint to *make a choice*."

"I didn't put the ring on the floor. It fell out of my pocket."

She stares at me. Then her eyes slowly form into slits. "Are we even getting a dog?"

"Yes, we're getting a dog. It's just..." I crawl over to her, feeling a fresh breeze where the pants are ripped. "The ring accidentally fell out of my pocket. And now I need a new pair of pants."

I reach for the box but she squeezes it to her chest, just out of my reach.

"You're telling me you've been walking around with a diamond ring in your pocket with no intention of proposing to me today?"

"That pretty much sums it up, yeah."

"And what if it had just *accidentally* fallen out in a parking lot somewhere? Or when you stopped to pump gas?"

"I didn't think it would fall out."

She's gaping at me wide-eyed and open-mouthed.

"Is this even for me?"

"Of course it's for you. Who else would I buy a massive diamond for?"

"I don't know. Maybe you're holding it for your sister's boyfriend and you were going to help *him* propose instead of… did you say you need a new pair of pants?"

"January, I do want to propose to you, but not like this. I was planning a big, epic thing you'll never forget."

"Well, I certainly will never forget this."

"I'm sorry. I screwed everything up. Why don't you give it back to me and I'll surprise you the way you deserve."

"No." She hugs the box closer to her chest. Meanwhile, the puppies are all over the place. Except Brownie, who made her way onto January's lap. "Why have it in your pocket in the first place?"

I shrug sheepishly. "I wanted to keep it safe."

"And you thought your pocket would be your best bet?"

I've come to realize the error in that plan. "Obviously I don't think that *anymore*."

She sighs and shakes her head at me. "You are unbelievable."

I hold out my hand. "I'll put it in my glove box."

"Are you crazy? No. The safest place for this ring is on my finger."

She plucks the ring out and snaps the box shut, tossing it at me. "Here. You can put *that* in your glove box."

The ring slides effortlessly on her left ring finger. It couldn't fit more perfectly if it had been forged by magic. She holds her hand out, admiring the bling. It's practically a disco ball.

"Does this mean your answer is yes?"

She raises one perfect brow. "Say yes to what? I don't recall you asking me a question."

I really am flubbing this up.

Scooting closer to her, rip in my pants be damned, I pick up Brownie and hold her close to my face. I pucker my lips and mimic Brownie's puppy dog eyes. With a squeaky little voice that is a terrible impression of a doggy woof, I wiggle Brownie's little paws.

"Will you mawie me?"

January ticks her head to the side and rolls her eyes. Taking Brownie from me, she gives her a scratch behind the ear.

"That was actually me talking, not the dog," I say, just to clarify. "I asked you to marry me."

She gives me a hard stare. "I'm wearing the ring, aren't I?"

"Aye! Mujer!"

Laughing, she kisses Brownie, then kisses me. I don't even care that her lips were on a dog. I'll take January's kisses however she wants to give them to me.

"Of course I'll marry you. Why do you have to be so difficult?"

"I was born that way."

She kisses me again, and a little squeak comes from the puppy between us.

"Should I keep Madison, or should I change my name to Mrs. Hot Bod?"

"Definitely Mrs. Hot Bod." I take her hand, twirling the ring on her finger. It really is perfect for her. "I'm sorry you didn't get a spectacular proposal."

She gazes at me tenderly, her smile shimmering in her eyes. "I don't want a spectacular proposal. I only want you… and Brownie."

Epilogue
part two
IGNACIO

The problem with owning your own catering business isn't family and friends wanting a dirt cheap deal on their swanky wedding. No. Au contraire. (Although, that does happen from time to time.) The problem lies solely in me and my inability to let a stranger prepare the meal on my brother's special day—not when I can do it better, healthier, and with more discretion.

I tried to stay out of it. I really did. But when I stumbled upon (spied, cough-cough) Enrique and January's list of potential caterers, I almost had an aneurysm. One guy was charging four grand a head for (get a load of this) soup! And I heard through the grapevine he cheats with canned broth. Another so-called chef had so much grease on his menu, the paper it was printed on almost clogged my arteries—and not a single mention of vegetables. I couldn't let that happen. My sister's a vegetarian. What would *she* eat?

So here I am, overseeing the reception with my best crew on the job. I promised Kiki I wouldn't do any of the work on the wedding day. And I'm not. Mostly. The thing is, there are a couple of new faces on staff. We had to hire some extra servers to account for those of us in the family not on the clock so we can celebrate with Enrique and January. I made sure background checks were ordered for every single new hire—we didn't need any psychopaths at my brother's wedding. A high-profile bride is stressed enough.

January does look radiant. More than usual, I think. It's the whole wedding day thing, and the way she looks at my brother. Her face lights up like a Christmas tree when he smiles at her, which reveals a hidden beauty not naturally present. Don't get me wrong, she's pretty, I guess. I'm not the one married to her so it doesn't make a difference to me. But my taste in women is a little less blonde and a little less skinny. I like a woman with curves. Something to hold on to. Which is why my gaze keeps skating over the new girl on my staff. Olive, I think her name is. It's a hot day and the servers wear black button-ups. I don't expect them to have the collar closed up to their chins. I'm not a monster. Two buttons undone is modest enough. But that girl... well. Let's just hope the strain doesn't pop a random button into the mascarpone figs. Not that I'm looking or anything.

"You can stop obsessing over every detail now." Mateo, my obnoxious younger brother, shoves a cocktail in my hand. "Relax. The fondue fountain isn't going to blow up if you have some fun."

"I'm not obsessing."

"Oh, really? What did Tío Enrique just say before he left us to attack the open bar?"

"I try to avoid anything Tío Enrique says. And did you instruct the bartender not to give him any booze?"

"Of course. And I wasn't listening to anything he said either. Too many hot girls to watch."

I grunt. Mateo doesn't need any encouragement to pick up women at a wedding. He has a master's degree in the subject.

"Cool your jets and get Mom a bottled water. I don't want her to dehydrate in this heat."

Mateo turns his head in time to see Mom cooling off her armpits with the ice cubes from Dad's vodka cranberry.

"Good call. Lord knows she'll need it after crying all day." He scoots away and I try to resist going over to check on the cook. It's only cocktail hour, but I'm worried he might not get the entree right for the sit-down meal. It's a delicate timeline, maintaining temperature without over-cooking the filet. The servers are passing around trays of hors d'oeuvres—seared ahi, Tuscan truffles, and coconut shrimp. I take one and pop it in my mouth. Quality check. Could use more orange marmalade sauce. I search through the crowd of wedding guests to flag another server but the only ones I see are at the other end of the garden. And that's when *she* catches my eye again. Olive. But this time it's not her large brown eyes that hold my attention, or the quirky smile she wears when she's offering canapés to a guest. The reason my gaze is fixed on her now, and why my jaw hits the floor, is because she's diving through the air toward Tía Lucy. And Tía Lucy is flying toward the cake.

Read about Ignacio and Olive in the grumpy/sunshine, fake relationship romcom, Nacho Boyfriend.

I have a secret bigger than my restaurant's burrito grande.

That girl everyone saw me fake kissing is not my girl-friend. Somehow a small favor turns into a recipe for disaster and the only way to fix it is to add a little spice, let it simmer, and serve it hot. We might be cooking up a fake relationship, but even pretend kissing Olive is muy delicioso.

*closed door

So much sizzle, you won't miss the sex.

FOMO?

Fear Of Missing Out can be a real bummer, right? Not to worry. I got you covered.

Get all the deets on future releases, first-look cover reveals, freebies, romcom book recs, current bookish news, and questionable inspirational quotes in my Sunday email blast.

Oh, and get a free book as a thank you gift, just for subscribing. Cool, huh?

https://BookHip.com/CKMQST

Social media more your thing? Follow me in all the places. (Hint: Instagram is my favorite)

Facebook: @gigiblume

Instagram: @gigiblume

TikTok: @gigiblumeauthor

BOOKS BY GIGI BLUME

BACKSTAGE ROMANCE

Confessions of a Hollywood Matchmaker

Love and Loathing

Secrets of a Hollywood Matchmaker

Driving Miss Darcy

The Friend Act

Pita My Heart

Dancing with the Cowboy

PRECIO BROTHERS

Messy Love

Messy Road Trip

The Hate Zone

Nacho Boyfriend

ACKNOWLEDGMENTS

Julie and Patty - thank you ladies for being my constant cheerleaders.

Thanks to my chat group of awesome romcom authors (The Most Amazing Women in the World) for calming me down when I was freaking out over everything.

Sophie, thanks for your help with the French lines. You're a way better source than Google translate.

Elaine York for challenging me to make this book better.

ABOUT THE AUTHOR

Gigi is a USA TODAY bestselling author and hopeless musical theatre nerd who has perfected the art of lolly-gagging.

Former professional wedding singer, Gigi lives in Southern California with her personal chef...er...husband and two weird and awesome teenagers.

When Gigi's not writing like a crazy woman, she likes to belt out showtunes, embarrass her kids, and spend all her free cash on books.